The Not-So-Old Man and The Sea

Adventures into the mind of

Ernest Hemingway

THE NOT-SO-OLD MAN
AND
THE SEA

Adventures into the mind of

Ernest Hemingway

A NOVEL BY

SAM BARLOW

PERIGREE PUBLISHING
PERIGREEPUB.COM

Barlow, Sam
    The-Not-So-Old Man and the Sea—Adventures into the mind of Ernest Hemingway by Barlow, Sam
p.cm.
Library of Congress Control Number: 2020944069

ISBN: 978-0-9703269-3-5

Publisher's Cataloging-in-Publication data
Names: Barlow, Sam O., 1966-, author.
Title: The not-so-old man and the sea : adventures into the mind of Ernest Hemingway : a novel / by Sam Barlow.
Description: Palm Harbor : Perigree Publishing, 2020.
Identifiers: LCCN: 2020944069 | ISBN: 978-0-9703269-3-5
Subjects: LCSH Swimmers--Fiction. | Hemingway, Ernest, 1899-1961--Fiction. | Philosophy--Fiction. | Conduct of life--Fiction. | Psychological fiction. | BISAC FICTION / General | FICTION / Psychological | FICTION / Magical Realism| FICTION / Literary
Classification: LCC PS3602.A7756235 N68 2020 | DDC 813.6--dc23

PRI Publishing/Perigree Publishing
www.perigreepub.com
245 Philadelphia Blvd.
Palm Harbor, FL 34684
(419) 869-7901
Email: proreach@aol.com
All quotes of Ernest Hemingway used with permission
Cover art by Artninja

Dedication

To my dad

and all the parents who never were

Concentrate on the stroke
Make each stroke better than the last
That is what perfection is
Better than the last
Better than what came before...
Each stroke more true to itself
Sam Barlow

CHAPTER *I*

*H*e was a not-so-old man who liked to swim in the sea alone. Or in a lake or pool. He did not like swimming in rivers because the currents were unpredictable and upset his rhythm. The rhythm was his luck, he thought. It gave him peace knowing what stroke was next, and it would be uninterrupted, and sure, and true.

The not-so-old man was not thin, but almost burly with well-defined but sleek muscles swimmers are wont to have and broad shoulders and thin waist. He hadn't swum in the sea for a long time—eighty-four days—but that didn't matter to him. He knew that once he touched salt water again and swam with sure and true strokes, his rhythm would return, and so would his luck.

There was no boy to help or encourage him, and this he regretted deeply. The boy had been taken away from him years ago by bad luck or fate or the devil—he had no way of knowing which—and he hated that with all his bones.

"The boy should be here," he often thought. "But I am just a man and cannot do anything about it. Still, there should be the boy."

The not-so-old man's mind drifted to the Cuban coast, where an old fisherman had launched his skiff in the chilly darkness before dawn, hoping to catch a fish big enough, worthy enough of his devotion: A noble fish that would break his long streak of the worst kind of luck—*salao*—that he refused to believe mirrored his advancing years and its inevitable frailty. Did the old fisherman know his hands would become so blistered and bloody he'd barely be able to hold the line taut? Did he realize that his fight against the giant marlin was in truth, a fight between his two inner selves? Did that old fisherman triumph in the end—as the story implied— or would it have been impossible for him to win simply because he hadn't had the boy by his side?

Perhaps the old man's real triumph was sailing back to the boy.

The not-so-old man pushed the car door open and climbed out of the car, his bare feet noticing the warmth of the parking lot pavement. He closed the door and then opened the back seat door and grabbed the beach towel he and his wife—now ex-wife— would lie on when they went to the beach and another towel he would use to wipe water from his face after a swim. Rolled up in the towel were goggles and blue-green latex racing swim cap. He wore cargo shorts with many pockets that were all empty except for the one that held his wallet and keys.

He closed the back seat door, and counting his steps, walked along the wooden planked walkway over the marsh grass to the beach. "... fifty-one, fifty-two, fifty-three," he mumbled under his breath. He descended the stairs to the beach and spread his blue and white striped towel on the sand between outcroppings of beaten white rocks. "This will do," he thought as he took off his T-shirt and sat on the towel. "Give it an hour and the sun will be going down and most of these people will be gone or leaving. Then I will start my swim."

He looked at the people: couples under umbrellas reading books or more likely playing on their phones; children running around teasing each other or building sandcastles or simply digging holes in the sand; teenage women in groups lounging on the jetty rocks. He watched people wade out into the gentle surf, which was really not surf at all but simply ocean water lapping the shore. This was Gulf of Mexico water, and unless a storm was brewing or the winds were unusually high, surf did not happen. He liked that. It was good water to swim in that was not unpredictable.

He saw a man and his son wade into the water, the boy no older than six or seven, and noticed they went out fairly far before it was up to the boy's chest.

The not-so-old man as a boy was no older than five or six, and his family was at a park on the north side of Long Island where you could wade out into the water seemingly for a mile before it got over your head. People from the city were always there in the summer to escape the heat since hardly anyone had air conditioning those days, and there'd be throngs of people wading out into the shallows to get to the deeper water to cool off. The not-so-old man's dad was a whale, and he was a shipwrecked sailor who found his dad's back to be his life preserver. His dad would lean forward into the water exposing his back and the not-so-old man as a boy would climb up on it and wrap his arms around his dad's neck and hang on as his dad doggy-paddled further out into the Sound.

Then his dad would call out, "You ready?" And the not-so-old man as a boy would reply, "Yes," and his dad would dive deep enough so they were both underwater for several seconds. The not-so-old man as a boy would close his eyes and hold his breath and hold onto his dad even tighter and count the seconds he and the whale were under. Finally, the whale surfaced, blowing out his blowhole, and the not-so-old man as a boy would open his eyes and take a deep breath. And he would call out in glee, "Again, Daddy! Again!" And the whale would dive again and the shipwrecked sailor would hold on. The not-so-old man remembered how smooth and slippery and warm and fleshy the whale's skin was and how safe he felt clutching onto it.

His mind kept wandering, back to the south side of the island where the true ocean met the sand, and the waves seemed to be stories high. His dad was out there now in his mind's eye, out past where the waves started crashing, floating, facing the shore, and holding his nose as a swell lifted him even higher and then let him down again. Each time a wave lifted him, he looked at the not-so-old man as a boy in mock surprise and grinned. The scene was so clear in the not-so-old man's memory—the look on his dad's face, the color of the overcast sky, the happiness and pride he felt seeing his dad do such a dangerous thing.

So it's not surprising that the not-so-old man as a boy became a swimmer and a champion swimmer at that. Crawl, butterfly, breaststroke, backstroke—it didn't matter. He accumulated medals throughout high school and college and even made it to the Olympics qualifier one year. But a slip on the wall as he flipped in his final turn cost him a second, so he didn't make it to the Olympics. All his friends and family said it was a shame and he should have gone because they knew he was good enough and one of the best swimmers there was. But time did not lie, and it would not lie to him for the rest of his life as much as he wanted it to or thought he deserved.

The sun was an inch from the horizon now, so the not-so-old man rose to his feet and pulled off his cargo pants, revealing his dark blue Speedo swimsuit. His wife would complain, saying it was just too revealing and not something an older grown man should wear, but it was the kind of swimsuit swimmers wore, and he just couldn't wear any other kind no matter how old he got. He threw his shorts on the towel and turned toward the water.

People were gathering on the beach to watch the sunset, some of them holding up their phones to take pictures of the sky. But there was a haze over the sun, and although the sky was streaked with orange, it wasn't a very pretty sunset—and not something worthy of taking a picture of and hanging on a wall. But still, the teenagers took pictures of it anyway. "They do not know any different," the not-so-old man thought.

"Now I'll start my swim," the not-so-old man said under his breath. "Everyone is looking at the sun in the west, but I will swim north-northwest so they will not notice me."

He picked up a corner of the towel and put his wallet and keys under it. "Not that it matters," he thought.

The not-so-old man had a peculiar trust in people—in humanity—despite being lied to and cheated many times in his life. In fact, he had come to the conclusion that although he was lucky in some ways—ways that proved unimportant—generally speaking, when it came to the more important things, he was not. Still, he believed that people, in general, were good. His sister once said about herself that she couldn't imagine others being unrighteous because she, herself, was not, and you tend to see in others what you are yourself. "Perhaps that is why I trust," he thought. "Or perhaps it is simply because I am lazy."

He walked down to the water and stepped into it, just up to his ankles. The water wasn't cold because it was Florida and September and wouldn't be cold for another couple of months. The gentle lapping of the water over his feet felt nice and had a rhythm to it, so it pleased him.

While he stood there, a little girl about two years old sprinted down to the water just a few yards away from him. She darted into the water up to her knees, turned around as if she had just seen a ghost, and sprinted back out of the water squealing. She stopped a few yards short of her parents reclining on a towel and looked at them briefly. Then the little girl turned and looked at the water for a couple of seconds, sprinted back into it, then turned around and darted back out, squealing again. The not-so-old man did not smile.

Instead, he turned around and went back to his towel on the sand, picked up its corner, and grabbed his wallet. He opened the wallet and pulled out a photograph, gazed at it for several seconds, and then replaced it into the wallet and then replaced the wallet under the towel. He thought to go back to his car and grab his cell phone to look at the photos he had scanned into it, but he didn't. Instead, he walked slowly back to the sea, watching the little girl as she continued to run back and forth from the water to the beach, squealing.

The not-so-old man stopped in his tracks. He turned and went back to his towel, removed the photo from his wallet, and without glancing at it this time, stuffed the photo under the elastic waistband of his swimsuit, so it pressed against his hip. He whispered to himself, "Ray Ray."

"Stop it!" he scolded himself.

When he turned around to go back to the water, he saw that the little girl had returned to her parents and all three were now busy building a sandcastle.

He walked back to the water and into it until it was up to his hips. He stretched the swim cap over his brown hair with some gray creeping up his sideburns and pulled the goggles over the cap facing backward. He didn't want them over his eyes until he got away from shore.

One short pause and he dove into the sea head first. He did the breaststroke underwater for a couple of minutes, heading directly away from the beach. Once he surfaced, he changed course to north northwest.

He crawled past the jetty and saw some of the girls still lounging on the rocks as his head turned up and down between breaths. One of the girls even stood up, waved, and called out to him.

"Always a Siren," the not-so-old man thought. "But I am too old and too tired to listen."

CHAPTER *II*

*H*e had not swum any appreciative distance for a week, and that had been in a pool doing laps. So the seawater, although making him more buoyant, was more difficult to swim in because it wasn't as flat as the water in the pool. There were very small swells—probably remnants of a wake from a boat or jet ski—with just enough slope to roll him slightly as they rolled in to shore. But soon he was in a rhythm, his mind settled, and he started not to think.

Keeping his goggles facing backward, he swam only at half speed, which was faster than most anyone else could swim at full speed. Years ago, his ex-wife—then-fiancé—would shake her head because she soon realized the not-so-old man as a young man was obsessed with speed, not just in swimming, but in almost everything he did. "You must have been a racehorse in a previous life," she would joke. "But now I am a raceswimmer," he would reply.

The not-so-old man had eaten a large meal of pasta that afternoon in anticipation of this long swim. After he failed to qualify for the Olympics and had graduated from college, he had taken to long-distance swims, mostly because he missed the competition of racing. He had even swum across the English Channel one summer. "Twenty-one miles and twelve hours of hell," he thought. "I never knew hell could be so wet." Pushing himself for distance instead of speed was his new competition. "But that will soon be over too," he thought.

He turned his head to the left instead of right to watch the sun as it sank below the horizon. Again, he noticed it was difficult to see the sun because of the haze that had accumulated right in front of it. But he saw the last sliver of it disappear.

Now, feeling no one was watching, he pulled his goggles around his head and over his eyes and changed course to due west, heading directly into the evaporating glow of the sunset. He swam the breaststroke for half an hour and then switched back to the crawl or freestyle stroke.

"The crawl uses 48 of the 639 muscles in the human body and is the most efficient stroke," the not-so-old man thought. "That's why when you see someone swimming for distance, you see them usually swimming freestyle. Then there's the breaststroke and backstroke. You don't want to do the butterfly because it's really hard on the body and uses the most calories." The not-so-old man liked thinking about swimming.

"The main propulsive muscles used during a swimming race are the latissimus dorsi, pectoralis major, and quadriceps. And you need good core muscles to pull through the water, stabilize the arm motion, and kick the legs. Those are the rectus abdominis, known as the 'six-pack' muscles. The external obliques, or side abdominals, stabilize the arm strokes, and the lower abs stabilize the kicking motion."

He felt satisfied he remembered this. The air was cooling, and the sky was getting darker by the minute. He kept swimming for another half-hour.

How far could he go? How long could he go? He pushed that out of his mind, turned himself over, and floated on his back.

"Feel the water," he said out loud. "Feel it hug you and flow around you. Feel how comforting and reassuring it is knowing you're doing the thing you do best."

The not-so-old man knew that talking would distract him. But it would also suck moisture out of him, and that would limit his swim. He stopped talking and thought his thoughts in his mind and tried to think only of swimming and the water.

But he could only concentrate on the motions of swimming for a brief time. Less than an hour later, he was talking to himself in his mind again. He thought about the land he had just left with its palm trees and mangrove swamps, flat land and beach grass, and sandy, sometimes rocky beaches that have never known snow. It was so different from the land he grew up on with its maples and oaks, soft and lush grass, gently rolling hills and rocky beaches on the north side, sandy beaches on the south, with fall and winter and spring. He wondered about who he would have been if he had grown up in Florida instead of Long Island—how the environment might have turned him into someone else and how different his life would have been.

He probably would have gone to a different college and married a different girl, and there never would have been Ray Ray or the boy who never was or the accident or divorce. If none of those things had happened, then maybe he would have been happier.

He could blame it all on where he grew up or his parents or teachers, swimming coaches, or college professors. He could blame it on things he had no control over—just a victim of circumstance or environment.

But as sure as him having brown hair and hazel eyes—things the environment had no part in creating—he knew one thing for certain: he still would have been a swimmer. He would have had swimming in his life no matter where he lived. Eye color, hair color, how big his nose was—those characteristics were always with him and went wherever he went, did whatever he did, lived wherever he lived. And the thought occurred to him that perhaps his luck was just like his hair or eyes or nose or the need to swim. It's everywhere he goes, and he can't escape it, whether it's good or not so good or just plain rotten—it would cause things in his life to be good or not so good or just plain rotten no matter where he grew up or lived or who he met or married. His luck was part of his essence, and his essence made his luck.

It was beyond his control, beyond his awareness, beyond his heart, emanating from his very being, his very soul. In a word, it was his destiny.

"But why?" he thought. "How is it part of me? Why is it destiny?"

He floated on his back.

"There are two, maybe three ways to look at this," the not-so-old man thought, hoping for a breakthrough. "It's either karma, or I'm supposed to learn lessons, or it's some sort of spiteful test. Maybe it was just meant to be, or it's genetics or fate, or it's already happened, and I'm just seeing it now…"

He looked up into the darkening night sky.

"…Maybe I'm somehow creating it all myself due to my deepest desires and twisted beliefs that it's what I really want or deserve. Maybe it's the devil working on me, or it's God abandoning me. Maybe it's just the continuation of something passed along from my father and his father and his father before that, or from my mother and her mother and her mother before that. Maybe it's about finishing some unfinished business, or I'm supposed to fumble around until I discover how to keep my thoughts right…"

The not-so-old man's head swam with the possibilities to explain and excuse his life, himself. He had never enumerated the possibilities before or realized there were so many. "And maybe it's a mixture of all of them or none of them at all." he thought. "Maybe I'm not even supposed to try and figure it out."

The not-so-old man's mind continued, "Is there a way to change your luck, your destiny? Can you change the size of your nose or the color of your eyes or your need to swim? No. The only way is to scrap it all and start from scratch—to begin anew. But to begin, you must first end."

The thought occurred to him, "And that brings me back around to where I had started, which does me no good at all."

He wished he had a radio to listen to the baseball.

An hour later, the small nimbus of light from Tampa and Clearwater Beach was insignificant, and there were no man-made lights within his range. There were no clouds, and the sky was remarkably clear since he was miles west of Florida now and over 800 miles east of Mexico, with nothing but ocean between. He shifted his goggles around, so they pointed backward, and he gazed with naked eyes at the virgin night sky above and around him for the first time in his life. It nearly took his breath away.

"Oh my goodness, God!" he whispered.

He remembered how he felt when he was a kid in a planetarium and the lights went down and a hush spread through the room and the dome above him lit up with stars. It was enthralling, captivating, and stretched his mind beyond its limit of comprehension.

But this! *This…!*

It had always been on the not-so-old man's bucket list to lie on the ground and look up at the stars from the middle of a desert. He had heard others tell how amazing and awe-inspiring it was to look up and see the Milky Way on a clear cold night when it seemed the whole world was asleep. Hearing that was one thing— but this!

This…!

He floated, moving just enough to keep his head above water. He marveled. He wondered. He pondered. He turned completely around—360 degrees—slowly, taking it all in. Then he spun around fast a couple of times to watch the stars whirl above him.

He gazed at the sky above the calm, mirror-like sea for a long time, hardly thinking at all and yet thinking more surely, more truly than he had ever thought before. He felt the *awe* deep inside—in his guts, in his bones. He felt like he was gazing into, and making contact with, the very soul of the universe. Everything was so still, so quiet, yet at the same time, it had a palpable vibration that insisted you realize what a precious gift it truly was.

"How many sailors have looked at the night sky like I am now?" he thought. "Sailors on the tall ships, waiting for the sun and sea breeze or rising tide to push them into the harbor. Sailors on fishing boats resting after a long, hot day of work. Sailors on battleships watching for the enemy and praying to make it through another night."

He noticed some of the brighter stars, "They're so bright! So clear and distinct. They're so close I could reach out and touch them!" He thrust a hand into the air as if to snatch a star out of the black sky.

"And so many! How many lights are up there? And what are they made of? Are they really other suns so far away? But they look like sparkles strewn by a magician on a glass ceiling of darkness that's just an arms-length away."

He saw a star shoot across the sky. He searched for constellations he knew. He found the Big and Small Dippers. "Easy stuff," he thought.

He remembered things from an astronomy book he had read in college: "The Big Dipper has seven stars in it and is often referred to as Ursa Major, but it also goes by the monikers Big Bear and Plough. Well, Ursa Major is the name of the brightest star of the seven, but when people hear 'Ursa Major' they automatically think of the whole constellation. But it's technically not a constellation, but an asterism, which is a group of stars smaller than a constellation. People get lazy and sloppy sometimes and lose the details amongst the devil."

His mind was churning now, remembering things he thought he had long forgotten, so it made him feel good. "Anyway, it's only visible in the Northern Hemisphere. The two outer stars of the bowl of the Big Dipper always point to Polaris—the North Star—and the North Star is always, always, always directly north of you, no matter where you are. That's the easiest way to find out which way you're going. Just find the two outer-bowl stars of the Big Dipper and see where the stars—referred to as The Pointers—point to. Once you find the bright star Polaris, which is a pole star directly over the North Pole, you're all set. You'll never be lost again.

"It's really cool because the position of the Big Dipper changes with the seasons: At midnight, in the fall (September 7), the Big Dipper is right side up and below the North Star. At midnight in the spring (March 7), it's upside down and above the North Star. At midnight in the summer (June 7), it's to the left of Polaris and points right. And at midnight in the winter (December 7), it's to the right of Polaris and points left. So if someone just came out of a coma and didn't know what season it was, all they'd have to do is look up at midnight and figure it out by seeing how the Big Dipper is oriented in relation to the North Star. And I'm sure that for anyone coming out of a coma, that's the first thing they think to do."

His mind was relaxing. He knew he was distracting himself, and he was thankful the stars were helping him do it.

"You can even tell time by watching how the Big Dipper turns around Polaris. If you pay attention, you can get pretty good. The Egyptians could predict to the second when the sun would rise based on watching the stars revolve. It's a little more complicated than the seasons, and I'm thinking hard enough as it is, you know, so I don't want to get into it right now. But it's like the song—the wheel in the sky, it keeps turning."

He focused on the Little Dipper. "The last star in the Little Dipper's handle is actually the North Star. And like I said, the North Star is always north of where you are. In fact, it's more accurate to use the North Star for navigation than a compass, since the magnetic fields vary sometimes. So there's that.

"Now here's a really cool thing they don't teach you in Geography class: You can also tell what latitude you're at by how high Polaris is above the horizon. The higher Polaris is above the horizon, the higher in latitude you are. That Jimmy Buffet song—*Changes in Latitudes, Changes in Attitudes*—that's how I remember latitude is up and down on the map rather than longitude, which is the long way around. People's attitudes change as you go from north to south—up or down latitudes: Yankee ingenuity and Southern hospitality and all that."

The not-so-old man heard the music and lyrics in his head as if he was listening to the song on a stereo. He was good at that. Some people have a photographic memory and can see things as if they were looking at them. The not-so-old man had an audiographic memory and could hear songs as if he were listening to them. But remembering the lyrics precisely—not so much…

> *I went off for a weekend last month*
> *Trying just to recall the last year*
> *All of the faces and all of the places*
> *Wondering how they all disappeared*
>
> *I didn't ponder the question too long*
> *I got hungry and went out for a bite*
> *Ran into a chum with a bottle of rum*
> *So we ended up drinking all night*

The not-so-old man thought the lyrics kinda, sort of, maybe pertained to him. But instead of trying to recall the whole year, he's trying to forget. Instead of drinkin' all night, he's swimming all night. He continued hearing...

I think about Paris when I'm drunk on red wine
And I wish I could hop on a plane
All of the nights I have dreamed of the ocean
God I wish I was sailin' again

But yesterday's over my shoulder
So I best not look back very long
There's just so much to see waiting in front of me
And I pray that I just won't go wrong

It's these changes in latitudes, changes in attitudes
Nothing remains all the same
With all of our running and all of our cunning
If we didn't laugh we might all go insane

The not-so-old man didn't laugh. Rather, the lyrics made him sad. He knew he couldn't stop himself from eventually looking back, and there was nothing but sea in front of him. He didn't have any rum or red wine to make him feel like he just couldn't go wrong, and he had concluded he was already insane. But his will to distract himself was still strong, so he made himself look up again into the night sky.

The moon was not there, or it was all black and new, or it had been swallowed up by his gloom, so he didn't see it. Instead, he looked down onto the black mirror of the sea and waited.

His eyelids were heavy—like when you've been driving too long and you have to fight yourself to keep your eyes open, because you know if you let them close, you might die. But his eyes closed anyway, and as they did, his mind latched onto thinking about his ex-wife, perhaps because their relationship ended up being not 360 degrees around, but 180 degrees opposite of what he had thought it would be. His memories of her were always bittersweet: Sweet because of her beauty and charm; bitter because of her heart and how it didn't mesh with his. There always seemed to be some kind of confrontation. Sometimes it was breathtakingly exhilarating, often gut-wrenchingly debilitating.

His eyes closed for more than a second, and his chin remained up and out of the ocean instead of dropping to his chest. He caught himself, and opened his eyes wide, and discovered his arms and legs were working automatically to keep himself afloat—like a fish beating its fins without having to think about it. So he let his eyes close again, and must have dozed off for several seconds, maybe even a couple of minutes, because he dreamed about another couple he knew of that had a similar kind of relationship...

The not-so-old man dreamed he was sitting at a bar in a bar where the air was warm and sticky and smelled like a sea breeze without the breeze and beer and sweat. He looked to his left and saw a man sitting in the last barstool beside the wall with a glass in his hand and a throng of people around him hanging on his every word. The man had a roundish, rugged face that was tanned from sun and wind, a brown mustache, and unkempt brown hair just over his ears with just a hint of peppering on the sideburns. He wore a bleached and stained cap tilted back on his head, and a khaki shirt that was weathered too with several stains scattered on it. Above his left eye was a scar just below his hairline about three inches long that was trying to fade into the rest of his forehead but hadn't yet succeeded, and probably never would.

The man proclaimed in a tipsy, boisterous voice, "We thought he was dead when we finally pulled him on board..." He took a swig of his drink, slammed the glass down on the bar, and added, "But once we got him on deck, the rascal started thrashing about like an angry tuna and was about to knock my boy out of the boat!"

His audience—typical flies you find in a typical bar—

responded with a hushed, "Uhhh... huhh."

One of the flies in the audience, who was wearing a tattered captain's hat, asked, "So what'd you do, Hem?"

"So what'd I do?" Hem responded.

"Yeah. What'd you do next?"

Hem puffed up his chest as he straightened himself in his barstool and blurted out as he slapped his hand on the bar, "I'll tell you what I did... I punched that fish right in the face!"

The barflies erupted in laughter, and a couple of them slapped Hem on his back.

As they were laughing, Hem shouted, *"... and knocked him out cold!"*

The barflies howled louder.

Just as the buzz started to wane, a blond-haired woman sitting at the bar several seats away from Hem called out above the noise, *"I doubt it!"*

The barflies were stunned. The buzzing stopped.

Hem turned to her, eyebrows raised, "And who in the world are you, little lady?" he asked calmly.

"Just a gal who's not little and who knows better."

The barflies let out a hushed, "Ooohhh..."

"And how do you know better?"

The barflies were waiting on *her* every word now...

"You're a fisherman and all fishermen lie," she said, looking him right in the eye.

The crowd was shocked. You could have heard a pin drop. Hem just looked down into his glass for a couple of seconds, then muttered loud enough for everyone to hear, "You're right. I lied. I didn't punch him in the face..." he paused two heartbeats, then shouted, *"I kicked him in the ass!"*

The barflies howled and buzzed even louder, and Hem was slapped on the back again.

Once everyone calmed down a bit, Hem said to the woman, "Come here, darlin'. Joe, give her your seat. What's your name?"

The barflies' ears pricked up again.

She didn't move. "Wouldn't you like to know."

"Yes, I would," he said sincerely. "I like feisty. What's your name? Never seen you 'round Cayo Hueso before."

The woman didn't look up from her gin and tonic but said gruffly and loud enough for everyone to hear, "Very clever, you know some Spanish."

"Si. ¿Cuál es tu nombre?"

"¿Cuál es mi nombre?"

"Si. ¿Como te llamas?"

The woman swung her hair across her face as she stood up from her stool, looked over the bar at Hem, and said over the silence of the throng, "My name...? My name is Martha. My friends call me Marti... You can call me Miss Gellhorn."

The barflies buzzed, "Ooooohhhhhh..."

Hem took the blow like a man. He punched back, "My name's Hemingway. My friends call me Papa... You can call me sweetheart."

"Aaaahhh Haaaa Haaahhhh..."

Martha sidestepped, blocked, and countered, "I can call you drunk."

"Ooooohhhhhh..."

"That may be, darlin', but I can call you..." Hem stopped mid-sentence and looked down into his glass that was now empty. The crowd was waiting on *his* every word again.

"What? What can you call me?" Martha asked indignantly, thinking she had him on the ropes.

Hem raised his head, looked her right in the eye, smiled a sly, mischievous smile, and said matter-of-factly, "I can call you a knockout."

A pause, and then... "Aaaaahhhh Haaaa Haaaahhhh..."

Martha smiled.

One of the flies watching all this jumped up on the bar, held an empty martini glass to his lips, and shouted, "Ladies and gentlemen! We have a split decision! In this corner, Hemingway with four left jabs. In that corner, Gellhorn with four right hooks! Rematch tomorrow night!"

The barflies buzzed, applauding, and laughing.

Gellhorn went and sat next to Hemingway. Papa ordered Marti a drink...

CHAPTER *III*

*T*he not-so-old man opened his eyes. He thought about the dream briefly, not giving it any significance. He had half-floated, half treaded water as he napped with no damage done. He thought it amazing, and it gave him confidence. But then he thought, "Who cares."

He had always found it interesting that his thoughts of the previous day or certain events of the recent past found their way into his dreams. He never gave much stock to dreams or that they could be messages to pay attention to like some people believe, mostly because they had never proved useful to him. But now, he didn't want to think about his ex-wife, as this dream was teasing him to do. He wanted to feel better, not worse. So he distracted himself by looking up once more.

He found the three bright stars in a straight line making up Orion's Belt, marking the waist of Orion the Hunter. He had memorized all the stars in Orion his sophomore year in college to impress a girl on a date. He told her while lying on a blanket one cool spring night, "Betelgeuse and Bellatrix mark the hunter's shoulders, and Saiph and Rige mark his knees. Orion's head is marked by the star named Meissa, and his belt, at a bit of an angle, is marked by three stars in a line: Alnitak, Alnilam, and Mintaka. Hanging from his belt is his sword, with the famous Orion Nebula as its centerpiece."

And right next door to Orion, the not-so-old man saw Taurus the Bull, which contains The Seven Sisters, also known as the Pleiades.

He saw a star shoot across the sky. It distracted him. His mind turned to himself again...

"Taurus the Bull," the not-so-old man thought. "I've been near bulls before, but not the kind with four legs. Yeah, I know what two-legged bulls can be like all too well."

Although he was a star athlete in high school and college and tough as nails, some kids thought he was a hair too smart and a touch too gentle. So they bullied him.

One time a kid pulled his books from his arms as he walked up a stairway, spilling them down to the landing. Another boy, who he thought was a friend, ripped his shorts during basketball practice. A different kid threw a basketball at him that hit him hard in the head. Then a few days later, the same kid did it again. They all laughed. In his senior year in high school, one of the 'cool kids' threatened to come to his house with a shotgun because the not-so-old man as a teenager was friendly with the thug's girlfriend.

In college, he got accused of beating up another student's girlfriend, who he had never met. Another time he came back to his dorm room to find piles of shaving cream all over his bed. He didn't think it right to retaliate. He just beat on, a boat against the current. A boat that had nearly sprung a leak.

And as it always was when he had depressing thoughts, he would feel that depression again and grow weary, and tonight, sleepy. He still had the strength to swim further, but his eyes wanted to close, perhaps to escape. It didn't make sense to him why he felt it important to get some rest, but he didn't try to figure it out. So he let his eyes close as he again stayed afloat with beating fins...

"Isn't that cute!" she cooed. "Come here, Marceline. Sit next to Ernest. I want to get a picture of you two dressed as twins."

Four-year-old Ernest was just starting to realize something wasn't right. He jumped off the couch and ran into the bathroom and locked the door. His mother was fast behind him.

"Ernest! Ernest! Open up! Come out here! Come out here this instant!"

The little boy saw himself in the mirror on the back of the door. He looked at the white, puffy, lacy dress his mother had made him wear and felt like throwing up. His little mind was confused. "She's such a pooey! Make her shut up! Make the pooey shut up!"

"You know, Ernest," his mother pleaded through the door, "This is what people do! This is the fashion. It's just for fun, Ernest. It makes your mama happy. Please come out, Ernest. Please?"

The little boy sat on the toilet, his feet not quite reaching the floor. What was he going to do? He wanted to rip the dress off and run away. "Yes, that's what I'll do!" he thought. He started to unbutton the front buttons.

"Remember, Ernest, Exodus 20:12—"

"Poo on her and all her Bible talkin'!"

"Honor thy father and thy mother: that thy days may be long upon the land which the Lord thy God giveth thee."

"Poo on her telling me what to do!"

"Ernest! Ernest! If you don't come out here by the time I count to five and sit on the couch with your sister, you won't be eating dinner tonight!"

"Poo on her making me have long hair and wear dresses!"

"One..."

"But who will feed me? Where would I go? Where would I sleep? I hate pooey!"

"Two..."

The little boy hopped down off the seat. He had no choice, really. Not yet, anyway. He wasn't quite sure about it and didn't really know what his mind was doing, but deep inside, somewhere, he was deciding to never be a girl, or be too close to a girl, and to show the world just how much of a man he really was.

"Three…"

"Poo on being her little Thweetie!" his little mind thought.

"Four…"

The little boy unlocked the door and turned the doorknob. The door sprang open right into his face, hitting him hard on the chin. His mother burst through the door, grabbed him by his hair, and slapped him on the buttocks. "Now get back on the couch and sit next to your sister... That's better... Now smile for the camera, my little Sweeeetie, my little Dutch Dolly!"

The not-so-old man's eyes opened. He knew who his dreams were about, and it didn't surprise him, and he was starting to get an inkling that these dreams were different than the ones he had while asleep in his bed on land. But that's as far as his analysis got because he was again distracted by the night sky.

The not-so-old man floated and wondered about the stars and how mankind has looked up to the night sky for centuries with the same wonder he was enthralled with now.

"They didn't have city lights to obscure the stars," he thought. "They didn't have TV or cell phones or the internet to distract or seduce them into thinking there's no need to look up and wonder. These people had to find some way to pass the time, so they looked up at the greatest show on earth and entertained each other with their imagination and stories."

So he looked at Taurus the Bull again and thought about its story.

"Taurus is the name of the bull that Zeus temporarily turned himself into to disguise himself to seduce the lovely and talented Princess Europa, daughter of Phoenician King Agenor. Just goes to show you—even gods can be suckers for a pretty face. And by the way, now you know who Europe was named after."

He kept remembering, knowing it was passing time and

keeping his mind off other things. "It's an interesting story. You see, Zeus was smitten with Princess Europa and wanted her. He wanted her bad. So he turned himself into a bull and mingled with King Agenor's herd of cattle to get closer to Europa and get her attention. Oh, what a god will do for a princess! The princess admired the bull and, when she sat on his back, he rose and headed for the sea. Zeus carried Europa all the way to the island of Crete. Once there, he did what any smitten god would do—he revealed his true identity and then lavished the princess with presents. And she took the bait.

"The two settled down in a three-bedroom ranch with a white picket fence up in the clouds on Olympus Drive and had three sons together, one of which became the king of Crete. Zeus later commemorated the bull by placing it among the stars. So that's how Taurus got up there. How's that for a story?"

He swam the backstroke. Another hour passed and he stopped swimming and just floated. He noticed the stars had shifted—having turned around Polaris as if they had turned around the hub of a wheel. He had noticed the Big Dipper turning around Polaris earlier, and even knew how to tell the time and seasons by it, but amazingly, his brain hadn't connected the dots like it was connecting them now. Now, it didn't make sense to him.

"How can the stars turn around Polaris when I'm supposed to be spinning around on a ball?" he thought. But it was undeniable. The small, barely visible glow of civilization at his feet and Polaris on his left were his reference points; and the Dippers, Orion, Taurus, The Seven Sisters, and every other star had definitely turned and turned together like they had been plastered on the underside of a beach umbrella that was slowly spinning around the hub of the North Star.

"Shouldn't they all be sweeping from east to west, just like the sun does during the day?" He wasn't angry with himself for pondering this but relieved something was keeping his attention from other things. "Must be a good reason for it," he thought.

"So because the stars are spinning around Polaris, I can tell time, direction, and season, just by looking up at the night sky. Kinda cool. What more could a caveman want?"

More swimming. Further out he went. The glow from the city lights was totally gone, and he started to feel his body a little, which was normal for not having swum a long distance for so long. It would take some time for his body to get back in the groove and realize it still had a long way and a long time to go.

He swam an easy breaststroke. "I still have plenty of energy to make it back to land," he thought. Then he laughed out loud.

He glanced at the stars again as he swam. "I wonder what it was like being a caveman, sitting around a fire outside a cave with my cavewoman wife by my side, maybe eating a roasted leg of lamb or something. After dinner, we'd sit on a bearskin or goatskin from a bear or goat I had killed the previous month using a spear, or a bow and arrow, or club, or my bare hands. And as the fire slowly died, we'd look up at these very same stars in their very same places and make up stories about the stars and who they were and she would tell me she thought they were angels watching over us. And I would say, 'I hope you are right.'

"We'd listen to the hissing of the glowing, orange embers and smell the nearby grass and feel the dew start to settle on us and maybe see some fireflies buzzing above us that almost look like shooting stars. We'd retire to the cave and its security, and I'd put the bearskin on the ground, and she would lay down, and I would lay down, and we'd cuddled together like two spoons, even though spoons had yet to be invented. I'd grab the goatskin from the bedside boulder, and drape it over my cavewoman wife and pull it over myself and then nuzzled my nose to her scalp and smell the fire in her hair and hold her close and not worry about hardly anything except if we'd survive another day or two.

"And we'd make love on that bearskin, as we did every night, not thinking there was anything wrong because making love back then gave you the feeling that you could guess what heaven would be like. Afterward, she would whisper, 'Gunga. Gunga gulunga,' which meant, 'We make cavebaby,' and I would smile. Contented, we'd drift off asleep to the sound of water dripping back in the cave, like the ticking of grandmother's clock, the faint echo telling us that the world is still here and this life is as good as it gets."

The not-so-old man lifted his head above the water and listened. It was quiet now since the sea breeze had settled with the night, and there were no waves or even swells, and the water was almost as flat as glass. There was no surf crashing against the shore and no radios from sunbathers playing in the distance; no screaming of children playing on the beach or drones of jet skis or motorboats skipping over the water; no gulls or even flying fish. "The fish must be sleeping," he thought. He closed his eyes and listened to the sea. The sea was silent and would not tell him anything.

He had noticed the calm silence hours earlier but there were small swells and ripples then and he was, for the most part, swimming and making his own noise. Then, the quiet was palpable. Now, as he motionlessly floated on his back, the silence was deafening. There were no distractions. But he wanted distraction. He kept swimming.

So he joked to himself: "Yeah... I'll be the first person to swim across the Gulf of Mexico—from Florida to Mexico. There's a little restaurant on Playa Bagdad just south of the U.S. border— *Restaurante El Pescador*. I've never been there but saw it on a map. I figure it's about an 890-mile swim. Piece of cake. *No problemo*. They'll hold a parade and I'll write a book and go on all the talk shows." He actually let out a chuckle as he swam.

"The world record for the longest ocean swim is 120.5 miles in 50 hours 10 minutes. Some guy from Croatia did it—I can't remember or pronounce his name. Fifty hours straight in the water. Over a hundred miles without touching a boat or person. So other people have done it. I swam the English Channel. I can swim the Gulf of Mexico."

The not-so-old man imagined approaching the beach—*la play*—and seeing a crowd of people waiting. There'd be tens of cameras pointing at him and pretty Spanish women news reporters with curled, bouncy black hair, and tanned, olive skin, waiting, inching closer to the water's edge as he got closer to land, holding their microphones in front of their eager lips, hoping to be the first to interview this brave and heroic man when he finally crawled out of the sea. There'd be a helicopter overhead, tracking his every move, every stroke. Once on land, he'd force himself to rise from his knees and stand on his wobbly legs to show he could, but he'd sway back and forth and begin to fall, and as he was falling, one of the women news reporters would drop her microphone and catch him in her arms—her soft and strong arms—and just before he passed out in her arms, their eyes would meet and both of them would feel the undeniable, overwhelming, and life-changing love-at-first-sight tingle that you see in the movies when it was meant to be.

Sure, there'd be some hiccups along the way—she wouldn't want to leave her family to move to Florida, and he wouldn't want to leave Florida for her family—but they would work it out. Maybe compromise to a Texas town near the border and Gulf. They would eventually get rich from all the endorsements he'd make from his world-record swim, and they'd travel the world together, and after that, maybe settle down on a Greek island or South Pacific island and have some native kids and eat coconuts.

The not-so-old man thought, "Yeah, I'll be a national

sensation. No! A *global* sensation! My achievement would be more incredible than Lindbergh flying solo from America to Europe or an old man catching the biggest marlin ever seen. It would reaffirm the courage and resiliency of the human condition. It would give people hope in achieving the unthinkable. Best of all, it would be sure and true and the best story I could write. Yes, I would show them all... and I would show *her!*"

He stopped swimming. He treaded water.

"Ray Ray," he thought. He put his hand on his hip and felt the photo. He took it out from beneath the waistband and looked at it. But it was too dark to see. He put the photo back under the elastic band. "Don't go there," he muttered. "Don't go there. You came to forget, so stop it. Don't think about her. Don't think about her. Stop it! Think of the stars. Look up and wonder about the stars again. That will distract you."

But when he tilted his head back to look at the stars, they were gone. Clouds had gathered and they were blocking the stars and the light they had been casting down on the sea. This intimidated him. He thought that a dark veil had been lowered on him which he had no control over. It would be the kind of omen the Greeks would have paid attention to, he thought.

"But the rhythm... The rhythm will restore my luck."

He resumed swimming, this time the elementary backstroke. Gliding on his back, he looked up at the sky, hoping to see a star poke through the clouds. But a star did not shine. Instead, all he saw was darkness.

He felt some rhythm return as he swam on his back. "Rhythm. The rhythm is my friend, my luck. Get in the rhythm. Then you won't have to think. Feel the water flow over your shoulders, across your skin, down your back, along your sides, and down your chest and belly. Feel the water resist as you kick with your legs and pull with your arms.

"Feel your legs kick through the liquid, the sensation of skin gliding through fluid. Feel your lungs expand with air and your diaphragm push it out once it's spent. Feel yourself shoot headlong through the sea, the deepening sea.

"Sometimes it's so easy not to think when I swim," he thought. "There's too much to feel about—too much to feel. Maybe that's why..."

He stopped abruptly and treaded water. Someone else might have taken it for granted, but he had never realized it before: "Maybe that's why I swim. I don't have to think about or *feel*, other things. Other things that pain me. Things that would make me sick to my stomach, sick to my heart, sick to my reason for being. Maybe I swim because... I... can't... handle... it."

His cheeks turned red. "I started this swim to forget her and the him who never was. I've been yelling at myself to stop thinking of the bitter, to forget my mistake, to keep my attention on my swimming and other sweet things."

He felt a creeping feeling inside, like an itch he couldn't scratch. The sea was still quiet, and the silence made the itch more pronounced. And as much as he didn't want to, he pushed himself to scratch.

"Swimming has almost been an obsession, maybe even an addiction. Some said it was, and for a very long time. It's an easy way to avoid things. It's an easy way to forget that I'm not number one in everything. An easy way to keep obnoxious people out of my life. It's an easy way to deny that my dad couldn't handle my mom. An easy way to make the pain, the heartache, of just about anything fade into the background. Being a *good* swimmer was really just an accident—I would have swum just as often and hard even if I had finished last."

He kept treading water. The sea waited.

"I don't want to face it, but now I have nothing to lose. All the pain will be gone soon anyway. This one time, I'm going to dive in and face it head-on. For once, I have to be true."

The not-so-old man's mind raced wildly forward—like he had taken one small step out of a forest and saw a clear open field unfold before him. "You swim not just for the exercise and not just for the competition. You swim to avoid facing the horror of your life."

It was like a cold, heartless slap across his face. He was stunned because he knew it was true. The silence of the sea kept egging him on...

"But even more than that, I obsess to avoid facing the obvious facts that life is deep and stormy and far from perfect; and I'm afraid of the deep, the stormy and the less than perfect. I've been afraid of it all my life, and never more so than after the accident. I swim because I'm afraid it might get too deep."

The not-so-old man kept treading water.

"Maybe life isn't a test like so many gurus and religions teach. Maybe you're not here to learn lessons, but simply..."

He spun around in the water to see if he could see the glow of lights on shore that he knew were no longer there.

"...simply to see how much crap you can handle. Maybe you get to heaven in one simple way," he thought. "You get to heaven if you can recognize hell and face it truly." He paused and stopped kicking when he heard his mind say, "And that hell is right behind your eyes."

CHAPTER *IV*

*H*e turned onto his back and swam the elementary backstroke.

"You hear that, ocean? You hear that sea? I heard your silent whispers. I heard you whispering behind my back, taunting me with your silence. Well, I did it. I see it. I understand. I've been weak and that made me miserable. It made my luck *salao*. Very *salao*. Fortune favors the bold, and I wasn't bold. I was weak. I was afraid. I turned my back on the truth by swimming away from it and then thought I was being brave in my swimming. But I can't fool you. I can't fool the sea. I get it. I get it. I did it and gave you what you asked for with your sneaky little whispers. So are you happy now? Are you? So just stop your whispering and leave me alone."

He floated on his back for a few minutes and then resumed swimming. But this time, he swam not to distract himself and forget; he did it because he loved it.

"Movement. Revel in the movement. Concentrate on the stroke. Make each stroke better than the last. That is what perfection is. Better than the last. Better than what came before. Each stroke more true to itself."

He noticed his strokes; how his body worked virtually automatically since he had been doing this for decades.

"The stroke. Sure and true. Each stroke better than the last. Each stroke more true to itself."

He swam for another half-hour on his back, hoping again for a ray of starlight to poke its little head through the clouds. But that ray didn't come.

"How do you do this? How is this stroke performed?" he asked. "Describe it to someone who's never swum before. Tell them how it's done."

He looked all around his field of vision, hoping to see light from a boat or ship. But there was no boat or ship.

"Okay. Here. Start by floating on your back with your legs stretched out and your feet together. Bend your elbows so your hands come up to your armpits. At the same time, bend your knees like you're a frog getting ready to jump."

The not-so-old man did this himself as he looked straight up into the black sky.

"Then thrust your arms out to your side and up so they look like a 'Y' while at the same time spreading your legs apart and straightening them."

He did this too making sure his form was correct.

"Now cup each hand with your fingers together and thrust your arms down to your sides, like you're doing a snow angel, and at the same time, bring your legs together fast."

He felt himself glide smoothly forward in the sea.

"That's right! That's it! That's how you do it, Ray Ray!"

His face flushed, his eyes watered. "Ray Ray! Oh, Ray Ray…"

The not-so-old man recoiled from his thoughts, "No! No! Not that! I can face many things, you stupid ocean, but I can't face that. So send me to hell if you want. I don't care. I can't think of her again. Stop it! Stop it! Stop it! I don't care about truly. I don't care about facing things. I don't care about heaven. I just want to take it back."

He started swimming freestyle as if he was in a race. He swam as hard as he could. When Ray Ray wouldn't leave his mind, he stopped and slapped himself across the face. It stung. He did it again. It stung again. He'd rather beat up his body than suffer his soul. He slapped again. It hurt again. He felt sorry for himself again. He slapped himself again. It hurt again. His right hand cramped for a couple of minutes. The pain drew his attention. He finally stopped thinking of Ray Ray.

His body was tiring. He expected it and even welcomed it. But his mind—his mind was weakening too. This bothered him. He had to be strong. He had to be a strong man who could push through the pain with his mind, his will.

"Pain is nothing," he thought. "Pain is nothing. Dying is nothing..."

He floated on his back.

"Pain is nothing. Dying is nothing. Will is everything."

A star poked its little head through the clouds for just an instant—just a flash of starlight. At least he believed he saw a flash of starlight.

"Remember," he thought, "A man can be destroyed, but not defeated."

His eyes closed as he floated, making little difference to what his eyes perceived since the stars were blocked by the heavy cloud cover. His arms and legs moved like fins again as he fell into a light doze...

He dreamed of the same man—Hem, Papa—younger and less worn than before, walking down a Parisian street pulling a hand cart filled with household and personal items. There were tears in his eyes that hadn't made them out of their corners yet, and he stared down at the sidewalk, sniffling now and then, as he trudged along. He mumbled, "Bumby. Bumby. Oh, Bumby. . ."

The items in the cart belonged to his wife and son, who had just left him. He was taking them to their new apartment five blocks from where they had all lived happily together until a few days ago. He and his wife had just been to Pamplona for *La Fiesta de San Fermín* with its traditional running of the bulls, bullfights, and wild parties. But the *fiesta* turned *pesadilla* when, during the second-to-last bullfight, Hem's wife announced she was leaving him. She had realized she was no match for the other woman—a friend of theirs—her husband was seeing. She wasn't going to be someone she wasn't, she said and left him standing on the platform once their train returned them to Paris. Hem mumbled, "Hadley. Hadley. Oh, Hadley… "

A tear plopped onto the sidewalk.

Hem turned a corner, the cart's wheels squeaking and looked up to see his three-year-old son break away from his *nourrice* and run to him. The boy called out, "Papa! Papa!" and ran into his arms. Hem hoisted him above his head and laughed, but the boy knew better.

"Pourquoi pleures-tu Papa?"

"Je me grattai la main. Voir?"

"Oh, Papa. Je vais vous aider."

The boy ran back into the building and returned with a bandage. He placed it over the small cut on the back of Hem's hand, and said, "Voir! Tout au mieux!"

Hem was on his knees, at the same level as his son, and cried even harder.

Bumby said, "Papa. Ne pleure pas. Maman pleure aussi. Elle est triste aussi."

Hem gave Bumby a hug. The boy said, "Je t'aime, Papa. La vie est belle avec Papa."

Hem's heart was melting fast, so he got busy. He brought the clothes and toys and a painting he had bought his wife that she liked up to their new apartment. She thought it best she not be there.

However, she had previously told Hem she would give him a chance to save their marriage: If he and the other woman stayed apart for one hundred days, and he discovered his infatuation gone, she would take him back. If he still couldn't live without her, she would divorce him. She even wrote it out as a contract and had both of them sign it. He was on his honor.

He watched his wife sign it. She held the pen out to him. He took it in his hand, looked down at the paper, felt a chill shudder through his body, and felt faint as he signed his name.

The not-so-old man shivered himself and opened his eyes. "Ernie. Ernie. Oh, Ernie… " he thought. "Poor old Ernie."

The water wasn't cold, and he wasn't cold despite the awakening shiver. Before he had started his swim—while waiting for the sun to set—he had covered himself with his own blend of porpoise oil and duck grease formulated to keep his body heat in his body instead of allowing it to be sucked out by the sea. Although the air temperature was close to 90 degrees F and the water temperature about 80 when he started his swim, he knew that was an illusion to his body. He knew that staying in the water long and into the night, the drop in temperature would cause his body to work too hard to stay warm. And if the body used energy to stay warm, it couldn't use it to swim.

He was hungry and thirsty but not too hungry or thirsty. He had experienced hunger and thirst in the past, and what he was feeling now was nothing.

It was years—twenty-one—years ago. Ray Ray had been gone for over two years, but that loss still stung as if it had happened thirty seconds earlier. He tried drinking his heartache away, getting drunk every night for a month. That didn't help because the buzz just made him slip into remembering his mistake more deeply. He watched movies late into the night, making him irritable at work and almost costing him his job. He bought a motorcycle and dirt bike and rode them like a bat out of hell without a helmet on. He tried rock climbing, hoping to make a fatal slip. He even dabbled in drugs—weed, blow, opioids.

Nothing worked. His wife watched his downward spiral without so much as a whisper of disapproval.

And the boy—losing him hurt just as much. But that wasn't his fault. It was nobody's fault. It was just stupid life. He could forgive himself for that, as much as he regretted it, but he would never forgive God.

So he did an about-face and tried to get healthy. He reasoned that maybe being of sound mind and body would at least give him the strength to carry on. He gave up meat, drank gallons of vegetable juice, grew his own garden and fruit trees. He went to doctors, chiropractors, got massages, suffered in sweat lodges, hiked in the mountains, worked out like a madman, and swam every day. He practiced karate and even got a black belt. And then he fasted. Like Moses fasting forty days and forty nights, he fasted fourteen days and nights straight, eating no food at all. But he didn't receive tablets with commandments or divine inspiration from God or Jesus or even Buddha or Mohammed. Going without food just made him look like a concentration camp survivor.

When none of that helped, he doubled down. He fasted again, but this time without drinking any water. That's called 'dry fasting,' and it's supposed to fix anything. But it didn't mend his heart. The only thing he learned that was of any use at all was that he could handle those things without dying. But he could not forget.

So now he swims to forget. "And maybe," the not-so-old man had reasoned, "if I forget, perhaps, I'll be forgiven."

Just then, he heard something—a swoosh in the water off his starboard bow. It wasn't close, but it was undeniable. And he knew what it was: A dorsal fin poking through the surface.

"I prefer you leave me alone," he whispered. "Dying is nothing, and you're just too stupid to realize it. But I've had enough pain in my life, so just let me die in peace." He wished he had a broken oar or rudder handle to beat the shark—the *galanos*—to death. But he didn't have a broken oar or rudder handle. All he had was his Speedo swimsuit, swim cap, goggles, and a soaking wet photograph of his baby-girl. And those would not help kill a shark.

"But if you must, if that's the way it has to be, bring it on. I will fight you with my bare hands and feet until one of us is dead. So bring it on, you spawn of the devil."

He didn't hear the fin again that night. At least, not in reality.

As the not-so-old man floated, he let his eyes close. He didn't nod off, but two poignant feelings surfaced in his disturbed mind anyway: He feared the shark, yes, but immediately remembered his dad's back.

He opened his eyes with a start, "Uhhhggg."

He remembered those thoughts and the feelings they evoked in the order they had come and realized how contradictory they were—one frightening, one reassuring. But that didn't surprise him. He was a Pisces, and the sign of Pisces is two fish swimming in opposite directions. Often he felt like his arms were tied to horses that were pulling him apart at the seams.

"Yeah," the not-so-old man thought, "I remember astrology. I remember it seemed to make some sense. I remember the shrinks, the psychics, the Gypsies, the Tarot, the hypnosis, and past life regressions. I remember the numerology, burning sage, placing crystals around my house, rearranging the furniture, and painting the bedroom a different color. It was all so inviting, so hopeful. Some of it rang true, and when things didn't work, there was always a plausible excuse. But even a broken clock is correct twice a day. They claimed it was all for enlightenment. But it was all for nothing."

When he saw his marriage falling apart, after Ray Ray and the boy who never was were gone, was when he became so desperate.

He tried everything to reconcile, to placate his wife, but the harder he tried, the more she shunned him. He spent a year sleeping on the couch. Then he fixed up the backyard shed so he could sleep in it and spent most of his time there, which proved to do nothing to improve their relationship. He even had cause to suspect her of having an affair. With that, he bought a little house on the other side of town without telling her.

"And just to show you, when I told her I bought a house and was moving out the next week, what did she say? She said, 'What'd you do that for?'"

The not-so-old man laughed out loud. "*What'd I do that for? What do you mean, 'What'd I do that for?'* You've been nagging me to get out of your life for almost two years! You blame me for something I regret even more than you, and you blame me for your heartache. I can't take it anymore, and I'm filing for divorce."

The not-so-old man believed he was justified. He reasoned that if she wanted him only when he was leaving, he'd never be able to satisfy her. "They only want you when they can't have you," he muttered.

But the not-so-old man wasn't that angry with his ex-wife. After all, as Scotty said, a woman's angst isn't always understood. "She was in hell too," the not-so-old man thought.

"Are you going to keep thinking?" he mumbled as he started side-stroking. "I told you, you came here to forget, so stop it! Concentrate on the movement. The next stroke better than the last. The next stroke more true to itself."

But he knew more thinking was inevitable. He knew that as his mind weakened from the lack of food and water and the exertion of staying afloat he would slowly lose control. But he reasoned to himself—as his sensei would tell him—"The nobility is in the try, not the do."

The not-so-old man had been in the water for almost ten hours. He stopped the sidestroke and floated on his back with eyes closed, trying desperately not to think. He listened to his breath and tried to feel his heart beat against the water, but he couldn't feel it.

He closed his eyes and saw the darkness and tried to study it. It was hard work keeping his mind from thinking of other things. He had practiced meditation seriously for several months years ago and he knew it helped settle not just his mind, but his life. Why he didn't make it a life-long habit, he did not know. The state he would get into when meditating was almost as calming as when he swam in competition: focused, attentive, consuming, unconcerned with outcome.

It was all about quieting the bossy mind so the whispering mind could poke its little head through the clouds. It was about forgetting the past for a while and not worrying about the future for a while and staying in the present—the now.

"Oh, now, now, now, the only now, and above all now, and there is no other now but thou now and now is thy prophet."

He could tell how well he was swimming by how focused and calm he was, and he would know before he touched the final wall if he had won the race or not. He was pleased when he won, even joyful, but he didn't feel like it was really him who had done it. It was, he said, kind of a buzz kill because doing it actually felt better than winning it.

"Is that truthful enough, Ernie?" he thought.

He feared trying to meditate now might relax him enough to cause him to nod off again, and he was getting a little weary of the dreams. So he started swimming again, this time, the backstroke, and concentrated hard on it for the next half-hour. Then the not-so-old man, as much as he was trying not to, thought again of his ex-wife.

"We met when I was studying for my MBA," he thought. "She was the prettiest girl in class, and once I saw her, I was smitten. One day after class, we happened to be going down the same staircase. She was a few steps below me. Without thinking, I caught up to her and said, 'It's about time we met. My name is Daniel.' She looked up at me and smiled. 'My name is Valerie. So nice to meet you.'"

The not-so-old man as a young man was usually not so direct, so self-assured. He took that as a sign that it was meant to be. She was part French, and you couldn't tell it when she spoke English, but when she spoke French, it was obvious where she'd been raised. He could still see her wearing one of his T-shirts, talking to her mom on the phone all curled up on his bed, almost in the fetal position. Her accent was sexy, seductive, infectious—and it infected him.

"Once we were married and after the accident, things reached a new low, a new tension. So I started grasping at straws, and thus, my escape into the occult. That's how I met Swami Jethro, a self-proclaimed expert in numerology, and told him I was having problems with my wife. "Let's run the numbers and see what in 'tarnation's goin' on!" Swami Jethro said.

"You see, it ain't no wonder y'all are always buttin' heads," he told the not-so-old man as a middle-aged man. "Both of you are 'one' life-paths. That means you both need to be number one in most every doggone thing you do. Both of you are always scratchin' and clawin' to be on top—King of the Hill—so to speak. It's how you're both wired, and it's not something y'all can change."

The not-so-old man as a middle-aged man had to agree with the swami. It explained his drive to win every race and be the number one producer in his business, and it explained his and Valerie's dissonance. He felt something wasn't right after they married. In fact, the first time he had felt it was on their wedding night.

He stopped swimming and floated on his back.

They had made love many times before their wedding night, mostly in the traditional missionary position. That was how he liked it the best and how he thought Valerie liked it. But after he had carried his new bride across the threshold into the hotel's honeymoon suite and after they had rolled around on the sheets for a while, she essentially insisted she end up on top. The not-so-old man as her husband relented, but it became a habit, and it made him increasingly uncomfortable.

"What's the big deal?" he thought at the time. "So what? You still love her, don't you? Get over it. Be a man, for Christ's sake, and let her be up there if she wants." But as he stuffed his emotions for this one thing, he found himself holding back his affection in others. That was his revenge.

"Neither of us wanted to admit we had made a mistake, so we avoided talking about anything of importance. It got to a point we hardly ever argued and hardly ever laughed. Sometimes there was such a stifling superficiality about us that I felt like I had been gagged and shackled."

He kept going backward in time in his mind about his ex-wife: "I should have known there was something not quite right from the very beginning. She was pretty and alluring, that's for sure, but she had something peculiar about her. She wouldn't say, 'How are you today?' or even a simple, 'Hello,' or any other normal greeting when we saw each other. She would say, 'So how are *we* doing today?' Sometimes even in a British accent. Other times I'd ask her how she was doing, and she'd say, 'Valerie's doing just fine,' or 'Valerie doesn't feel good today.' I know it's not a big deal. There are stranger things people do. But when someone talks in the third person, I get suspicious. Why must they be so different?

"She would slip into the third person now and then, especially after she had a glass of wine or got excited about something. It's just one of those things that bug me. Funny how a little thing like that can be such a big deal. Yeah, relationships aren't so much about liking the things someone does, but not having to put up with things they might do that you just can't stand."

The not-so-old man stopped swimming, treaded water for a few seconds, then spun around to see if any part of the horizon was getting lighter. He didn't notice any change to the dark sky.

"So I looked it up. You can look up just about anything these days real easy. Used to be you'd have to go to a library and thumb through a card catalog and ask a librarian for help. Anyway, I looked it up and found out that people who talk in the third person tend to be narcissistic. And in a back-assward way, they're trying to command your respect. They're adding weight to what they're saying to detach themselves from reality because they can't face their deepest emotions. They perceive themselves as a larger-than-life character, yet, if forced to talk in the first person, emotions might erupt that would ruin them."

The not-so-old man resumed swimming, now doing the breaststroke.

"It's like someone writing in all capital letters. That's annoying as hell. It could mean, and it kinda looks like, the person is shouting. He writes that way for emphasis, so people will hear what he's saying. But it means more than that. I looked it up on the computer thingy a while back—didn't even have to go to a library or ask someone. I just asked the computer thingy.

"So all capital writing means that the PERSON IS HIDING SOMETHING and they don't want anyone to KNOW ANYTHING ABOUT THEM! Did you like that? Did you like me shouting like that? I can be a jokester sometimes. Ray Ray loved it. My wife, not so much."

The not-so-old man realized he was tired and was talking like he used to when he got drunk. But it felt good. It always felt good to babble on with no restraints, even to nobody, as unmanly as it might appear.

"Have you ever noticed that advertisements on TV or in magazines or whatever most of the time use ALL CAPITAL LETTERS? Sure, they're doing it for emphasis, to command attention. But perhaps they're doing it to hide the fact that in reality their product or service SUCKS or is OVERPRICED.

"Did you know they've done studies that prove it's more difficult to READ ALL CAPITAL LETTERS! That's right. A capital letter usually comes after a period, and a period is a stop sign to the brain because it signifies the completion of a thought. When your mind sees a capital letter, it's accustomed to pausing between thoughts. Just a fraction of a second, but that's still a pause. So in CAPITAL, the brain actually pauses seven times. In Capital, just once. It's just faster.

"But maybe these advertising people know all this and just want to make your eyes hurt. Speaking of hurt...

"Back to what I was saying about my wife: She would say, 'So Valerie wants to know, how was *our* day, sweetie?' Like dragging nails across a chalkboard. I should have just walked away then. But we had already made love (with me on top) and that was so amazing, I let the chalkboard thing slide. Bad idea.

"Sometimes it got so bad that I started looking for other women to talk to just so I wouldn't have to hear that third person whine. I never cheated on her, but can't say I didn't think about it.

"Don't get me wrong, we had some good times: That cruise around the Caribbean, vacation at the Outer Banks, Miami, Key West, and Clearwater Beach when Ray Ray was just a tyke. It wasn't a vacation unless there was an ocean involved..."

The not-so-old man turned over onto his back and floated. His eyes closed again and fell into a half-sleep as his arms and legs worked involuntarily to keep himself afloat.

He half-dreamed, half thought about: swimming the length of Skaneateles Lake; swimming the English Channel; fighting the crashing waves on the Outer Banks; his first swimming lesson in the community pool; his boyhood room; summer vacation on Virginia Beach; swimming in the Nationals; holding Ray Ray. Memories mixed with wishes floated before his eyes. They all seemed so real, so important.

He opened his eyes. The sky had lightened behind him, but the sun was still not rising.

"Ray Ray," he whispered. "I promised not to think of you. But I will think happy thoughts of you now, so that's okay."

He thought of her on their vacation to Clearwater Beach when she was just a year-and-a-half as he noticed the smallest sliver of sun poke over the horizon.

"It was Rachel's first time on a beach and she couldn't have been happier..."

It was a cool, breezy April day and the beach was virtually deserted. His wife was getting her hair and nails done, so the not-so-old man was in charge of his daughter. Ray Ray was dressed warmly in a pink and white sweatshirt with her swimming suit underneath and a little pink knit stocking cap. The not-so-old man as a young father carried her in his arms from the parking lot to the sand, put her down, and let her go.

She sprinted ahead on her little bowed legs without thought or care, squealing a little in delight. She ran. Just ran.

The not-so-old man as a young father followed a few steps behind and didn't yell at her or admonish her—there was nothing there that could harm her. Ray Ray saw a gull and ran after it, causing it to take flight and fly away. She paused briefly, watching, and then started running again.

The not-so-old man treaded water. The sky was getting brighter as the full sun was now visible just slightly above the horizon.

He reached down and pushed his fingers under the elastic band of his Speedo and found the photo. He remembered Ray Ray running on the beach to a playground off to its side: A teeter-totter, a slide, and swings. The not-so-old man as a young father picked her up and lowered her into the plastic cup-like swing made for babies and toddlers. Ray Ray looked confused for a moment—she had never been on a swing before.

"Ready?" the not-so-old man as a young father called out. Ray Ray giggled.

The not-so-old man held the picture of Ray Ray in front of himself, taken at the apex of one of the arcs of her swing. Her face—with its little button nose and tiny giblet teeth amongst full pink gums and puffy baby cheeks and her stocking cap crooked across her forehead, almost covering a dark brown birthmark on her right temple—was as happy a face you'd ever see, beaming in delight as the swing swung up and down.

The not-so-old man gazed at the photo and thought, "This must be heaven."

The not-so-old man as a young father picked her out of the swing and put her on the ground. Immediately, she started running again, this time straight toward the ocean.

He caught her before she got to the water's edge. He asked her if she wanted to go into the water. The child pulled him closer to the water.

"Okay, okay," he said. "Here, let me take off your sweats and cap. It's not too cold. You can see what the ocean feels like."

He picked her up and dangled her over the water for a few seconds as she mumbled in anticipation, "Uh, uh, uh."

The not-so-old man as a young father lowered her into the water, her legs kicking. Ray Ray squealed a little louder, "Uh, Uh,

Uh."

The water was cold but not that cold, but that didn't matter to the little girl. Once her feet met the sand below the water, she pulled her dad until the water was up to her waist.

The not-so-old man as a young father was delighted. "She's an adventurous one, that's for sure," he thought. He felt satisfied that she trusted him enough to push herself to the limit knowing he would save her if needed.

"It's going to be a blast watching you grow up," he told her. She kept trying to get further into the water. "I'll teach you all sorts of things and protect you and love you forever," he said.

The not-so-old man kept looking at the photo, tears in his eyes. "Stop it," he muttered. "What's done is done."

It hurt too much. He put the photo back under the elastic waistband over his hip. The image was burned into his brain, however, and all he had to do was think of it and it would appear in his mind's eye and he would feel happy to see her and crushed that he never would again. He swam the breaststroke, trying to get her image out of his mind. He looked across the horizon for boats or ships. There were no boats or ships.

CHAPTER V

*H*e turned to the sun on the eastern horizon and swam the sidestroke so he could watch the sun rise higher into the sky. "Looking over the sea, over the flatness with no hills or valleys, the horizon, they say, is..." He paused, trying to recall the formula for figuring out how far the horizon is, knowing that it depends on how high the observer is: The higher you are, the further you can see.

He used to know the formula—he learned it years ago when he first started long-distance swimming in lakes to prepare for swimming the English Channel. He thought since there were no waves or even swells as he was swimming now, he'd be able to see the farthest horizon possible.

He wondered if Ernie ever knew the formula. "Are you kidding?" he thought. "Ernie knew everything. He probably knew it because it helped him figure what trajectory to set the big guns at to bomb behind enemy lines. He knew it to figure out how long it would take him to sail to the best deep-sea fishing spots. He knew it to figure how far the next mountain peak was so he could decide whether to climb it to ski down it the next morning.

"Ernie had a mind 'like a rat trap,' his son Patrick said and remembered stuff like it happened yesterday. He could recall whole conversations that took place years before at the drop of a hat. And he read voraciously—and I mean voraciously—since he was a youngster. His sister Marcelline said she and he read the classics like Dickens, Thackeray, Stevenson, Kipling, and Shakespeare that adorned the shelves in their home. They both read Horatio Alger in the third and fourth grades. Reading was a daily ritual for him, and for most of his life, Ernie read at least a book a day and several newspapers. He would take a duffle bag of books with him on trips. In addition, he could speak four languages, and I don't believe he ever took a lesson. Having a mind like a rat trap helps in that regard too. Yes, sir. A good memory helps you know a lot of stuff. It helps a lot.

"So, what's the formula, dummy? Prove to me you know stuff." The not-so-old man paused.

"Okay… It's something times the square of the distance in meters... Something. What's that something? Wait! I remembered it by thinking it had something to do with prime numbers, even though it doesn't. Prime numbers... The prime numbers are 2,3,5,7,11,13... Now I remember! It's 357. But not really 357. It's 3 *point* 57. That's how I remembered it!" The not-so-old man was proud he remembered.

"It's 3.57 times the square of the distance in meters to get how many kilometers away the horizon is. So as I'm swimming here my eyes are just a few inches above the sea. How many meters is that? Maybe point one meter? Then what's the square of point one meter? But I want it in feet. There's 3.28 feet in a meter..."

The not-so-old man's mind wasn't working well enough, and he knew it. "Aw hell. Let's just ball-park it. After all, it'll be close enough for government work." He laughed in his mind because his dad used that expression, and he had worked for the government.

"Anyway, let's just say my eyes are one meter above the surface. The square of one is one. So one times 3.57 is 3.57. So the horizon, when I'm one meter above the surface, is 3.57 km away.

"Now let's get that to miles. I don't like kilometers. I don't like the metric system at all. I don't care if they use it in France or Spain, or even Cuba. It's silly. It might be more efficient, but I don't care. I was raised on the British system of weights and measures, and that's good enough for me. Why can't the rest of the world think like I do, in feet and miles and pounds and cups? People are stupid. If only I were king..." He kept looking at the horizon and the rising sun as he swam the sidestroke.

"Aw, shut up about the metric system. You whine too much. Just use your brain and figure it out. And why do you do this to yourself anyway? Who cares how far the horizon is. Does it really matter? Is it going to bring world peace if you know how far away it is? What difference does it make?"

But his mind wouldn't let it go. "This is not so hard, dude," he scolded himself. "Figure it out. A kilometer is less than a mile, but more than half a mile." He kept swimming the sidestroke as his mind searched for the conversion number. "It's something like point 6 something. Yeah, now I remember—point 62 something. Close enough. Close enough.

"So it's 0.62 times... Uh... what was the first number I figured?"

His mind was grinding now. But he knew it was okay because it made the time go faster and took his mind off his swimming and distracted him from the pain he was trying to forget.

"Oh yeah. That prime number thing—3.57. So 3.57 times... uh... point 62."

The not-so-old man shook his head. "Where's my calculator? Where's my phone with the calculator in it? Where's technology when you need it?"

His mind drifted again: "I remember when I was a kid, I saw this thing on Johnny Carson with these Korean girls who used their fingers somehow to do simple math and they challenged Johnny that they could figure things out like adding and subtracting and even multiplication and division faster than he could on a calculator. It's called Chisenbop math. Funny the things you remember sometimes.

"So they gave these girls some problem like 234 times 456 or something, and sure as spit, they figured it out faster than Johnny on a calculator. The audience went wild. Of course, Johnny's jaw dropped and he looked like he had just swallowed a cat.

"The girls told everyone how to do it, and I knew how to do some of it for a while. But I had a calculator in college, so I grew dependent on that and soon forgot the Chisenbop. But it's wild what you remember sometimes."

There was almost a smile on the not-so-old man's lips now.

"But enough of that. I'm gonna figure out how far the horizon is in miles if it kills me. I've got all day to do it, and what else is there to do?"

The not-so-old man imagined writing the numbers 3.57 above 0.62 with a line underneath on a chalk-board and started figuring: "Two times seven is fourteen, carry the one. Two times five is ten plus the one is eleven, carry the one. Oops, now what was that first number again? Three, or was it..."

This went on for a good fifteen minutes as he kept forgetting some of the numbers and had to start over several times. But eventually, he got it, or thought he had.

"Two point two one! Two point two one!" he yelled out in a dry, hoarse voice. "The horizon I'm looking at is roughly, ball-park, close enough for government work, 2.21 miles away!"

"How do you like me now, Ernie?"

The not-so-old man felt better—the best he had felt since he left his house the day before when he headed to the beach. In fact, he felt better than he had for several weeks. He was proud, but should he be? It was something simple. Very simple.

"The simple things in life," he thought. "Simplify. Simplify."

Then, "Wait a minute there hot-shot. When I stand on the beach at the park, I can easily see the high-rise buildings on Clearwater Beach. I measured that once on the computer map, and they're about five, maybe six miles away. How can that be if the horizon is only two or even three miles away? Isn't the horizon supposed to be as far away as you can see? And I've even seen the bottoms of the buildings, not just the tops when I use my binoculars or zoom in with my camera."

He pondered this for a while. It bothered him. Then he dismissed it, "Well, I guess I may be farther away from land than I thought. So I've got that going for me, which is nice."

He turned his attention to the sky. It was turning bluer with every minute as the sun climbed.

"No matter, No matter. I'm not turning back anyway. I still want that parade and those talk shows."

The not-so-old man knew that he was further from land than just a few miles. He hadn't seen the light of a boat, and he knew he was swimming west because he tracked himself using Polaris at night and the sun as it rose.

He remembered it took him about twelve hours to swim the twenty-one miles of the English Channel. Now he'd been swimming west and floating to rest sometimes for over twelve hours. If he had swum about seventy-five percent of the time, he figured he was at least sixteen miles from land.

So he knew his goal for this swim was going to happen no matter which direction he swam. He knew that his fantasy of swimming across the Gulf of Mexico wasn't only a crazy fantasy, but just another distraction. He wasn't sad and didn't regret. He was just a little shocked that what he set out to do was going to be realized no matter what: He was going to die alone in the sea.

"There are worse ways to go," he thought. He kept swimming west.

He thought of his marriage again, then quickly remembered his dad and what he endured. But endure it he did. His dad explained to the not-so-old man as a middle-aged man that once he made a promise and commitment, he would never break it. "What's done is done," his father said. "I knew what I was getting into, and I stand by my word."

The not-so-old man as a middle-aged man admired his dad for his fortitude, but couldn't understand why keeping a promise that proved to be obsolete was so important. So after the not-so-old man had finally divorced his wife, he felt a little guilty. But just a little. "Dad never had to endure what I have," he reasoned.

The not-so-old man thought as the sun climbed, "It's all prideful ego. My dad had his pride that he would never waver. The old man had his pride that he was born to fish. And I have my pride that I was born to swim."

In the past, he had swum to see how fast he could go, and later, how far he could go. This time he was swimming to see how long he could last. "But what good is a record if no one hears about it?" he thought. "If a tree falls in the forest and nobody hears it, does it make a sound? If a crazy person sets the record for lasting the longest in the sea before he drowns, and nobody knows about it, does he hold the record?"

He stopped swimming and treaded water. "It'll all be over very soon, Daniel. So stop your worrying. Nothin' to worry about. It's over. It's as good as over. Gotta get out of here. Say goodbye to Mom. Say goodbye to Dad. Say goodbye to Sis. Say goodbye to Valerie. Say hello to Ray Ray and the boy who never was."

The not-so-old man floated on his back. He saw the full sun high in the sky. "It's over..." lingered in his mind. "Gotta get out of here." His fins kept moving, his chin stayed up, his eyes closed...

"Hey, Ernie! Wait up!" the teenage boy called out.

Ernie slowed but didn't stop walking. When the boy had caught up to him, the boy said, "Pheww! Man! What a day, huh? Can you believe it? It's over! We're finally done with school! Yessiree,

Bob! It's all over! We graduate this Saturday!"

"Yeah," Ernie replied,

"So what're you gonna do, Ernie? You goin' to Northwestern like your parents want?"

"Nah. Don't want no more school There's too much to see out there."

"Yeah, I know what you mean. But my pop, he won't let me. Says college is too important so you can get a good job later."

"Maybe. I don't care. I want to see the world."

"But how you gonna make money?"

"Don't know exactly. I'll figure it out. My dad's brother Tyler said he can get me a job at the *Kansas City Star* since I wrote for the school newspaper and all."

"*The Trapeze?* You know, Hem, all the guys on the football team thought you were a cad for writing for that rag and calling yourself Ring Lardner, Jr. And they said..." the boy stopped abruptly.

"What else did they say?" Hem barked back.

"No. I better not tell you. You'll be sore."

"No, I won't. Tell me."

"Promise we'll still be friends?"

"Sure. We'll still be friends."

"Well... One of them said that writing is for sissies."

Hem stopped in his tracks and punched the boy in his arm.

"Ow! Hem, I didn't say it! Harry did. What'cha hit me for?"

"He's a dope. Writing isn't for sissies. I'll make sure of that. I'm gonna write tough. Tough and mean. You'll see."

"Ok, Hem. I believe you. We still friends?"

"Yeah, sure. It just makes me sore. Sorry for punching you."

"That's okay. Didn't even hurt. Anyway, I heard Kansas City's a dump. Just stay here, Hem. Oak Park's a nice place. No slums, you know. We can stay friends that way, too."

"Naw, I gotta get out of here. My dad's depressed half the time. Can't figure out why. He's got money and everyone thinks he and my mom are swell. But my mom, with her constant nagging and Bible-quoting! She's driving me nuts. Can't stand it. Gotta get out of here. The only good thing is going to the lake every summer huntin' and fishin.' That's the best."

"Yeah, you really know your onions on all that stuff."

"Guess so. That's the kind of stuff I'll write about. Huntin' and fishin' and shootin'. That sure ain't sissy stuff."

"No, it ain't. Okay, Hem. Here's my house. See you Saturday at graduation..."

The not-so-old man's eyes opened. "Can't stand it," lingered in his mind. "Gotta get out of here."

The sky was now blue with no clouds and the air was hot. He swam the backstroke for half an hour trying to shake the cobwebs from his mind. He knew he was crazy. Here he was, pushing himself for no reason. Making himself hurt, for no reason. Continuing to live, for no reason.

"So you might as well go down swinging," he thought. "Even if you're the one taking the swings at yourself."

But he took a perverse kind of solace knowing that in the end, it's all the same for everyone. Your life ends and all the dreams are over. All the hopes and fears become moot. In the 1920s they called death the Big Sleep. "Maybe my nodding off is just practice, just getting me primed for the real thing," he thought. "Yeah, that's as good a reason as any."

The not-so-old man saw a fish fly up and splash down. It made him think of fishing, and that made him think of deep-sea fishing, and that made him think of the old fisherman, and that made him think of Ernie again. Suddenly, he felt a little better.

CHAPTER VI

"Hey Ernie, how you doing? How've you been? I hope you're doing well," the not-so-old man thought. "I know you don't like the name Ernest, so I'm going to call you Ernie, if that's alright. Calling you Ernie makes me feel like we're friends, and I'd love to be your friend. You can call me anything you want. You can call me Daniel, or you can call me Dan, or you can call me Mr. D or even just Hey You. Whatever you want."

The not-so-old man called Ernest Ernie out of respect. But he called him Ernie out of contempt, too. He admired Ernie for his abilities and achievements, his writing skills, story-telling abilities, and profound perspectives. But he envied him for his life: All the adventures he had, all the women he loved, all the drinks he drank and meals he ate, all the strolls around Paris and bullfights he saw, the battles he witnessed, the mountains he climbed, and friends he troubled with.

And the not-so-old man hated Ernie not so much because he had not had a similar or even close to a similar life. He hated Ernie because Ernie's extraordinary life highlighted to him how wrong his own life had become.

Mostly, he hated Ernie for being called Papa. He hated Ernie for having three sons.

As the not-so-old man tried to rationalize his contempt by calling it respect, he felt anxiety grow within him. That anxiety grew slowly, gradually, but relentlessly until suddenly it turned into anger. Anger he had to control, contain, tuck away into crevasses—cold, frozen crevasses like the kind Ernie would ski around schussing down the Austrian mountainsides with Hadley right behind him—to subdue it before it exploded out of him and caused him to destroy.

The not-so-old man caught his anger as he had done so many times in the past and tucked it away. It wasn't that difficult. It had become a reflex. Instead, he forced himself to think. But these thoughts were not strong enough to hide some of the feelings that had not yet been tucked deep enough into a crevasse.

"So I envy him. So what? I have every right to. And I'm not the only one. Millions of others have envied him too, whether they'd admit it or not. Then, when he was still writing, and now, almost a century after his first novel. His rough and tumble thrill-a-minute life and revolutionary writing that changed the world of prose begged for a mystique. And so it began. And the wonder and jealousy continue.

"Yeah," he thought. "I envied him enough to go to Paris after I swam the English Channel to see where he had lived and retrace his steps. I wanted to imagine what it was like in the early and mid-1920s after World War I when everyone smoked, and everyone drank, and they were all just happy to have survived as they clumsily tried to live life to its fullest."

The not-so-old man's thoughts rambled to Ernie and Hadley and Mr. Bumby and their time in Paris before the rich pilot fish came and ruined it all and them going to the horse races out in the country and how they had to be so careful with their money because Ernie was a writer and that's what he wanted to be so he kept at it no matter how many rejections he got or that Hadley lost all his earliest, unpublished stories in the Gare de Lyon train station in Paris on her way to meet Ernie in Switzerland where he was covering the Lausanne peace conference for the *Toronto Star*. She had packed up all the stories, including the carbon copies in a suitcase, and left it on the train to get a bottle of Evian water before the train departed. When she came back, the suitcase was gone. The stories never showed up. Ernie was crushed. Hadley was inconsolably miserable.

Even so, the not-so-old man had a crush on Hadley because she was cute and supportive of Ernie and called him the pet name Tatie, and she believed in his dream of being a writer and skied when she was pregnant even though it was risky and she cared for their son nicknamed Mr. Bumby who had a cat named F. Puss who was his guardian babysitter sometimes and she played the piano and told Ernie she loved him. She and he would smell the wood smoke from the fireplaces and woodstoves floating in the air around Schruns and would wake up way before dawn and carry their skis and knapsacks out into the light, crisp snow that squeaked when they walked on it in their heavy black leather boots that went up above their ankles with black socks folded down over their tops to start the climb up the mountain because there were no ski lifts to get them up to the slopes they wanted to ski. Hadley didn't mind and even liked learning to ski behind the Taube Inn where they stayed; and once she got the hang of it, hiking up the mountain on snowshoes with Ernie along with their ski instructor Hannes and the small, gnome-like porters who helped carry their food and wine and wood to burn to stay warm at night in the high base Hütte called Madlenerhaus.

And after a warm and filling dinner with wine and conversation, Hadley and Ernie would retire to their room with those wide windows and open them up to let the night air in so the room was cold and crisp and invigorating, and it would be a little shocking, but still feel good, when they climbed into bed between the cold sheets and feather quilt naked, and they would wrap their arms around each other long enough for the sheets and quilt to warm up. They would lay on their backs, with their heads propped up on pillows so they could look out those wide and open windows at the stars shining above the snow-covered mountain peaks and the stars would feel so close—so close and bright and imaginary and then eternal. They would talk a little, whisper a little and hold each other's hand and play with each other's fingers while looking out the windows at the stars the whole time. And they would feel like everything was so real and so good and so truthful that it felt like a fantasy come true that they wanted never to end. And it would be so—after the hard climb up the mountain that got their blood pumping and their muscles pleasantly sore— that making love beneath the stars and under the newly warmed feather quilt with the one and only love of your life was simple and easy and so utterly natural and right that it would be impossible to even imagine anything else being so sweet.

Climbing the mountains would build muscles that were needed to ski down the steep slopes safely and smoothly, and they would also climb to the Lindauer-Hütte or Wiesbadenez-Hütte and pay for the wood they would use to heat the hut and drink the wine they had carried up in their knapsacks and wake up the next morning and ski down the mountain and climb up the next one and find the next hut where they could warm themselves and drink again and sleep again.

He thought about them riding in trains and buses to get to Austria from Paris and how they had to carry heavy leather luggage and how when they got to the mountains they carried wine in sacks and their favorite books too that they were renting from Sylvia Beach and her Shakespeare and Company bookstore at 12 rue de l'Odeon in Paris so they would have something to read up in the mountains in the evening after they skied.

The not-so-old man liked the photo in the book of Ernie standing in front of the bookstore when he was about twenty-two or three years old—years before he was famous—with an "awe shucks" look on his face and some dumb-looking bandana on his head (or, was it a bandage from having a skylight fall on him?) so the not-so-old man had his picture taken in front of the store that was there then and he imagined Pound and Joyce and Stein chatting away in Gertrude Stein's apartment at 27 rue de Fleuries.

The not-so-old man liked the photo of Ernie and Hadley together, her face in profile looking into his eyes with a questioning yet confident look on her face. Now, as he floated in the sea, he saw those photos in his mind, and he liked that. He liked that he could think about the book and the life they led and see the photos in his mind any time he wanted, no matter where he was. The movable feast that is Paris book was to him the movable feast of a bygone era when everything was simple and natural and sure and true. There were no cell phones, cell phone towers marring the landscape, TVs, ATMs or credit cards, computers or internet, no ten-lane highways full of cars going nowhere with drivers pondering nothing.

Instead, there were horses still around that people rode or used to pull carriages, and cars had been around for a while but were mostly open tourers in the early 20s, so if it rained, you got wet. Many didn't even have headlights. There were plenty of Model T cars, but as people got richer, they wanted not just a roof on the car, but better and fancier. After all, this was the roaring 20s and fancy meant status. So there were Hudsons, Packards, Nashes, Studebakers, and Chryslers in America; and in Europe, Peugeots, Renaults, Fiats, Mercedes, and Rolls Royces. It's ironic because since most of the roads outside of towns were dirt, that turned to mud when it rained, and if a car got stuck in it—which happened all the time—they had to use horses to pull the stuck cars out.

Telephones were a luxury and used only wires, and when you picked up the earpiece, you got an operator—a real human being—not a dial tone or busy signal or voice mail menu where you'd have to choose option one or four and then two or six and then seven or nine and then have to leave a message for someone who would never call you back. It was a super-big deal to get a long-distance phone call, and it made the person who got the call feel like a hot-shot. People sent cables and wrote letters on paper with pencils you had to sharpen, and people mailed them in envelopes with stamps, and you had to wait for days or even weeks to get them. And when someone received a letter he or she would read the letter and read it again and maybe a third time, and write a reply, kinda like texting back and forth, and then would save the letters as they saved things in a scrapbook because these letters detailed their life, thoughts, and feelings and most people want to remember their lives, thoughts, and feelings.

There'd be crowds at train stations anxiously waiting for the train that was delivering the latest magazines with short stories or serials by the popular writers like Fitzgerald or Anderson, and they'd read the stories and talk about them with their friends as we do now with movies and TV shows because, you see, reading was entertainment. There was no TV, remember, or internet or iphones, so people would read books and stories and entertain themselves all the time by reading, which made popular writers akin to what movie stars are now—revered and envied and thought of as cool by all the cool kids.

People rode in buses and trains that served dinner and had sleeping cars in them, and they met other people who shared their cabin during the day who talked about their own adventures. The men played cards at night and gambled even though some of them didn't have the money to gamble, but the not-so-old man didn't really know what the women did when their husbands were playing cards and, of course, drinking and smoking too. He guessed they would take care of the kids or knit a sweater or something. Ernie never said.

Ernie told of the nightly card games he would have with the

owner of the Inn, the ski instructor, a banker, and captain of the Gendarmerie of the town, and how, since gambling was against the law in Austria, when they heard the regular gendarmes making their nightly rounds outside the door of the hotel—where they had the doors locked and windows shuttered—they would stop their game, be silent, and wait for them to move along. "Typical," the not-so-old man thought,

When you stayed in a hotel, you'd be sure to tip the bell boy who carried your luggage up to your room because you knew you might need him to fetch a thermometer and aspirin for a fellow writer named Fitzgerald who thought he was sick but wasn't sick at all except maybe a little sick in his head and who worried about the size of his manhood because his wife Zelda said it wasn't enough to satisfy any woman since she was jealous of him and wanted to destroy him even though he was a talented writer and some even say a literary genius. Poor Scotty—later dead from a heart attack.

The not-so-old man was nostalgic and sentimental, and Ernie said in one of his short stories about Fathers and Sons that a sentimental man is unlucky and often betrayed and the not-so-old man knew it was true. But the not-so-old man was sentimental, and he couldn't help it as much as he couldn't help the color of his eyes. The story said the sentimental man starts out sentimental but often ends up cruel because being sentimental opens a man up to abuse. Suffer enough abuse, and a man turns cruel. The not-so-old man wasn't cruel. He was just cruel to himself.

He thought he'd like to experience those by-gone days and go back to see Ernie and Hadley and Bumby and F. Puss and talk to them and find out if Ernie admired swimmers—hopefully, the same way he admired bullfighters—and watch them hike up the mountains or stroll around Paris and hear them laugh and worry about money.

The not-so-old man thought that someone should invent a theme-park where different eras were replicated, and you could stay for a week in the 1920s or 1950s or 1970s. There'd be no cheating—you would have to give up your phone or Game-Boy or headphones. There'd be no TVs, except in the 70s and they would be black and white with no remote control and only three channels. "Maybe the people would want to go fishing or hiking or play cards with friends to pass the time," the not-so-old man thought.

He thought he would like to go back to each era—the 70s to see what his early childhood was like; the 50s because he'd like to see what his parents experienced around the time they were married; and the 20s, to experience the roaring extravagance before the crash.

He remembered after swimming the English channel and going to Paris and walking down the Rue de Cardinal to get to number 74 and looking up at the fourth-floor windows overlooking the street that Ernie and Hadley had looked out of and heard the clippity-clop of horses hooves in the morning pulling wagons of vegetables or horse-drawn tank wagons that collected toilet waste and how the smell would float up into their apartment on hot days. In the evening they were serenaded with accordion music coming from the dancehall on the first floor.

He found rue Morfetard where the Café Amateurs was, which is now the Café Delmas, and had a cup of coffee there where all the bums, drunks, and hookers hung out back in Ernie's day and which was the café Ernie avoided because of all the rabble and smell. But the no-so-old man as a young man wanted to experience the rabble and the smell, but it was no longer there— civilization had overtaken it. Then the not-so-old man as a young man took the route Ernie took past the Lycée Henri Quatre and ancient church of St. Étienne-du-Mont and Place du Panthéon to the Boulevard St. Michel past the Cluny and the Boulevard St. Germain to a café on the Place St. Michel where Ernie would escape the cold of his apartment during the dreary Paris winters and write. The not-so-old man as a young man thought at the time, "There sure are plenty of saints in this town."

This one day in Ernie's story, Ernie ordered a café au lait and wrote a story that took place in Michigan on a similarly cold and windy day. He drank a rum St. James that he said tasted wonderfully and warmed his entire body and noticed a pretty girl walk in and sit down to wait for someone and Ernie thought, "I've seen you, beauty, and you belong to me now, whoever you are waiting for and if I never see you again, I thought. You belong to me and all Paris belongs to me and I belong to this notebook and this pencil." He returned to his writing and got lost in his story and wrote without thinking about anything else but the story, and when he looked up, the girl was gone. Ernie said, "I hope she's gone with a good man, I thought. But I felt sad."

The not-so-old man as a young man also went to the Arc de Triomphe just to do the tourist thing and also because Ernie mentioned it in his book and the not-so-old man as a young man thought he might as well see it while he was there.

Then he found where the apartment above a noisy sawmill at 113 rue Notre-Dame des Champs would have been where Ernie and Hadley had also lived. They had left 74 rue Cardinal Lemoine in September 1923 to move to Toronto because Hadley got pregnant (which Ernie wasn't thrilled about—he said he was too young to be a father) and where Ernie took a job as a journalist at the *Toronto Star* for a lofty $125 a week. He felt obligated to support his wife and baby-to-be in any way he could, and he had heard that Toronto was a good, safe place to have a baby. Hadley gave birth in October while Ernie was away on assignment—an assignment his boss sent him on purposely so he'd miss the birth of his son because he and Ernie, well, they didn't get along too well. Ernie knew he had to write a novel to become great and that being a journalist again was just wasting his time, so after discussing it with Hadley, they high-tailed it out of Toronto (after Ernie received his Christmas bonus) under the cover of darkness and moved back to Paris in January 1924. That's when they moved into the apartment over the sawmill. Again, it was cheap.

The not-so-old man as a young man liked seeing all these places and thinking about Ernie during those times, but he didn't like all the long names of streets and hotels and shops and everything else, especially since they were not in English. "How do these people remember them all?" he wondered. "And it takes so long just to say them... 'Excuse me, madam. Could you please tell me how to get to one-hundred-and-thirteen rue Notre-Dame des Champs?' It's ridiculous! It's so much easier to say something like, 'one-thirteen 7th Ave.,' like in America."

He found another café called La Closerie des Lilas where Ernest would go to escape the cacophony of the sawmill outside their upstairs apartment window and the screaming baby inside the window where he first read his friend Scott's *The Great Gatsby* and wrote much of his own first novel there. He gossiped with Ford Madox Ford about other writers and artists at an outside table. Their conversation went something like this...

"Did you see me slash him?" Ford asked. "*Did* you see me slash him good?"

"No. Who did you slash, Ford?"

"Belloco! *Did* I slash him!"

"I didn't see," Hem said. "Why did you slash him?"

"For a hundred good reasons in the world," Ford said. "*Did* I slash him though!"

Ford was a kind man most of the time, Hemingway said, but was apparently a bit senile and sometimes bitter and had a stained mustache the not-so-old man figured was stained from smoking.

The not-so-old man as a young man learned that these once-famous talented people were just as messed up and sometimes even more messed up than regular people, and this made him feel better since he was certainly not famous and only sometimes talented.

One evening, an hour or so before sunset, he went to Les Deux Magots in the heart of the Saint Germain-des-Près neighborhood, another one of Hemingway's hangouts where all the intellectuals gathered back in his day. He sat at a table on the sidewalk that pointed out into the street on the corner of Boulevard St. Germain and Rue Bonaparte and ordered a beer and an appetizer and sat there and tried to imagine what it would have been like almost a hundred years ago. The sun was just over the top of the buildings now, and he had drunk one beer and was already feeling a little tipsy and felt the warmth of that summer's evening all over himself. He felt the evening and felt the birds chirping their last chirps of the day and saw people enjoying themselves in a lazy, contented way leaning back in their chairs at their tables and others leisurely walking along the street. He was trying hard to imagine, to *feel* what it was like, so he ordered another beer and thought that getting drunk might help because that's what they did back then. He wanted to talk to friends sitting at his table who were artists and writers and activists in the 1920s and he thought in his tipsiness he should hire actors to play the parts of Ernie's friends so he could have conversations with them and know what it was like to sit on the sidewalk of a Parisian café on a summer's evening where everyone smoked and everyone drank and were happy to just have survived the war. And he would love them all as a young child loves a new kitten or puppy.

By chance—or was it fate—a woman came along and sat down at another table near the not-so-old man as a young man, and she looked like she was waiting for someone, and she ordered a coffee, and that was all.

The not-so-old man as a young man sipped his beer and nibbled on his appetizer and watched people walk by, some couples hand-in-hand, and watched people order drinks and then food and he wanted to pretend it was 1926 and Hadley was sitting next to him and across the table sat the Murphys and on his other side was his good friend John Dos Passos, and sitting kinda behind Dos was Harold Loeb, the Jew, who Ernie played tennis with sometimes. And he was hoping Pablo Picasso would show up.

The not-so-old man as a young man glanced at the woman who was waiting, and she looked at him and smiled, and then got up and went over to him and said with a shy but coy smile on her lips, "Êtes vous un Américain?"

The not-so-old man as a young man smiled and motioned for her to sit down, which she did, and he said in English, "Is it really that obvious?"

The woman laughed briefly, nodded her head, and asked him, "D'où venez-vous en Amérique?" She didn't wait for him to question her French, saying in English, with a forced and silly British accent, "That means, Mr. America, 'Where, in America are you from?'"

The not-so-old man as a young man held up his glass, winked, and said, "Dame de France, I am from a place near Lake Michigan called Oak Park, Illinois, and I swam here just the other day."

He was feeling funny now and quite lucky to have met her and was hoping for witty repartee, partly because he was sure that's what Ernie and his friends had back in 1925 or '26 (or both), as they sat on the same sidewalk, maybe at the same table on the same summer's evening. And suddenly, he was hoping for witty repartee because a bold and lovely woman such as she intrigued and excited him.

Boosted by liquid courage, he talked to her effortlessly for several minutes and he admired her class and charm and full, rosy cheeks and ample body he knew was soft and feminine yet strong and resilient. He couldn't help thinking that she was his Hadley, there, being a friend and enjoying his company and the café and the sidewalk and sunset. She was one of those few people who were as good as spring itself, he thought, and this made him a bit dizzy in the head.

Suddenly, the woman shot her arm up into the air and jumped up and waved and called out to someone across the street; and they saw her and came and sat at the table too. She introduced the not-so-old man as the young American who had just swum across the Atlantic Ocean and English Channel and an old friend from long ago, and he felt even happier when she did that.

Her friend was a clean-shaven man wearing a French beret with a full, but round, soft curving nose and receding hairline and who talked in a staccato, abstract sort of way. A few minutes later, he too jumped up and waved at a couple walking along the sidewalk, and they also came and sat at the table after having the waiter get another chair. These two were apparently quite rich because they were dressed impeccably and gave off that "I am quite rich" vibration the not-so-old man had recognized in other quite rich people before. One more man, with dark hair and thick, round-rimmed glasses, also joined them a few minutes later, and they all crowded together around the small round table that was growing more congested by the minute with empty or half-full glasses and a few plates with crumbs on them. Each of them talked and laughed and sometimes made funny faces or playfully punched the other's arm.

Pablo, the man wearing the beret, ordered a round of drinks for everyone in French but with a Spanish accent. The not-so-old man as a young man was on his fourth beer and was, in fact, on his way to getting drunk, which made him think of Nick Carraway saying he had been drunk only twice in his life and this was the second time. But he smiled and listened to the banter, and thought of Ernie saying something profound like, "You may talk and I may listen and miracles might happen." He held up his hand to stop the chatter at the table and stood up, held his right hand over his heart, and said those words out loud in a serious reverential way, and everyone laughed, and Pablo even slapped him on his back.

Someone inside the café was playing the accordion, and the music drifted outside onto the veranda where they sat. The not-so-old man as a young man enjoyed the French music and the chatter of the patrons and his new friends and the warm air and smell of escargot with garlic sauce. He liked watching the waiters being polite in their black and white waistcoats and dickey bow ties and large, white, linen napkins draped over each of their left forearms as they worked hard enough to work up a sweat. He imagined he knew the waiters by name and they were always happy to see him because he always left a good tip, and people generally like you when you give them something.

He enjoyed watching people walk by, sometimes with children in tow or pushing a stroller, and he enjoyed the sun going down and the air cooling as it did and the streetlights coming on and the horns of cars sounding in the street and even the occasional profanity from an angry taxicab driver. And he thought to himself how wonderful. How wonderful it is to be alive and feel all this and live all this and be here and how wonderful it would be to be able to do it often like Ernie had done, with friends who were as good as spring itself. He looked at the woman and smiled, and she smiled back, and he knew they were friends and would always be friends even if tonight was the only time they would be together.

After Paris, he had wanted to go to Africa and Mt. Kilimanjaro and fly over it and see its snow-covered square top as he figured

Ernie had done and then wrote a story about a man in the African jungle near the mountain who scratched his leg and didn't treat it with iodine soon enough, so it turned into gangrene which killed him. But that trip would have to wait for another time, the not-so-old man as a young man thought back then.

The not-so-old man kept swimming. The sun continued sweeping across the sky.

The not-so-old man didn't want to go back to the war to end all wars that Ernie was in in 1918, but he would go back to Milan, Italy, to see where Ernie convalesced after his legs were torn up. Ernie was an ambulance driver and was delivering chocolate and cigarettes to men on the front lines when he got almost fatally injured, but still helped pull injured Italian soldiers to safety. He later received the Italian Silver Medal of Bravery. The injuries to his legs were so severe he didn't have to go back to the War. But instead he stayed in Milan, recovering in a hospital for six months where he met Agnes, a nurse he fell in love with. The no-so-old man thought it would have been cool to be a fly on the wall of the hospital behind Ernie's cot to hear what Ernie said to the nurse and listen to their conversations as he and she fell in love...

"So, Agnes, what are you doing after work tonight? Wanna come over to my place for a drink?"

"We're already at your place. Your place is in this cot, Hemingway. You can't walk yet, remember?"

"Who needs to walk when there's angels like you flittering about."

"Don't you ever give up, Hemingway? You're just a kid and you know nothing. I told you a hundred times, your charm won't work on a nurse my age."

"But you're as young as a cherry blossom, Agnes."

"Stop it, Hemingway. If you keep it up, I might just end up liking you. And you think your war wounds are difficult."

Agnes turned to leave, but then turned back and said, "Speaking of drinking... I found a couple of empty bottles under your cot. Where'd you get them, Hemingway? You know you can't drink in here."

"I know, I know. It won't happen again."

"Sure it won't."

"You can't deny a wounded soldier a little comfort every now and then."

"Every night is not 'every now and then.'"

"Oh, Agnes. Let's not argue. None of that's important." He reached out his hand. "But here... I need you... my bandages need fixing. Come fix my bandages, Agnes. Come fix my bandages, my angel."

"Hummmph... Hemingway! Why must you do this? You know I can't help myself when you smile like that. Okay. Up you go. Stop fidgeting. There..."

"You'll see Agnes. I may only be nineteen, but I've seen more in my not-so-long life than most men. I've seen the incontinence of the Kansas City slums and ridden in cop cars to crime scenes to report first hand. One guy died in the hospital after getting his skull crushed in a fight. I saw that and wrote about it."

"That's nice, Ernest. Here, move your leg..."

"You know, I would work so late at the *Star* sometimes I was too tired to go home and slept in a bathtub using towels as my mattress."

"That's nice, Ernest. Now the other leg."

"I used to eat chili con carne from an all-night lunch wagon while waiting for a story to develop as a cold wind from the Missouri River Valley swept snow down the street. I won't even tell you what happened to the boy who came into the hospital one night and asked the doctor to fix him so it'd be impossible for him to sin again.... if you know what I mean."

"That's nice, Ernest. All right. All done."

"So I've seen a lot, Agnes. More than most men in a lifetime."

"I'm sure you have."

"So Agnes... now take them all off."

"Stop it, Ernest! You're too..."

"I can't Agnes. Not with you around."

"Good night, Ernest."

"Good night, my angel."

The not-so-old man saw a picture of Ernie in the hospital lying on his cot on his side, looking into the camera with a very charming and contented smile on his face. They planned on getting married, but once Ernie was discharged and back in the U.S. still recovering, she wrote him and said she had fallen in love with another man—an officer in the Italian army—and would be marrying him instead. Ernie was crushed, and some say he became defensive with women and abandoned them before they abandoned him to avoid more heartache. Hadley, Pauline, and Martha were his wives and were all left for the next. Mary was his last wife, and he left her when he killed himself.

The not-so-old man didn't want to go back to the Spanish Civil War where Ernie went as a reporter. He didn't like war.

He thought about the sea and Ernie's novel, the *Old Man and the Sea,* and remembered he read in a magazine once that the old man in the story was modeled after an old man in real life who was a fisherman named Gregorio Fuentes. He couldn't remember if Gregorio had really struggled with a giant marlin for a couple of days and, after he killed it, tied it to the side of his boat and watched sharks attack the marlin with wide-open jaws to devour it as he fought them off with a broken oar handle and tiller handle. But he often wondered why the old man in the story didn't cut the marlin in half and load him into his boat or at least cut the meat off him and load that into the boat so that the sharks couldn't get it. At least the old man would have gotten something for his efforts. "But that would have ruined the story," he thought. And as Frances said talking to Robert Cohn, "But remember, it's for literature. We all ought to make sacrifices for literature... Don't you think?" The article said Greg loved Ernie and didn't believe he was an alcoholic or mentally deranged, as the article implied.

The not-so-old man believed there's a fine line between madness and genius and figured if Ernie had some issues, it was to be expected. He liked thinking he had a dose of that too—it helped him believe that what he was doing now was justified.

The books he liked the best were about Ernie's life in Paris in the years after the war—where the people Ernie wrote about were often young and confused and searching. The *Lost Generation,* Gertrude Stein called them.

He wondered if he liked those stories mostly because the people were young and that had a way of making him feel young too. Would he have liked the stories as much or at all if the characters did the same things—or sort of the same things—and said the same things—or sort of the same things—but were in their seventies or eighties?

What if Brett was seventy-five and on a respirator instead of thirty-four smoking cigarettes and been married four times and Jake was seventy-six, not thirty-five, and had lived with his war wound alright until he needed a wheelchair and had never found a woman to have him? He doubted he would have liked the stories as much. And he doubts anyone else would have either.

He especially liked the parts where they were doing young things like skiing and hiking and taking trains to new places or Ernie and Scotty riding in a car through the rain that didn't have a top, so they got all wet and had to stop under trees to wait out the storm. He didn't really like all the talk about different kinds of drinks and drinking and being drunk, or 'tight,' or 'slow on the uptake,' mostly because the not-so-old man never got drunk except for that one time he drank to forget, but that was only for a month. Besides, he was always training to be a faster swimmer. So he didn't know about apéritifs or even what an apéritif was and how it went down smooth or not or which wine was good for its price. Ernie had said that to be a good writer, you should write only about what you know. The not-so-old man figured Ernie knew a lot about drinking.

The not-so-old man liked the parts in the stories that made him feel crisp and clean—like sleeping in the winter with the wide hotel windows open and feeling the stars so close.

He liked the parts about hiking for miles over the Spanish countryside up and down hills and through forests and over log bridges over streams to get to a good trout stream and catching trout and putting them on fern leaves in his satchel and then taking a nap next to the cold running stream.

Crisp and clean things—like fresh crisp lettuce in a salad or just ripened blueberries that were not mushy with age or fermented from spoiling but just turned sweet—made him feel crisp and clean too. He liked thinking young thoughts even though he knew he would never be young again and could never erase the scars from the past—the past that came after his crisp and clean years. And as long as he didn't look at himself in a mirror, he could let himself feel young for a long time.

The not-so-old man had read a couple of Ernie's books in high school and college only because he had to, and he didn't like them or understand them until someone explained them to him, or he read the CliffsNotes. He read more of them while in business school and after that mostly out of obligation because he wanted to be well-read, for a reason he never fully understood since he was a numbers and business person.

It might have been because, when he was just a boy, he had

learned about Leonardo Da Vinci and Michelangelo and how they were considered Renaissance men who were great at just about everything they did, from painting and sculpting to architecture to philosophy to engineering. And since as a young impressionable boy and in need of role models and because he was partly Italian, the same as Lenny and Mikey, he felt a sort of obligation to his Italian heritage and mankind in general, to become a Renaissance man too. "Who knows what I might turn up," he thought.

He never really stopped to consider that he was doing it— reading all the Russians, Austrians and Germans like Tolstoy, Kafka, Nietzsche, and Dostoevsky; and English and American writers too like Dickens, Paine, Conrad, Melville, Fitzgerald, Emerson, Faulkner, Hawthorne, and Twain—out of pride. But truly, he didn't do it out of pride. He just had a thirst to challenge his mind and go where the books would take him—mostly into hard and depressing places. "But that must be life," he thought.

It wasn't unlike his thirst for swimming and pushing his body to the limit through the resistance of the water. With these books, he had to push his mind to its limit through the resistance of heavy thoughts. He didn't always like doing it while he was doing it, but he would feel the satisfaction later when he reaped the benefits of those mental workouts in heightened awareness and self-confidence in knowing.

The not-so-old man, as he swam now, remembered reading *Crime and Punishment* by Dostoevsky, where a young man, for no particular reason, killed his lady landlord. After he had read the part where the man actually murdered her, he paused and discovered that the passage was like ten or twenty pages long and the half-hour it took him to read it, felt like two minutes. That intrigued him. It was similar to the feeling of swimming a race that was many meters long but was over before he knew it.

For a while, he even tried writing himself and started like Ernie had with a few mock news articles and then a couple of short stories that he never submitted for publication but wrote just for himself to see if anything clicked. It did not. So he gave it up. "I'm a swimmer and will always be a swimmer," he consoled himself. His Renaissance man dream was over.

Yes, Ernie had it click for him when he was writing stories in the Parisian cafés where he would disappear into the story and lose himself as he wrote; much the same as the not-so-old man would disappear into the water and lose himself as he swam.

And Ernie had a style. It wasn't the flowing, effervescent prose of Fitzgerald or the insufferable misery of Tolstoy or Dostoevsky or the meandering aphorisms of Nietzsche or the twists of Dickens. Ernie's writing was simple, almost too simple. It was like Ernie would beat you over the head with a club into liking him.

"There is never any ending to Paris... We always returned to it... Paris was always worth it... But this is how Paris was in the early days when we were very poor and very happy."

The not-so-old man had read that whole book—slogged through all the strolls around Paris with all those long street names and all the conversations with once-famous people he had never heard of before and all the apéritifs and beers and wine just to get to that ending: "...when we were very poor and very happy." And when he read those words, it was like all the mundane suddenly came alive and suddenly made sense. That simple little sentence stuck in his craw like a bird getting a seed stuck in its gullet. But when that seed was finally, laboriously swallowed, it germinated inside of him, and blossomed into something still simple, yes; but also shakingly and pleasantly profound. He loved Ernie for that. But he hated him too.

And "Isn't it pretty to think so."

Another provocative line. Another slap-you-upside-the-head ending. Isn't it pretty to think Jake and Brett could have had a wonderful life if only man and his war hadn't gotten in the way?

The not-so-old man floated on his back.

He thought about the book he had read of Ernie's in high school about Ernie in Paris and Spain, which was supposedly fiction, but the not-so-old man figured it was more like an autobiography. Ernie took a vacation to see the running of the bulls, and this is where the not-so-old man's mind went.

His mind galloped over the French and Spanish countrysides as he retraced Ernie's trip on his way to Pamplona through the forests and over the streams and fields of grass with cattle grazing. He remembered stopping in Burguete where Ernie and his buddy had taken a detour on their way to the bullfights to go fishing. They had to take a bus to get there and rode on the roof of the bus with luggage and peasants who only spoke Spanish and who offered them wine out of a wine sack, showing them how to squeeze the sack just right so the wine shot into their mouths from an arm's length away. They rode up and down hills and through forests as tree limbs passed above them and then over barren land as the hot sun shined down on them. When they got to the mountains where the fishing was, in the restaurant, it was so chilly they could see their breath—so his buddy played the piano to stay warm.

In Pamplona, he watched the running of the bulls and two bullfights. As he sat in the stands, he imagined looking across the arena and seeing Brett, Mike, and even Robert Cohen, with Mike cheering with his fist and Robert cringing and Lady Brett Ashley mesmerized as she watched the ballet of man against beast play out below her. He heard her explain herself to Jake, remembering the quote in a way that was close enough for government work:

"Because I'm really gone, Jake. I'm crazy about that Romero boy. I think I'm in love with him. Yes... I just can't help myself. I've never in my life been able to help myself."

"Then, Ernie," the not-so-old man thought, "another classic..."

"How did you go bankrupt?" Bill asked.

"Two ways," Mike said. "Gradually, then suddenly."

CHAPTER *VII*

*T*he sea was like going bankrupt that day. Small swells came slowly, almost imperceptibly. Then suddenly, large, almost white-capped waves were upon the not-so-old man that knocked him out of his rhythm. The not-so-old man thought, "Now, for sure, my luck is *salao*."

He bobbed up and down in the swells, no longer swimming, but just floating and treading water, trying not to swallow sea. He saw the horizon all around him was the same—no boats or cargo ships visible. His mind was getting weaker and weaker, but his will was still there.

He had fought it until now. But now the sea wouldn't allow him to avoid it any longer. The turbulence stirred it up in him and made what he so desperately wanted not to think about beat against his head.

His imagination took over. He imagined what could have, what would have been if he had listened to his wife years ago and hadn't put Rachel in the car to go to a new playground across town. Although Ray Ray loved going to new places, and he loved watching her face light up when she discovered one, he could have easily convinced her that playing in the backyard would be fun too.

The not-so-old man as a young father would have put her on the rope swing that hung off the oak tree in their backyard and she would have smiled and giggled as he pushed her up and down. He would have put her on her new tricycle and guided her gently as her little feet and legs furiously pedaled down the sidewalk to the corner and then all the way around the block.

They wouldn't talk much because Ray Ray was busy taking in all the sights of the neighbor's yards with flowers blooming in the flower beds, and she would have talked to the birds sitting on a white picket fence and pointed at this and then that like she was narrating a story. He would have quietly guided her along and thought how lucky he was and that his wife wasn't that bad after all since she gave him Ray Ray and how they'd find a way to fall in love again when their next child was born.

They would have taken Ray Ray to her first dance recital and her first day at kindergarten, and both his and his wife's heart would have broken a little having to let Ray Ray go to school by herself without them. He imagined he would have carried her in his arms, her little head on his shoulder, maybe even drooling on his shoulder, asleep after a day at the carnival where she would have delighted in all the lights and games and rides and music. He imagined reading her a bedtime story and tucking her in bed and kissing her on the forehead and telling her he loved her and her saying she loved him too, and he would have turned out the light and would have thought, "I'm the luckiest man alive." He imagined her going through grade school and having to comfort her when some boys made fun of her because they thought she was cute, watched her cheer on the football team as a cheerleader, taught her to drive, taken her to college, met the boy she would marry and given her away at her wedding. He envisioned it all, from the time after the accident to her raising her own kids and him taking his grandkids to ball games and spoiling them at Christmas and then having her and them pay visits to him in a nursing home.

The not-so-old man kept fighting the sea as the waves got even larger and more violent, stealing his luck by making him imagine how good his life could have been.

He imagined his son being born normally and alive and how he would grow up normal in a normal family. He would have shown him how to hold a plastic baseball bat right after he had learned to walk, placing his little hands on it correctly and moving his arms as he should to swing at a Wiffle ball. And the boy who really was would have looked up at him with wide and joyful eyes as he started to realize he could do it.

The not-so-old man as a young father would have taken him to Little League and Mets games, and the boy who really was would have loved the stadium and the green grass field and the hot dogs and drinks and Mets ball cap the not-so-old man as his father would have bought him. And the boy who really was would have had fun wearing it and rooting for his favorite players. They would have grown up together—the boy for the first time and the not-so-old man as his father for the second—and they'd always have baseball in common, and both would learn the game and learn lessons of life through the game as they did with other things like swimming.

The not-so-old man as a father would have shown the boy who really was just as much attention as he had paid his daughter who was the firstborn because he knew first hand that after the first child the parents forget about the next ones some and he didn't want the boy who really was to feel like he had been forgotten as he himself had been.

As a young father, he would have helped the boy who really was learn the multiplication table and English grammar and even a foreign language and would have watched his boy play baseball on the high school Varsity team. He would have taught him to drive and would have taken pictures of him going to senior prom with his girlfriend and warned the boy about sex and told him how to treat women and that a good woman was a gift from the gods to cherish and treat with respect but to have a firm and guiding hand with and he would have taken him to college and been his son's best man at the young man who really was's wedding.

The not-so-old man as a young father would have taught his daughter and son how to swim, and they would have put a pool in their backyard and gone to the ocean and spread a towel on the sand and plant an umbrella in the sand and build sandcastles and swum in the sea together and bob up and down in the waves together.

He would have leaned over and have his little girl and boy climb on his back and wrap their arms around his neck— sometimes one at a time and sometimes both together when they were really small—and he'd call out, "Ready?" and they would yell, "Yes!" And he would dive down, so they were all underwater, then come back up and hear them scream, "Again Daddy! Again!"

The not-so-old man and his wife would have grown together instead of apart and her idiosyncrasies that had bothered him either would have disappeared on their own because she was happy instead of sad, or they wouldn't have bothered him any longer, or he would have grown to think they were endearing because he was happy instead of sad. Together they would have welcomed their children with their children home at Christmas, and they would have all gone skiing on a winter vacation and seen each other on the 4th of July holiday and sat on a blanket on the town square's lawn and watched the fireworks light up the sky.

The not-so-old man's imagination was driving him now, taking him places he had never let himself go before. And it hurt. It stung him in the heart, like a barb from a stingray, and its poison was spreading into every cell of his body.

He hated. He hated himself for not listening to his wife and feeling now for the first time what he had missed. His imagination was betraying him, stinging him, killing him. The years of distraction and suppression had piled up, gathered strength, and were now beating on him like a tsunami and exploding out of his soul like an atomic bomb.

Tears didn't flow. Instead, he thrashed at the water in a violent, foam-at-the-mouth rage he had never before let himself feel. He beat the waves of the sea with his open hands and closed fists, turning them swollen and red. His right hand clamped shut so it would no longer open. And as he thrashed, he knocked the goggles off his head and didn't even try to save them as the waves pushed them away.

The wind blew hard and whitecaps appeared on the sea. Foam slapped his face. Seawater splashed into his nostrils.

"Blow!" she said.

The not-so-old man as a little boy blew.

"Harder!" she commanded.

He blew harder.

"You've got to get it out or your nose'll stay congested. Do it again."

He blew his nose again. "But it hurts."

"More. You've got to get it out. Do it more or you'll be sorry."

But to do it more, you need more time, and to get more time, you need to speed up the now to get to the more—the more that never ends.

And it was now that he hated and it was now that he hated more. Hatred regurgitated up from the pit of his stomach into his throat and out through his nostrils and eyes. He hated everyone and everything. He hated his mother, his father, his sister. He hated his brother, but he never had a brother. He hated his ex-wife and all his ex-girlfriends. He hated his teachers, his coaches, his friends, his enemies. He hated money and debt and affluence. He hated pride and humility, health and sickness, good people for not being bad and bad people for not being good. He hated strength for its flaunting and weakness for its clumsiness. He hated all of his past and all of his future. He could not stop hating.

The only things he didn't hate were Ray Ray and the boy who never was.

He realized that he had done the right thing by taking this swim. He had to end it. He had to take responsibility. He had to die. The hatred had to end.

The sea kept beating on him, taunting him.

"What more do you want?" the not-so-old man whimpered when he finally became aware of himself bobbing up and down in the roughening sea. "Haven't I given you enough? I spilled my guts all over the deck, and you still want more?"

The not-so-old man heard his thoughts tell him what he was feeling: "You think I'm gonna give in? You think I'm a patsy? You can go to hell, you stupid ocean. Go to hell, where it's wet like the English Channel. You think you can beat out my sorrow? You think you can wash away my grief? I'll never leave them. You hear me? Never. I can't. I can't. I can't let them go. It wouldn't be fair. They never had a chance. They never had a chance. It was all my fault. All mine. I can't let them go. I have to hold onto them so they can forgive me... you understand? It's only right. It's only fair to them. They have to realize I never wanted this to happen. They have to forgive me... but I should never be forgiven. I can't let them go. I can't. So do what you want. It doesn't matter. I'll die before I give in to you and your taunting."

The ocean paid no attention, and the not-so-old man's imagination wouldn't relent. It took hold of him again as if it knew better than him and took him deeper—perhaps as penance, perhaps as revenge—and instead of seeing the raging sea before him, he saw a raging bull. For a second, the not-so-old man felt like the bull being taunted by a swinging red cape, huffing and puffing his frustration out his nostrils into the dusty air. But then suddenly, his mind switched positions, and he was the matador holding the cape and swinging it in front of the bull, taunting him, egging him on to get angrier and angrier.

The bull pawed at the ground, stirring up dust, then his tail went up, and he charged huffing and puffing at the cape. The not-so-old man swung the cape aside as the bull's horns just missed his thigh. Swoosh. Again, the bull passed by his side. Swoosh. Again, around this time, around his body the bull chased, trying desperately to get to the cape and destroy it. The not-so-old man felt the muleta in his sweaty, dirty hand as he maneuvered the cape, stiffened with dried blood from a previous fight, in front of and around the bull.

He felt it all, lived it all in his exasperated, fantasizing mind that wouldn't relent to the sea but did. For several minutes he felt like he was the master bullfighter Romero showing off in front of Brett. But more importantly, he was experiencing the essence of a fight he had always been afraid of experiencing.

The bull didn't relent. He kept charging and chasing, charging and chasing, getting more frustrated with each failure to conquer the cape. The crowd in the arena kept moaning and cheering, ooh-ing and ahh-ing, as the passes got closer, faster, tighter—then slower and still tight but more dangerous with the slowness.

The not-so-old man felt sweat roll down his forehead, down his cheeks, and saw it drip onto the dust-covered ground next to his black leather matador boots. He smelled the odor of the animal, so majestic in its presence, its strength, its cockiness, so noble in its single-mindedness and stupidity. He heard the cheers and felt the exhilaration of the crowd and their approval, their approval, their approval, and then their envy. The rabble wanted to see death cheated and held at bay, to be controlled and mastered, to have saliva spit authoritatively in its face, and yet, they wanted to see the death of something greater than themselves to prove to themselves that they are as great and even greater. But they—as he was now—are only greater due to deception and guile which is not noble, but wicked.

The not-so-old man felt the bull's flank as it brushed his thigh as the bull passed, then the side of his head as it came the next time around, then the brush with a horn and a small rip about the size of his pinky in his skin-tight matador pants—just enough to elicit several drops of blood—as the crowd ooh-ed with the brush and ahh-ed with its completion as the muleta swung up over the bull's and then the matador's head with the showmanship of a master.

The crowd rose to its feet in delirious approval. Their applause and cheers made the stones of the arena tremble.

The not-so-old man cringed. He knew it was time. Showmanship was over. Flaunting was forgotten. Now came the dying. He found himself looking at the bull, sighting down the sword, measuring where he should plunge it. The bull charged. The not-so-old man sighted along the blade, became one with the blade and then the bull, and plunged the sword in high between the bull's shoulders. He felt it himself, in the hump just below where his neck ends, and his upper back begins—a sting, like a bite from a wasp or bee, right there, on his spinal column—he felt the dagger slice in.

The bull crumbled to his knees and paused, suspended, his eyes wondering what, how, why? Then as if he had been gently nudged by a pinky finger, the bull fell over sideways onto the dust-covered ground with a thud.

It was over. The not-so-old man felt sick. And as if he had been gently nudged by a pinky finger, he fell to his knees. He struggled to look up into the crowd. There was Brett. All he saw was Brett, applauding with tears in her eyes as roses fell around him. The cheating had been realized; the dying approved.

He was on the Serengeti. It was before dawn. The bait had been set the night before for the lion to smell and eat. The not-so-old man slung his rifle over his shoulder and followed his safari guide, Philip, one of the Great White Hunters, out of camp and across the plain.

"The average male is nine feet long and about four hundred pounds, you know," Philip said and then spit on the ground. "The female is eight feet, maybe three hundred pounds at most. Of course, she doesn't have the mane of the male, so we want a male to put on the wall as your trophy."

There was still time. The sun wouldn't rise for another hour. They hiked further into the plain.

"A lion can get up to thirty miles an hour in a sprint, you know," Philip said. "So we have to be careful. A well-placed shot might be all you need since a lion has hair, which is just one layer, and not fir, which is two layers, so the bullets do more damage. They only live about twelve years in the wild, twenty years in the zoo, you know, and eat about fifteen pounds of raw meat a day." Philip laughed. "So it's a good thing the wildebeest and hyenas multiply like rabbits."

He paused again and spit on the ground. "The king of the jungle sleeps a lot, you know. I guess when you're king, you can do that. Up to twenty hours a day. And those buggers can make a ruckus, you know. You can hear a lion roar up to five miles away."

They walked quietly on the reddish-brown dirt that was dried and hard and sometimes loose and dusty, around the tufts of drought-burned grass forward towards the lightening sky. Ahead they saw a herd of wildebeest, thousands strong, migrating north to cross the Grumeti River where the grass was green, and the water flowed.

"They say over 250,000 wildebeest die every year making the five-hundred-mile migration, you know," Philip broke the silence. "Over six thousand die just crossing the Mara River. Too bad wildebeest can't swim. It's a pity instinct can kill you."

The not-so-old man slowed his pace as he gazed across the land. Miles. He could see for miles. Miles of very little, just some grass, a few trees here and there, dust on the ground meeting the pastel of the sky as it lightened. He looked to his left, then right, then turned around and walked backward several seconds just to see behind himself and he felt alone and small and he felt like he was just two eyes and nothing more. The plain stretched out in every direction and he thought it might just stretch out forever and maybe it was endless—an endless plane—vast and gigantic and overwhelming and real. It was real. Hard dirt, clear sky, boots on the ground. The scent of raw nature and earth diffusing into every pore of his body. He took a deep breath.

They hiked around an acacia tree and through the gloom of dawn saw another tree in the distance with a couple of giraffes grazing on it. "Not long now," Philip said. "Get your rifle ready."

The not-so-old man pulled the rifle off his shoulder. It felt familiar. He knew how to use it. "We need to make sure we stay downwind. If he smells us first, it's over." They walked in silence for a while. Philip stopped abruptly and said, "There's three times you're afraid of a lion. First, when you see his tracks. Then, when you hear his roar. Then when you see him. Look down, matey," he pointed to the ground in front of him. "There's your first lion track."

The not-so-old man looked down. He shuddered but was exhilarated.

"You're either the hunter or the hunted, matey," Philip said. "Now, we're the hunters. Let's keep it that way."

The not-so-old man and Phillip saw three Rüppell's vultures circling above where the lion tracks lead. When the three birds dove, they heard a roar that would rattle windows. The not-so-old man shuddered again, this time, more intensely. Their eyes followed the vultures down, and now they could see the sun starting to rise, and right in front of the half-circle of gold, they saw the lion. It was male.

The lion shook his head at the birds and roared again, and the birds aborted their dive and flew to the nearest tree. The lion looked around briefly, then put his head down and opened his jaws wide. The not-so-old man shuddered a third time but was entranced at the animal's beauty and presence. The lion looked content, gnawing on the bones of the carcass Phillip's helpers had left there the night before.

The guide licked his finger and held it up. "He's distracted now," he whispered. "This way. Quiet now. No more talk."

They stooped down and quietly shuffled right so they'd be south of the lion. They squatted behind a toothbrush tree. The lion stood up, walked around the carcass as if he were on a midnight watch, then sat down again facing the other direction, and resumed eating. "He's looking the other way," Philip whispered. "Come."

They quietly moved through the grass towards the lion. The not-so-old man's breath was fast and hot, and his stomach churned. The normal sweat on his brow from the early morning heat had tripled in intensity.

They were directly behind the beast now and saw his spine with the ripples of hide over its thirty-three vertebrae—the same number as a human—in a line from his tail to the back of his head that almost looked like ripples in a calm sea, and the flanks of his stomach bulging up from the ground like gently inflated light-brown balloons, and his shoulders, broad and angular and powerful. Flies were buzzing around him, and the lion's tail waved automatically and rhythmically—almost like it was conducting an orchestra—to keep them away.

If the lion turned his head in either direction, he would see them. "And then what?" the not-so-old man thought. "He'd charge us, that's what he'd do. At thirty miles an hour! A roaring lion coming right at you at thirty miles an hour! A target that's much harder to hit than a sitting one. Should I run now? Should I turn and run now?"

He stayed next to Phillip's side and matched his slow, quiet steps as they inched closer. "My God, we're so close I could reach out and touch him! Turn and run, Daniel! Turn and run, you fool!"

Two more steps closer. "What am I doing?" the not-so-old man thought. "This is madness. Turn and run!"

Two more steps closer. The not-so-old man was shaking. When they were forty yards away, Philip said in an authoritative whisper, "Now."

The not-so-old man froze—half out of fear, half out of respect for the animal. Could he really shoot this amazing creation sitting innocently in front of him? Something wasn't right. Something made him question the whole affair. "All this time and trouble just to kill nobility?"

"Now!" Phillip whispered again with more urgency.

Phillip's voice was so authoritative, so sure, so knowing. That demanding confidence put the not-so-old man's mind into a kind of trance where it was no longer his own, but just an instrument of the authority's desires.

He raised his rifle, and got the lion in the rifle's sights; his finger wrapped around the trigger. But without Phillip saying anything else right away, quickly, his doubts returned. The not-so-old man did not squeeze the trigger.

"Now!" the guide demanded in an angry, hostile tone as he raised his rifle too.

When he heard the order, the not-so-old man's mind no longer thought but obeyed. He squeezed the trigger. He felt the recoil on his shoulder and heard the explosion of gunpowder hard against his eardrum. The bullet hit the lion on the side of his neck. The not-so-old man saw blood spray out and the lion's head waver from the shock.

The not-so-old man's mind had been blank as he squeezed the trigger, but once he saw the animal was hit, he immediately thought it could not have been him who had done it. It must have been Phillip! He glanced at Phillip, but Phillip had not fired.

The lion raised his head, saw the two humans, and roared—or tried to roar—but the sound was limited and spastic. The not-so-old man felt different now. He felt sorry. He wanted to take it back. He wanted to run to the lion and gouge the bullet out of his neck and stop the bleeding with his handkerchief and stroke his forehead and tell him everything was going to be okay. He wanted to take the lion home and nurse him back to health and release him back into the wild and wave goodbye.

The lion charged. Phillip screamed, "FIRE!"

Again, the not-so-old man's body acted on its own. It squeezed the trigger. The bullet missed and kicked up dust in front of the charging lion. Then a loud BANG right near his ear. Philip's bullet hit the lion in one of his ears and a chunk of it flew off. The lion paused, then kept coming.

The not-so-old man saw the lion and could swear the lion was looking directly at him, and he thought the lion had it out for him and that the beast—that majestic, noble work of art—would not stop until he had run him down and killed him. Rightfully killed him. What had the lion done to *him?* Nothing. He was just eating breakfast, much the same as the not-so-old man had done a couple of hours ago. The not-so-old man felt a shiver through his entire body. "He's looking at me! My God! He's looking right *through* me!"

The not-so-old man dropped his rifle, or really, shoved it away from himself towards the charging lion. He turned and ran. Another shot. He didn't turn to look. Then another. After he had run many yards, the not-so-old man finally turned and saw the lion sprawled on the ground, his face pressed straight down into the hard, dry dirt, with a pool of blood already forming around him.

Philip stood just a few yards in front of him, his face flushed and somber, still pointing his rifle at the beast. The not-so-old man fell to his knees, panting. Phillip shot the animal one more time. The animal didn't move a whisker as the bullet entered his back at the same level as his heart. Phillip looked up and turned towards the not-so-old man. He saw him kneeling and catching his breath. Phillip just shook his head, and then spat on the ground.

The concussive explosions were not just from machine guns firing at them; they were also from mortar shells and grenades exploding amongst them. The not-so-old man felt the weight of the metal helmet on his head and rucksack on his back, but he didn't have a rifle—he was only an ambulance driver. He had dropped the chocolates and cigarettes he was bringing the troops on the front lines a few seconds earlier when the attack had started.

There were soldiers to the left and right of him, barbed wire thirty yards in front. The soldiers were yelling. "Ritiro! Ritiro!" Men scrambled out of the trenches and ran across the field away from the barbed wire. The not-so-old man held his helmet down and ran with them.

"Ritiro! Ritiro!"

"What the hell?" the not-so-old man thought. But hidden behind his fear was the notion of, *"It's about time!"*

He felt the mortar shrapnel rip into his legs in over two

hundred places. He went down and lost consciousness for a minute and felt death and then woke up. He realized what had happened and started crawling across the field when another soldier—an Italian infantryman—was shot in his leg. The soldier flinched as blood shot out of his thigh, and his rifle flew high into the air as he fell right next to the not-so-old man. "So this is how I die," shot through the not-so-old man's mind. "Then I will die with dignity."

He pushed himself up while holding the leg with the most shrapnel in it to minimize the bleeding, and stumbled to the downed soldier. Without a word, he bent down, wrapped the soldier's arm over his soldier, and with a quiet grunt, lifted him up.

"Cosa fai?" the soldier mumbled. "Sono già morto. Lasciami e salvati."

The not-so-old man started carrying the man away from the mayhem.

Then, the machine gun bullets. Three or four pierced into his right knee and foot. He hardly felt them but stumbled from their impact as he hobbled with the man on his back. After a few whirling steps, he fell on his face and the soldier fell on his shoulder.

He looked to his left. Another soldier was crawling. He realized his own legs were shot to hell, so he started crawling too. He looked forward and saw the remains of a bombed-out house. "Thank God," he thought. He crawled on his belly and dragged the wounded soldier along by his shirt collar over a hundred yards of withered field grass, discarded firearms, and scorched earth.

His legs were virtually useless, but his hands and arms were strong and true. He used them to grab the ground and pull himself and his soldier forward. He used them to push aside rocks and twisted rifles and the occasional lost limb so he could pull himself and his soldier over the hell of the battlefield and through mortar shell craters towards the safety of home. It took a long time and felt like forever, and he thought that this is what hell must be like.

At times, the shelling and shooting let up for a few minutes but never stopped completely. Then they'd intensify again and he'd hear bullets whizz over his and his soldier's head and slam into the dirt beyond them or a rock or some metal sticking out of the ground and his soldier would let out a moan or a sigh and a few times a whimper of defeat, but the not-so-old man didn't stop pulling him away from the front line.

As he crawled, he inhaled the pungent and choking smoke and dust of the battlefield. It stung his nostrils and made him cough up phlegm. But he couldn't stop breathing. To pause now meant certain death—not just for him, but for his soldier.

"Siamo quasi arrivati, amico mio," he said loud enough for the soldier to hear. "Non ti lascerò morire."

"Ma potresti morire provandoci," his soldier replied, choking on his words.

"Impossibile," the not-so-old man grunted. "Sono già morto una volta oggi. Il fulmine non colpisce mai due volte."

Then, KA-POW!

Another shell landed and exploded just a few yards in front of them. He felt the explosion deep down in his bones. If he and his injured soldier had been running, they would have been blown to smithereens.

Once inside the skeleton of the bombed-out house, the not-so-old man ripped his shirt off, tore off the sleeve, and wrapped it around the soldier's bleeding thigh. He tightened it and tied it into a knot.

"Grazie," the soldier mumbled. "Grazie mille," he whispered hoarsely and then passed out.

The not-so-old man looked at his own legs. His trousers were blown to shreds, exposing cuts and gouges where the shrapnel and bullets had entered. But he wasn't bleeding too badly. Dirt had been rubbed deep into his wounds that sealed them nicely, and some of the pain soon turned to numbness.

He saw another soldier stumble toward the house and fall on his face in the dirt. The not-so-old man crawled out of the house, grabbed the soldier's collar, and yanked him through the battered door opening and behind the concrete wall of the house. As he entered the house for the second time, he noticed a colorful sign written in a fancy script that read, "God Bless This House" in Italian.

Suddenly the gunfire stopped, and the mortar shells stopped falling. He let himself lie down on the ground.

Then someone was leaning over him and cutting off the shreds of his pants with a Swiss army knife. The not-so-old man closed his eyes and winced as whiskey was dabbed up and down his legs. It stung like hell, but he didn't mind.

CHAPTER *VIII*

As it is after sparring with a bull, a successful hunt, or battle for survival, an unexpected yet welcome sort of relaxation sets in. The not-so-old man's mind was blank, totally blank for several long minutes—long minutes of reset, recalibration, and renewal—as he instinctively stayed afloat in the roiling sea. Water kept beating on him. Beating on him like it was gushing out of a fire hose, washing his resistance away and exposing what he had unconsciously piled on to save himself.

Then finally, it came. Finally, the cleansing...

She was due in a month and a half. They had refused ultrasound because they wanted to be surprised if it was a boy or girl. Valerie had bumped into the corner of the kitchen table one evening and thought it was nothing. But the dull pain was even worse the next morning, so she decided to play it safe and go to the hospital. The not-so-old man as her husband had already gone to work, so she went alone. She and her husband barely spoke anymore, and she didn't tell him any of this. But when the doctor showed her the ultrasound with the umbilical cord wrapped around the fetus's neck, she called him.

It had been two years and five months since Ray Ray had died, and both of them were still shell-shocked and anxious about having another child. They both felt cursed because of what had happened to Ray Ray, but they both felt blessed in a way and that another child was meant to be because, during the time since Ray Ray's death, they had had sex only once.

As the not-so-old man as Valerie's husband drove to the

Emergency Room she started having labor pains. They were normal pains, the doctor told her, but there were other problems. The fetus's heartbeat was weak, and an ultrasound showed that the umbilical cord had a knot in it and was wrapped around the fetus's neck. Plus, there were signs of velamentous cord insertion, causing umbilical cord prolapse. He recommended an immediate C-section. Valerie agreed. By the time the not-so-old man as Valerie's husband arrived, she was about to go into surgery.

The not-so-old man as the husband insisted he be allowed into the operating room, and the hospital's policies allowed that. Valerie wanted him there. She was looking into his eyes and holding his hand when the epidural went into her spine. When the cut was made, the not-so-old man as Valerie's husband looked away. They were both scared. He could tell she knew something, and he knew it too.

As the doctor squeezed his fingers into Valerie's womb to pull out the fetus, her blood pressure dropped hard and fast. She fainted. The fetus's heart stopped as the doctor pulled him out. The not-so-old man as Valerie's husband squeezed his wife's hand firmly as the nurse put the oxygen mask on her face. The not-so-old man as Valerie's husband watched the doctor pull his son out of his wife, and saw the cord with a knot in it wrapped twice around his neck. The baby did not cry.

The nurse cut the cord and unwound it from the baby's neck, and the doctor furiously performed CPR. The not-so-old man as his father watched his son never be his son as the doctor and nurses worked. Valerie didn't regain consciousness until five minutes later when they officially pronounced her and her husband's baby dead.

The not-so-old man as the father that wasn't stretched out his arms, and without a word, the doctor placed the lifeless fetus into his hands. The not-so-old man as the father that wasn't looked down at his son, streaked with blood and covered in gelatinous goo: his eyes closed and a little fuzz on his head; his little mouth slightly open as if he was about to cry for the first time; and his little hands and feet—with all their digits fully formed—there in front of him with his arms and hands outstretched as if yearning to give someone a hug.

He had been so close, so close to making it into this world and making his father a father again, and helping two broken hearts mend some. Valerie regained consciousness and whimpered. She glanced at her husband holding her son, and then quickly looked away and fainted again.

The not-so-old man as the father that wasn't fell to his knees while pressing his little son to his chest. Silent tears streamed down his cheeks and fell onto the floor. He leaned over and braced himself with one hand on the floor while he pressed his son who never was fast against his heart with the other hand, and vomited.

The not-so-old man floated upright in the sea. It enveloped him, rolled him, defied him, and mercilessly tossed him about. There were tears in his eyes now as it crashed back down on him. He felt sick to his stomach and wanted desperately to die, but his arms and legs kept treading water. Clouds had gathered above his head, and the memories kept beating on him, breaking him apart, reaching deeper into his past, deeper into his gray matter, deeper into his soul, back to where the worst damage had been done. He couldn't take it any longer, but he couldn't stop it either...

It had become a battle of egos and supremacy. Master or slave. He'd be damned if he was going to be her slave. So when she insisted, even demanded, he not take Rachel to the playground as the little girl so enthusiastically wanted, it was the final straw.

He moved the child safety car seat from her Lexus to his, packed some water and snacks in Rachel's little backpack, and led her by the hand to the car. The tension was palpable and almost physical as he strapped Rachel in, her eyes wide with confusion as if to say, "Why isn't Mommy coming too?"

Valerie held herself in check, knowing that an obvious display of anger and hostility toward her husband wasn't what she wanted her baby-girl to see. But her feelings were obvious anyway.

The not-so-old man as a young father pulled out of the driveway without so much as a wave and immediately shifted Rachel's attention away from the tension and her longing for Mommy. "So which playground do you want to go to today?" he asked. "Do you still want to go to the new one I told you about?"

The not-so-old man as a young father often wondered why he and Val had this background static in their relationship—like when you can't tune in a radio station, and there's a constant rasping behind the music. It had started soon after their engagement when they got in an argument about dinner rolls, of all things, on Thanksgiving Day. Valerie was preparing the turkey and everything that went along with it, but she had forgotten to make dinner rolls. The not-so-old man as a young man said, "We're eating by ourselves, and I don't care."

"Well, Valerie does! Please, go get some."

So he drove across town to the only grocery store open and brought back a tray of cafeteria grade dinner rolls.

"What's this?" Valerie grumbled.

"Dinner rolls," the not-so-old man as a young man said bluntly.

"You call these dinner rolls?"

"Yes. It says so right on the label."

All she said after that was, "Idiot!"

The not-so-old man as a young man's jaw dropped, but he didn't say a thing. He went into the family room and resumed watching the football game on TV.

They ate that dinner alone—him watching the game in the family room and her brooding in the kitchen—and in silence, neither of them willing to concede defeat. But later that evening, after both had cooled down, one thing led to another, and they ended up making love on the couch with the TV off. Neither of them had apologized. And he never did eat his dinner roll.

Eventually, it became a fight for who was King of the Hill except for the few months before and after Ray Ray was born. Valerie would insult him and push him down to the bottom because she knew he was too polite to react. But he would gather strength and make a charge, like a flag bearer leading his troops up the hill, with a surprise counter-attack when she least expected it. That seemed to settle her down, almost like she finally respected him. But later, she would insult him again, and the pattern would repeat.

The waves kept coming. The not-so-old man kept fighting them.

And it kept coming, harder and deeper...

They had stopped at a light a block away from the new playground. Ray Ray had fallen asleep in her car seat. The light turned to green, but the not-so-old man as a young father didn't notice since he had been looking back at his daughter sleeping. A toot of the horn from the car behind him made him realize the light had changed, so he waved to the driver and pulled ahead.

He felt the jolt as the speeding garbage truck that ran the light slammed into the passenger side of the car. Its bumper and grill smashed through the back seat door, right where the car seat was fastened, and Ray Ray slept.

The not-so-old man as a young father grunted with the initial impact. Ray Ray screamed. Glass shattered and rained like sleet in the car. The sound was like a bomb had gone off with the screeching of metal on metal. The car was thrown across the intersection all the way into another car that was waiting to make a turn, crunching the not-so-old man as a young father's door and pinning it shut.

The not-so-old man as a young father's head banged against his window, shattering it. He saw stars but didn't lose consciousness. His hand instinctively went up to hold his head, and he turned around and looked at Ray Ray. What he saw horrified him.

The door had been smashed in almost two feet, shredding it into metal daggers pointing inwards and right at and onto Rachel's car seat. The safety seat was strapped tightly to the regular seat with the seat belt, so it held fast against the crashed-in door. The seat was twisted sideways toward the other side of the car and arched from a dagger pushing into it from behind.

Ray Ray's back was bent back and sideways, and her sleepy eyes were open and afraid. There was a cut across her forehead from the shattered glass, and her arms were bruised. She moaned softly as if there was no air in her lungs to scream. But she finally mumbled, "It hurts, Daddy."

The not-so-old man as a young father unbuckled his seat belt and reached behind for his little girl.

"Daddy. It hurts, Daddy,"

"I'm coming," he said. "I'm coming. It's gonna be alright."

He could reach the car seat, but the strap that held Rachel was contorted such that it was wrapped around her with the release buckle behind her, between her back and the smashed door. Her little body was twisted toward him, and he could clearly see her sleepy, pain-filled eyes looking at him for help.

He saw the metal daggers more closely now and could see that one was pressing directly into the back of the car seat, putting a dent and bend in the plastic.

Someone outside screamed to call 911. Someone else was trying to push the other car the Lexus was pinned against away from it. The not-so-old man as a young father pulled at the door latch to open the door and get to his daughter in the back seat, but the door wouldn't budge.

The not-so-old man as a young father tried to climb over the front seats, but the way the door was smashed and the car seat pushed up and in, there was no room for him to get there. The garbage truck was pinned to the right side, the other car to the left. He was trapped. Someone outside yelled, "Back up! Back it up!"

He grabbed the belts that encircled and pinned his daughter. He could bend his wrist to get his fingers to the button to release the straps, but no matter how hard he pushed on it, it wouldn't release. He grabbed the straps and pulled on them, twisted them, pried at them, and pulled on the car seat with all his might, but nothing would move. He tried to get to one of the belts with his mouth to chew it in half, but he couldn't reach it.

"It hurts, Daddy. Daddy, it hurts."

He was blind now with panic. He flailed like a fish just brought up in a boat thrashing on the deck, beating the life out of itself. He tried to open his door again, tried to open the passenger door, tried to climb over the seats to get a better angle.

"Back it up! Back it up!"

"Daddy. It hurts, Daddy."

He heard the garbage truck's engine roar and the screech of metal as it backed slowly away from the Lexus. Then the snap. The not-so-old man would never forget that sound. As the garbage truck pulled back from the car, part of the door that had been smashed in and caught on the car seat released, plunging its knife-like shard into the plastic back of the safety seat, through it, and into Rachel's back. He heard her gasp as the air escaped her punctured lung. Then a gurgle. Then silence.

The not-so-old man as a young father refused to believe the truth he had just heard and quickly pushed the passenger side door open and crawled out of the car. He pulled the mess of metal away from the back door and reached inside. Ray Ray's head was down, chin on her chest, mouth oozing blood, eyes open but lifeless.

He yanked and pulled and twisted until he finally released the buckle on the car seat and pulled Rachel out. He couldn't look at her. Instead, he held her to his chest, kissed her on the top of her head, fell to his knees, and vomited. The rest he did not remember.

The not-so-old man was still treading water amongst all this as the sea continued to rage. His hand was still cramped. The clouds above him were high and white and billowy. Tears washed down his face into the sea, and he wailed loud, slow, pain-filled, heart-pounding, and gut-wrenching wails that bounced off the white-capped waves and turned back upon him amplified, as if he was in an amphitheater of pain. His heart tightened and ached, and for a moment he thought he was having a heart attack. Then he felt his hands and fingers red and hot like they had been plunged into a blast furnace, and he felt his stomach being twisted like a wet rag would be twisted to wring out all the water—but it wasn't a rag being twisted and squeezed, but his guts. He heaved. He heaved again. Nothing came out of him, but he heaved again, and then a little teaspoon of bile gurgled up into his throat and sat in the back of his mouth that tasted like bitter, pungent metal and felt like slime you'd scrape off pond water infested with algae.

He didn't just feel, but in reality, *was,* empty, alone, forsaken, and forgotten. He had been left alone and forgotten by his ex-wife and his sister, he had no real friends, and anyone who showed interest in becoming a friend quickly learned there was something about him that would best be avoided. His parents were close to death, and he felt more alone when he was with them since both of them couldn't remember who he was most of the time anyway. He never stopped to consider that it was he, in fact, doing things to push people away—and he was doing those things to punish himself for a mistake he thought was all his own.

He kept floating. When his body calmed down and his mind

settled some, he found it hard to believe he was still alive after being in the sea so long. And he considered it even more amazing that he hadn't found a way to die—or hadn't already committed suicide—after all that had happened in his life.

Yet, after all this, he felt a strange sort of release he had no conscious role of creating. He hadn't cried since his son's death and hadn't allowed himself to fully feel the pain of losing the boy and the girl, and now that he had, he felt lighter.

He thought of his mother, there, in the nursing home, calling him by her brother's name, asking if Pops was still alive. He would reply no, he passed away. How about Mom? she would ask. And Andy? another one of her brothers. She sat in her easy chair as he sat on the side of her bed, tucked in a corner of her room, the window showed snow outside, and a church steeple in the distance. The nurses had to lock the closet in her room because she would take all her clothes—what was left of her clothes—and pack them in the one suitcase left and tell everyone she was going home: "I want to go home," she would say. "I want to go home." "Is Pops still alive?" "How about Mom?" And she took his hand and held it. He never remembered holding her hand, even as a child. Tears made their way out of the corners of his eyes now as the sea raged around him. Mournful, sentimental, bittersweet tears dribbled down his cheeks and dripped one by one into the sea below. Her hand, her skin, so soft and fragile and cool to the touch. Her asking him if he needed anything—a drink, a snack? Asking him if he could stay the night. He could sleep on the bed and she would sleep in her easy chair. If only she had been so soft and kind when he was growing up, he would think. "But at least she remembers my name this time. At least she hasn't turned mean like some others." And as he drove away, she was there, waving through the side windows of the locked main entrance door, waving, waving goodbye to him, frantically waving goodbye. She knew she had little time left. She knew that. And he knew it too. And finally, he hated that. Finally, he wanted mommy. And he would have to stop the car once he got on the road to cry like a baby and wipe away the tears and get a hold of himself and think of something else before he got on the highway back to his other house, his other home, his other excuse for a home.

He thought about his dad—the times he showed toughness, the times he came to his rescue, then the times he had a catheter to hold his pee because his bladder was too weak to push it—the chair beside their bed, holding the plastic bag. His hero, his pal, his father, this sweet, sweet man who answered the phone, "Shoot, it's your nickel," in his jovial, welcoming voice. Sitting in the family room, looking at a book with pictures of fields and streams and beautiful landscapes, and remarking to the not-so-old man as a not-so-old man, "This is quite a book! Have you seen these pictures?" and two minutes later, saying, "This is quite a book! Have you seen these pictures?" His heart ached with the memories. But his heart shattered every time he remembered his dad not being able to sleep, getting out of bed and gingerly walking into the kitchen, holding the bag, and mumbling, "Mama. Mama. Mama." Shattered, broken, wrecked, he was. The last time he would see him. But as painful as those memories were, the not-so-old man always came back to remembering his dad during the good times: the times hiking with the sun going down, the time in the rowboat he saved his sister from drowning, the times he showed him how to use a saw and a file and rasp so he could make a toy boat out of some discarded pieces of lumber, the times they played catch and the times his dad sat in the bleachers watching him play ball. The times people gravitated to him, laughed, listened, wanted to have him as a friend.

The sea took the not-so-old man's tears as if they meant nothing, swallowing them into the trillions of other's tears that had come before his.

Then he whispered, "It wasn't all your fault. She knew how you responded to demands. She knew you would defy her just to defy her. She knew no good ever came of her being that way. And yet she persisted in her need to be right and to be obeyed. Neither of us realized how our greedy egos would hurt someone else.

"And truly, all she had to do was ask. Just ask me not to take Ray Ray. I wouldn't have gone. I wouldn't have taken her to the playground. I would have stayed. I would have. I would have. I would have stayed. Just having her ask me instead of ordering me would have quelled my stubbornness enough to listen. It wasn't just my fault. It was her fault too. It was her fault too."

The not-so-old man opened his tear-filled eyes and looked up into the heavens. "I'm sorry, Rachel. I'm sorry for my stubbornness and fear. I'm sorry about your mom's stubbornness and fear. We didn't know it would hurt you so."

He kept treading water.

"And son, I'm sorry you never had a chance. You would have been terrific. You had *salao*, and it just wasn't fair."

The not-so-old man had tried his best in both situations. He had tried to accept that but never understood how. Now he did, and his heart, to some degree, did too.

His tears stopped. Several minutes passed as his mind, body, and soul lingered in the new sensation. It was strong enough to deflect away any feelings of guilt he might have had for feeling better, or more precisely, not feeling as bad as he had for decades.

And the minutes passed.

How do you get out of bankruptcy? Two ways. Gradually, then suddenly. The waves subsided as quickly as they had come.

Chapter IX

*T*he not-so-old man noticed himself. He noticed he was floating on his back in the sea, all alone, under a blue sky strewn with billowy clouds. He realized his body was very weak and would not last much longer. He had been running on adrenaline too long. Power that should have been going to his brain was being diverted to his muscles for simple survival. Life does not want to die. It is pesky, unrelenting, and covetous. It will push aside almost anything in its way to survive—except a stronger will to die. He still had that will. His mind kept returning.

He thought about a part of Hemingway's story where the old man hooked a dolphin, and he pulled in the line, and eventually pulled the dolphin up into his skiff and watched the mammal toss and thrash and convulse wildly trying to get free and trying not to die. The dolphin didn't want to die; he hated to die. And yet, the not-so-old man here, now, was hoping for death and wanted to die but was still alive anyway.

"Yes," he thought. "There is clearly something wrong with me."

Then a thought occurred to him which he really didn't want to think because it was hopeful, and he had learned to hate feeling hopeful.

"What is hope, anyway?" he thought. "Is it not just a specious delusion? A delusion that everything's going to get better, everything's gonna be alright? Whoever invented hope was desperate, I tell you. Desperate to believe things are going to change—to *improve*. But isn't it just the conscious admission that whatever you have isn't good enough? Hope melts reality away, distracts you from the present moment. It convinces you to ignore the problems and live for tomorrow. It's like candy for the broken; A sweet morsel to excite the downtrodden that numbs the torment of a lusterless path. You lose yourself in that sweetness and deny the present, and that, my hopeful friend, is what caused all your problems in the first place. So forget it. Spit it out and forget it…"

The not-so-old man was suddenly proud. Proud of his ability to deny himself, to spit it out as if he were too noble to swallow it. But, as with life itself, the compulsion for some sweetness—that was manifesting inside of him as an original thought—was too strong to deny, and his next thought (that his reflection of Hemingway's story was creating) was, "Inside everyone, dolphins included, is the desire, the will, to live and keep living. That's your natural state. If you want to kill yourself, then something went wrong. It isn't you who wants to die, but it's the problems of your life that are too painful to face that want you to die.

"It's not you," he thought. "It's your stupid life that's the problem. Deep inside, you really want to live."

He paused, then whispered, "Nice try, wise guy. Nice try. Problem is, you're wrong. I want to die, and that's all that matters."

He floated on his back and thought his mind was done with its silliness, but that candy was sweet and he couldn't resist…

"If life wants to live, and I am alive, then by thinking I want death, am I in actuality, just deceiving myself?"

A fish jumped out of the water and splashed down beside him. The not-so-old man didn't flinch.

"The old fisherman said he didn't understand sin and couldn't decide what sin was. Perhaps deception is a sin. Perhaps deception is the only sin."

And with that thought, he stopped thinking. He kept floating on his back and looked at the sky.

The not-so-old man had often wondered—when he was contemplating how to do it—how many people, after they had taken that fateful step off the bridge or high-rise and were plunging to their deaths, thought on their way down, "Oops! I should have thought this through a little more."

He had wondered too if he would think the same thing just before he went under for the last time. But now, at the very least, he was hoping that since he had found a way to forgive himself to some degree, his suicide wouldn't be a sin, but a blessing.

The sun was waning. The clouds had drifted to the horizon.

He thought about Ernie and wondered if, as he squeezed the trigger and felt the subtle yet irreversible strike of hammer on firing pin, "Oops! I should have thought this through a little more."

The not-so-old man's mind and body floated aimlessly. "I don't think you really killed yourself, Ernie. Somebody else did it. Maybe the FBI. Maybe they wanted to show that even heroes have flaws, and you can't count on anybody but the government. Maybe an ex-wife or jealous husband. Maybe the KGB. Maybe an old friend that decided you were too rich and was jealous of your success.

"Or maybe you just wanted out of the rat race and decided to retire somewhere in peace where you no longer had to live up to your macho-man image. Your son Greg said that you often complained about how hard it was being a man. 'It's hard, son. It's hard,' you would tell him. 'It's hard being a man.' Perhaps those words were part of the reason Greg—nicknamed Gigi—became a transvestite.

"That's kinda sad, Ernie. But back to you… Maybe you made a deal with the FBI where you would write their news stories for free if they gave you a new identity. They were watching you, weren't they? People thought you were paranoid, but I believe you. And hey, Ernie, I just thought of something. How could they pull that off? By not needing to show a body—it would be too gruesome. So who's to say what was in the coffin, Ernie? Maybe there was just a sack of potatoes weighing it down. Your suicide happened in Idaho, didn't it? So they hustled you out of the country to some faraway island to live happily ever and drinking cocktails with little umbrellas in them.

"Dying in an airplane crash would do the same. No body to show. You know, Ernie, I like music so I follow it some. Did you know a whole bunch of musicians and singers have died in plane crashes? Buddy Holley, the Big Bopper, and Ritchie Valens all died in the same crash on February 3, 1959. That's what the song, *American Pie* was about—'The day the music died.' John Denver, Patsy Cline, and Jim Croce all died in plane crashes. Who knows? Maybe they all have new identities and are living in luxury somewhere. Maybe Tahiti. I wouldn't mind retiring in Tahiti.

"I know I'm being stupid, Ernie. All I can say is that you'd better hope that all that stuff about burning in hell for eternity if you do certain things on earth aren't true. It wouldn't be right that a guy who won the Nobel Prize and Pulitzer and made all that money and entertained so many people with his thoughts and words would have to spend eternity down there. You lived more in one lifetime than most people live in fifty. Maybe we should ask for a pardon for guys like you. You know, get a 'get out of hell free' card. Or maybe we could petition God to rewrite the rules. He could do that. Truly, he could.

"You see, Ernie, buddy, we have much in common with this suicide gig. But I'm just a little more thoughtful than you. Maybe it's because I don't get drunk and hardly ever did except for that month I was trying to forget. Were you drunk when you pulled the trigger, Ernie? Have one too many apéritifs that morning? Have trouble finding just the right word for one of your short, declarative sentences? Get brain-freeze from your Iceberg Theory? Get motion sickness from your high/low strategy? Maybe you blew your brains out because you realized you had already written about everything you knew, so what else is there to life without drinking? I couldn't finish *Islands in the Stream*. Sorry, Ernie, I'm just being truthful. I know you hated negative criticism and would complain and get downright petulant when the critics missed your point or heaven forbid, negatively criticized your writing. But you can't have honesty without that possibility, Ernie. I'm sure, you understand.

"My suicide may not be as declarative as yours with buck-shot through the skull, but it's much cleaner and cheaper. I'm simply swimming out to sea to get thoroughly exhausted, so I have no choice but to drown. Less work for everyone and zero expenses— no hiring someone to clean the walls and pick up the pieces of my brain, no ambulance, no body bag, no coffin, no funeral director, no digging a hole and putting up a tarp in case it rains, no priest or donation, no post-funeral buffet, and no time lost from work. The fishes will eat me and save everyone the bother. I hope it's a marlin that eats my body—maybe a descendant of the Great Marlin the old man hooked and killed. That would be some kind of payback, don't you think? That would validate karma, don't you think?

"It would save loved ones from having to make a politically correct statement like, 'Untimely death,' or 'Unexpected death.' In your case, your wife at the time said immediately afterward that you shot yourself by accident cleaning the shotgun. Later, however, she admitted you pulled the trigger on purpose and said she wasn't in her right mind when she said it was an accident. But in my case, there'll be no politically correct excuses needed for my death. I'll simply not show up to work Monday morning. 'Where's

Daniel?' they'll ask. I did make one tactical error, though, by leaving my wallet on the beach. I should have thought things through a little better.

"But still, it's better than blowing my brains out at 7:30 in the morning in the downstairs foyer while my wife was sleeping like you did. Maybe the tide will come in and just wash my wallet out to sea. Or someone will find it and hopefully keep the money and credit cards for themselves and have some fun since I have no one to pass anything on to. But some good person might find it and that would be a clue. Then they might search the beaches and troll the ocean for a body for a few days. No big deal. But for all anyone would know, I could have been kidnapped or moved to Paris or Key West just to leave it all behind since I often complained I just wanted out of the rat race. Then the few people who knew me and even fewer people who would give a rat's ass could console themselves thinking I'm still alive and well and living the life of Riley.

"But seriously, Ernie. Who would care about me? My ex-wife will be happy I'm gone since she hated me for ruining her life for over a dozen years. She remarried and even had a kid. Had a normal birth through the birth canal and everything. Had a little boy. He's sixteen already. I've never seen him. Couldn't bear it.

"I have a friend who I swim and play basketball with at the Y in the winters. He's an okay guy—puts up with my sulking. He might come to my funeral if I ever had one. Kinda makes me think of what happened to James Gatz… you know, the Great Gatsby who entertained the whole city, and then nobody came to his funeral? But I am not in his league. My secretary at work is okay. She even seems to like me, but I never let her in.

"You see, Ernie, my suicide would harm pretty much nobody. My parents are both gone—figuratively and soon to be literally. My sister might take it hard for a few days, but she's always been resilient and convinced that everything happens for a reason, so she'd be okay in the long run. We hardly ever speak anymore anyway. I should have written her a goodbye note, though. I owed her that.

"Even though our methods differ, Ernie, the outcome is the same: we killed ourselves. So when I meet you in hell, I hope we can be friends, maybe even best buds. It would be nice, don't you think, if we got along? We should give it a shot. Oops. Sorry. Didn't mean to remind you.

"Speaking of friends... Tell me truly, Ernie, what really happened with you and Gertrude Stein? The woman you said was, big and tall and built like a peasant woman, and who guided you to appreciate art and painters—especially Cezanne with his heavy brush-strokes you thought you could model your prose after somehow—and who coached you and chatted with you about writing and introduced you to other writers, artists, and publishers.

"Did you tire of her because she thought you were *inaccrochable?* Or did you resent her for calling you part of the *Lost Generation* who used alcohol, parties, and sex to distract yourselves from your aimless lives? Isn't that what *The Sun Also Rises* is partly about? And while other writers infesting Seine's Left Bank were desperately trying to be avant-garde by writing nonsensical gibberish...

> *Would he like it if I told him if I told him if Napoleon.*
> *Would he like it if Napoleon if Napoleon if I told him.*
> *If I told him if Napoleon if Napoleon if I told him.*
> *If I told him would he like it would he like it if I told him.*

"...you went back to the basics, the fundamentals. Not only did you read all the Rrrroooosians, as your drinking buddy Erza called them, you got as fundamental as you could—you went to the Bible for inspiration for the title of your first novel:

> *One generation passeth away,*
> *and another generation cometh:*
> *but the earth abideth forever.*
> *The sun also ariseth,*
> *and the sun goeth down,*
> *and hasteth to his place where he arose.*

"Yes, your generation too did pass. As will mine.

"I don't blame you for resenting having your generation being called lost. I remember what you wrote, 'I thought of Miss Stein and Sherwood Anderson and egotism and mental laziness versus discipline [acquired in war] and I thought who is calling who a lost generation?... I thought that all generations were lost by something and always had been and always would be.'

"Ernie, I figure your generation got lost after the war trying to cope with PTSD by anesthetizing yourselves, feeling survivor guilt, feeling there's no meaning to life, and just as importantly, getting lost in the death of dreams that had yet to be dreamed. The next generation will get lost in the extravagance always seen after a war. Then the next will get lost in the next war, and so on."

The not-so-old man had figured that to keep the extravagance coming, the thing to do would be to be at war all the time. Not big wars, but a succession of small ones. Then every generation would have the extravagance of war and would be at the same time automatically lost—lost enough to keep agreeing to go to war. He called it his Perpetually Lost theory. He figured that someone had already figured that out. "But I think crazy," he mumbled.

"Yes, Ernie, I want to hear all the dirt. And how could you cheat on that angel Hadley? Come on Ernie. Not cool. But at least you gave her all the royalties from your first book *and* its movie. That was big of you. But why did you come down on Fitzgerald? He had a gift too. He just had issues with drinking and his crazy wife Zelda and the size of his you know what.

"After all, Ernie didn't Scotty give you advice about cutting some stuff out of *The Sun Also Rises* before it was published that saved the book? If it had been published with the first two chapters you originally had that sophomorically dwelled on the wonton life of Lady Brett Ashley, they would have thought you were playing for the junior varsity and weren't ready for the big leagues. And he even introduced you to Max Perkins who ended up publishing it. So give old Scotty a break. I really liked his *The Great Gatsby*, especially the beginning when Nick talks about what his father told him that ended up molding his character because I have the same characteristic—which is probably really either weakness or laziness or both—in myself.

"But you were never weak, Ernie, until you blew your brains out, that is. But like I said, I don't believe it because not only were you *inaccrochable*, but you were also a bull-fighting *aficionado*. And the chicks—they dig it.

"After all, Ernie isn't suicide truly a relative term? I mean, most people do something that's slowly killing themselves; whether it's drinking too much (And what's too much? Some think *any* alcohol is poison.) or smoking or taking drugs or doing extreme things like riding around on a dirt bike like a bat out of hell without a helmet on. All these compulsions to distract ourselves.

"The complicated things in life. Compulsify. Compulsify.

"We all know better, Ernie than to do those things. Take Scotty for example. He drank way too much and died way too early because of it. He knew better but did it anyway. So if we do those things and know they're going to shorten our lives, isn't that just a slow form of suicide? Yes sir, Ernie. I can rationalize with the best of them.

"Do you think Mademoiselle Stein would mind if I called her

Gertie? Probably. That's too diminutive for a lesbian. But maybe she let her girlfriend Alice B. call her that during playtime. Just imagine them talking after you left Gertie's apartment for the last time when they were arguing: 'Come here, Gertie, sweetheart. Now that that *inaccrochable* Hemingway is gone, we can have some real *inaccrochable* fun of our own!'

"And about your buddy Ezra—he helped you with your writing, so in return, you gave him boxing lessons:

"Okay, you ruffian," you said. "You're right-handed, right?"

"Yeah, Hem. I'm right and I'm feeling all tight... err... all right too."

"We're not talking drinkin' now, Ezra. We're talkin' defending yourself."

"All tight... Did I just say that again? Damn! I mean, right you are, buddy boy!"

"Oh brother. Listen. You stand like this: left foot forward, right foot back. Weight even between the two."

Ezra shuffled his feet the wrong way.

"No! The left foot forward! Not *that* left foot! The other left foot!"

"Oh! Okay."

"Now hold your left fist in front, about as high as your chin."

"Like this?"

"No, Ezra! You're making a fist like a girl. The thumb goes on the outside or else when you punch someone, you'll break it."

"Like this?"

"Yeah."

"That feels strange, Hem."

"Of course it does. Get used to it. Now the other hand. That's better. You're catching on. At least you know which one is your other hand."

"I need an-other drink."

"That comes later, Ezra. Focus! You've got to focus!"

"Okay, Hem. Don't get sore. I'm just a poet! A sensitive poet!"

"I know. We gotta toughen you up. Now put your right fist back a little near your chin. Yeah, that's it."

"Hey, this is easy."

"We haven't done anything yet, Ezra! Now *I* need a drink."

"Agreed. Let's go to Le Dôme. There's a cute waitress there I want to impress with my new self-defense moves."

"You're hopeless, Pound. Okay, we'll go. But tomorrow, we work on footwork. Footwork is very important, Ezra."

"Is that anything like running? Wouldn't it be easier if I just ran away from a fight?"

"Here's your beret, you degenerate. Let's go before the rains come."

"Right you are, Hem. Thanks for the lesson. I feel much more confident now."

"Oh, brother!"

"I feel better with my beret on anyway. You know, Hem, it makes me look like a beatnik writer who's different like a cat on the prowl so nobody should cross my path or I'll write a pithy poem about them and their bourgeoisie attitude that got us into all this trouble in the first place and makes all the…"

"Yeah, yeah, yeah. Watch the curb, there Ezra…"

The not-so-old man was amusing himself now, so he looked up high and noticed a new cloud in the sky, and strangely, it looked like a spitting image of Elvis from the neck up—mullet hairdo and all.

"Ernie, did you ever see Elvis on stage? Did you ever meet him? I bet you and he would have been great friends. You could have taken him on safari, and he could have shown you how to grow a mullet. Oh, what fun Ernie. Such fun you and Elvis on stage. He could sing, *You Ain't Nothin' but a Hound Dog*. I bet your ex-wives would sing right along."

The not-so-old man tried to find a cloud that looked like Ernie in his golden years, with a full white beard, thinning white hair, tanned bronze-colored skin, and pensive frown. There was no such cloud.

"I guess you and Elvis never met," he continued. "And Ernie, I used to think that maybe the war wound Jake got was the same as the wounds you got in the war, you know since you write so autobiographical and all. Once I looked into you a little deeper, I found out it was your legs that got messed up. But for the longest time, I figured that because you had kids—John with Hadley and Patrick and Gregory with Pauline—perhaps the milkman had paid them both a little visit. I know, Ernie, my imagination is rotten sometimes.

"And along with a crush on your first wife, I also fell in love with one of your grandchildren, Mariel. I saw her in the Woody Allen movie *Manhattan* and was instantly smitten. D'em some lovely genes you passed along, Ernie. And you would be proud of her because she's faced the Hemingway Curse head-on and has tried to help people with depression. She said that when someone talks about their depression it helps them overcome it. So that's my excuse.

"But Ernie, you would probably empathize with me about marriage. For a wild man like yourself, it's hard to settle down like they say they want you to. They want you playing house instead of roaming the open range and being the cowboy you truly are. But if you squash your needs and do what's expected, they end up disrespecting you for it. After all, every girl loves the bad boy, but teacher's pet, not so much.

"You see, Ernie, for me, acting domesticated wasn't so bad. Although I like to be number one, I know that being part of a winning team helps me be number one.

"One problem with my wife, though, besides needing to be on top and talking in the third person—and this new annoyance didn't happen until after the accident—was her need to one-up you. She became what I call a 'one-upper.' If you said the sky was blue, she would say something like, 'Not as blue as yesterday.' If you said the traffic was bad, she'd say, 'Yeah, but you should see it in CHICAGO.'

"I would bite my tongue for as long as I could, but eventually I couldn't take it anymore, and I would defend my opinion, and that would start an argument. I kinda think what happened to Rachel and then losing her baby made her that way. And I don't blame her. But her one-upping me all the time drove me crazy, and my mood would swing from strained acquiescence to bitter hostility. And that's not a good rhythm to be in.

"But Ernie, I had a daughter. Rachel. My little Ray Ray. The joy returned to our marriage, and my wife and I had so much fun teaching her to walk and hearing her first words, and even wiping her little nose or changing her diaper. My wife changed for a while when it was all new, and I changed too. But just to show you, do you know what Ray Ray's first words were? 'Da Da.' That's right. 'Da Da.' I was King of the Hill again. I know. I know, Ernie. I'm a bum.

"And hey, I didn't mention it before—it's funny sometimes what you forget—but while we're speaking man-to-man, I thought I'd tell you that you and me, we're *sympatico* in a way. We're both, according to numerology, a 'one' life-path.

"I don't know if you'd put any stock in that, but maybe you would, considering how you kept a rabbit's foot in your pocket to the point of rubbing off all its fur and you carried a good luck stone and recommended your friends carry one too. You even had good-luck stones and trinkets scattered throughout your house in Cuba—that are still there, by the way—in dishes and glasses and whatnot since you had to leave all your possessions behind when you fled the country when Castro came to power.

"Yes, Ernie, you'll be happy to hear they restored your house to its former glory after taking pictures and even samples of the paint and stucco to make sure they brought it back to exactly how it had been when you lived there. And because it was infested with termites and mold, they had to strip it down to its studs and rebuild it from there. You probably would have cringed.

"It took *mucho pesos* to restore, Ernie, so that just goes to show you how much people appreciate you. Then they put all your things back just the way you left them and turned it into a museum. Tens of thousands of tourists from all over the world come to see it every year, Ernie. Even people from China love you, even though I heard you didn't like China.

"People can walk around and peek in the doors and windows but can't go in since they want to keep it all just the way you left it. So there they are—the plates and silverware set on the dining table and the liquor bottles still sitting on a table between two easy chairs in the living room and the heads of animals you shot hanging on the walls and over nine thousand books on bookshelves that seem to be in every room, sometimes reaching up to the ceiling, and over three thousand photos, some of which are under glass on table and desktops.

"They restored thousands of documents using tweezers and magnifying glasses that included personal letters, drafts of stories, and manuscripts they found in the damp, moldy basement. Then they took pictures of them and digitized them and sent them to *The Hemingway Collection* at the JFK Library in Boston since Kennedy's wife Jacqueline loved your works and wanted to preserve your stuff.

"You worked on *For Whom the Bell Tolls* and *The Old Man and the Sea* during the twenty-one years you called that house and

Cuba home (you lived here longer than you lived anywhere else), and you said you wrote better in Cuba than anywhere else in the world.

"There are framed drawings and paintings and bullfighting posters from Spain hanging on walls or resting on shelves, and a shelf with all sorts of knives and hatchets spread out on a blood-red tablecloth. There's a wall in your bathroom they didn't tear down to the studs because they found your handwriting on it. You wrote your weight there to keep track of it since you were kind of obsessive about it...

3/24/1950 – 215 ½ (after big lunch)

July 24, 1960 – 190 ½

("Some people snicker, thinking that the last thing you wrote in Cuba was something on the bathroom wall, since you had to flee soon thereafter—July 25th, I believe it was.")

"I saw an interview with one of your employees at the house who said the stories of your drinking were way overblown, and she never saw you drunk and that you treated all the help with kindness and generosity and was a wonderful person. I also heard similar interviews of people who knew you in Idaho. George Plimpton interviewed you in 1958 and reported you typically wrote when the sun came up until noon and took a half-mile swim every day. That's heartwarming for me to hear, Ernie, for obvious reasons.

"You had furniture made to order using the best Cuban mahogany, and your old *Royal* typewriter is sitting on a dictionary on a bookshelf in your bedroom since you preferred writing standing up, sometimes barefoot.

"There's an animal skin on the floor where you'd stand and bang out your stories, and although I don't remember what animal the skin came from, I do remember you hid letters from other women under it so your wife wouldn't find them. (You dirty dog, you.) Some of these letters were undoubtedly from a nineteen-year-old beauty of Venetian nobility you met while on a duck-hunting trip in Italy. Her name was Adriana Ivancich, and you made no effort to hide your infatuation, even from your wife, Mary. And from December 1948 to December 1955 you had what some considered a platonic (plus the hugging and kissing) relationship with her.

"She and her mother visited you in Cuba and stayed at your house from October 1950 to February 1951. You took her fishing and to your favorite downtown hangout, the *Floridita Restaurante Bar,* and showed her around and showed her off. One of the main characters in your novel, *Across the River and Into the Trees,* was modeled after her, and she did the artwork for that book cover and the book cover for *The Old Man and the Sea.* Apparently, she was your muse—your inspiration for both. But Ernie, I have sad news: She hung herself in 1983 from an olive tree in her backyard.

"On a more cheerful note, I'm sure you'll be happy to hear that they also restored your boat, *Pilar.* In fact, that was the very first thing they did, and it's sitting in dry dock down in the garden, looking brand-spanking new with its dark green hull and rich, dark mahogany wood. Yes, I know you left the boat to Gregorio, the man you modeled the old man on in your Pulitzer Prize-winning novel, but the Cuban government confiscated it, saying they needed it for the tourist money. I'd better keep my mouth shut about the government, you know, Ernie. Good thing I don't drink. Anyway, Gregorio was also the first mate of *Pilar* after Carlos Guttierez—*Pilar's* first, first mate—was hired away by one of your women friends, Jane Mansfield. because she was sore at you for fooling around with Martha. Women! You can never tell now, can you Ernie? They sure are a conundrum.

"I know you put your heart and soul into that boat, Ernie, and I know you believed in the soul since when you got shot-up in the war, you said your soul left your body and then came back. You once had a long talk about your soul with a woman you picked up in a Parisian bar—a dancer in the *Folies*—who was wearing only her birthday suit under her mink coat on the sweaty, hot dance floor. (When asked why she was wearing it, she replied, 'A girl's gotta wear something!') Surprisingly, your conversation was pretty deep and centered on how both of you believed that too many 'cruel vibes' in this lifetime would offend the soul and drive it out, sending it off to a better place—meaning, it would leave you and your body, causing death. You were worried about what you did to Hadley. So to make amends with your soul, you gave Hadley the royalties to your first novel and its subsequent movie.

"And just like at your home when you lived in Key West, celebrities would come to 'Papa's Hideaway,' they called it, and swim in the swimming pool and hang around and eat and drink with you and your fourth wife, Mary. Movie stars like Eva Gardner, Katharine Hepburn, Errol Flynn, Gary Cooper (who was slightly taller than you), and Spencer Tracy came, and even the Duchess of Windsor, and I heard tell that Ms. Gardner liked to swim in the pool naked. I doubt you objected, however.

"Then you'd take them to the *Floridita* to have a game of Bingo. Or was it Yahtzee? The history's a little murky on that. Of course, you'd admonish your guests—as you always did—not to muddle their thinking by drinking since it might cost them the game. You spent a lot of money at that bar, and the owner and people who worked there were very grateful. And they're grateful still since it's one of the stops on the Hemingway tour around Havana and anyone who's anything of a tourist has to go there and have a Papa Dobles (a daiquiri with a double shot of rum [but no sugar—you the man, Ernie], your favorite drink that they named after you) or two (or would that equal four?). In fact, to show their appreciation of you (and the business you brought them), they had a life-size bronze statue made of you, and you're sitting on a barstool with your left elbow leaning against the mahogany bar with your right hand on your hip as you list slightly to port with a subtle yet endearing and very satisfied grin on your bearded face. I guess that bronze daiquiri went down pretty smooth. Makes a great photo-op by the way.

"Speaking of smooth...

"...Oh yeah... I was talking about your rabbit's foot. Please forgive me, Ernie. I know I get off track and go off on tangents, but there's just so much of you to talk about it's hard to say it all at once. I'm doing the best I can. Truly, Ernie, you know I love you. So back to the rabbit's foot...

"So when Hadley got pregnant, you told her you could tell if it was a boy or girl with your rabbit's foot. You suspended it over her face and told her if it moved left, the baby would be a girl, and if it moved right, it would be a boy. And sure as spit, that rabbit's foot moved and moved to the right. And sure as spit, the baby ended up being Mr. Bumby. Pretty cool, Ernie. Of course, 50/50 ain't bad odds.

"I think you eventually gave the rabbit's foot to Scotty when he was stressing when Zelda—who is considered to be 'the first American *flapper*'—was in a mental institution, or should I say multiple mental institutions. It didn't seem to do him or her much good, though—she was schizophrenic and died in a fire in one of those institutions, and Scotty died at the tender-is-the-night age of forty-four. Someday, maybe I'll go by Scotty's and Zelda's graves in Rockville, Maryland, just for a visit. Oh, wait! I'm dying in just a few hours, so I won't be able to make it!

"And then there was that part in *For Whom the Bell Tolls* about the strong and wise, but ugly, peasant woman turned fighting guerrilla, Pilar, reading Robert Jordan's hand, you know, like a palm reader. You implied she saw his future, and it wasn't good.

But it might have shown that you, Ernie, could have believed in that stuff. But that wouldn't have gone along with your macho-man image, so you put it down in the part of the iceberg that's below the surface. That's clever, Ernie. My personal opinion is you gave some credit to the supernatural, and there's times when it can be accessed. That makes us *sympatico* in that way too, Ernie, which pleases me.

"But who's to say about all that stuff? Maybe we find out about it as we're floating up to heaven... or sidestepping our way into purgatory... or falling into hell. It's so much easier to sink than to float, don't you think? And it's so much easier to tumble down a hill than to climb one. So who are the truly weak? It takes guts and stamina, persistence and patience, to keep your head above water. Lord knows I know that as fact. But the weak ones—just like alcoholics—will turn everything upside down and make themselves out to be right and the sober to be wrong and drag you down with them if they can. ('Come on! One more! One more and you'll break your record of sixteen Papa Dobles in a row! You can do it, Hem! You can do it! Just one more!') And that's becoming more evident as time goes on, wouldn't you say, Ernie? That's entropy for you. Yeah, that's order into chaos. How do you like d'em apples, Ernie?

> *Would he like it if I told him if I told him if*
> *Ernie Hemingway.*
> *Would he like it if Ernie Hemingway if*
> *Ernie Hemingway if I told him.*
> *If I told him if Ernie Hemingway if*
> *Ernie Hemingway if I told him.*
> *If I told him would he like it would he like it if I told him.*

"Oh God, Ernie. I'm really losing it. Now I'm paraphrasing Gertrude Stein!

"The bottom line, dear Ernie is you had to be number one in most everything you did, which you were. You were a master tracker, hunter, boxer, fly-fisherman, deep-sea fisherman, big-game hunter, poker player, skier, journalist, short-story writer, novel writer, bullfighting *aficionado*. On the sober side, though Ernie, one thing you were not number one in, was being a devoted husband. But nobody can be number one in everything. I hope that doesn't stop you from floating.

"So you are my confidant now, Ernie, and I love you for it. Talking to you is keeping me alive. Not that it matters in the grand scheme of things, but I'm kinda getting into this crazy talk. Maybe Mariel was right. *Lo que es bueno.*

"And may I quote you, Ernie? 'Everyone needs to talk to someone...' Pilar said as the bell was about to toll for Robert Jordan. 'Now for everyone there should be someone to whom one can speak frankly, for all the valor that one could have one becomes very alone.'

"Lord knows, I know what it's like to be alone. And I like to think I have *some* valor, Ernie. But maybe not."

The not-so-old man floated as his mind kept rambling.

"Ernie, I'm telling you things I never told anyone, maybe even myself, before. You see, Ernie—I don't have a giant fish to fight, I only have myself. And where the old man at least had a chance against the fish, I have none against myself. And that is as truthful a statement I could ever make."

The not-so-old man floated on his back, feeling loose, looking at the billowy clouds above. He felt better. Almost good. It was part delirium, part catharsis.

"I didn't mean to get all philosophical on you, Ernie. I know how you like things cut and dry and simple. But I'm not plain and simple. I'm a twisting, winding road that usually ends up meandering in circles or ovals or octagons. And that gets tedious.

So forgive me this one time. Indulge me, please, Ernie, because I will be dying in just a few hours. So at least you can give me a break this one time. Isn't that what friends are for?"

The not-so-old man came off his back and treaded water. His hand was still cramped, and he thought to talk to it as Santiago had done to his cramped hand, but he really didn't care anymore. "What's the use?" he thought. He thought he heard something off in the distance, but turning 360 degrees around proved that nothing was there. He started swimming the elementary backstroke.

"While I was cruising through your books, I noticed you acted like a true journalist: reporting events you had witnessed or heard about. No twisting plots, no clever mysteries—just the facts—changing the names but not even changing the places most of the time—just reporting as a good journalist would:

"*The Sun Also Rises*: Your time in Paris and trips to the bullfights, and hotels and meals and drinks and fishing.

"*A Moveable Feast*: Your early years in Paris with Hadley and Bumby and the expats, most of whom were drunk or hungry or confused and disparaged.

"*For Whom The Bell Tolls*: Your experience in the Spanish Revolution.

"*A Farewell to Arms*: Your life as an Italian ambulance driver during WWI.

"*The Snows of Kilimanjaro*: Your trips to Africa and other short stories.

"Stories about hunting and fishing. Stories about women. Stories about war. Stories about depravity. Stories about heroes and dignity and dying. Stories about Nick Adams. So really, Ernie, many were good stories and in some ways better knowing they were historically correct, or at least close, and somewhat autobiographical; but at the same time, disappointing because they required little imagination to create. Or maybe I'm missing something. Probably am.

"And that's quite a beard you've grown. Was it from your last safari or when you moved from Cuba to Idaho? It's so hard keeping up with you, Ernie—you're always into something.

"I went by your house on Key West one time. I got there too late to go inside, but I saw the outside and the fence around it and the sixty-foot long swimming pool in the backyard. You might have guessed I like really big swimming pools. One passer-by local person mentioned that it cost a ton of money to put that pool in because they had to dig it by hand. You wanted to blast away the underlying coral rock, but the city wouldn't let you, so it took a year and a half and twenty grand to dig that hole and build that pool. Is all that true, Ernie? We all know that twenty Gs in those days would be like two billion dollars today.

"You used to entertain all your hot-shot movie star friends like Spencer Tracy, Gary Cooper, and Ingrid Bergman at that pool. They loved the pool. I think they loved you too. And it was obvious you loved cats. They were all over the place. Some of them even got kinda famous since they were polydactyl with six or seven toes. They were all descendants of your original pet named Snowball. But I digress...

"I found out your dad committed suicide too. He was a medical doctor who suffered from diabetes, heart disease, and depression, worsened by bad real estate investments in Florida. So he shot himself in 1928 at the age of 57 with his father's Smith & Wesson Civil War pistol just before the letter you wrote telling him not to worry about expenses arrived in the mail. Bad timing. Damned Postal Service. Should have sent a cable. Wasn't your dad worth a cable?

"After hearing the news, you wrote to a friend, 'I'll probably go the same way.' You had a feeling, didn't you? You could feel the future, just like me. And then I discovered Hadley's father killed himself in 1903. Your dad, Hadley's dad, then you. Lots going around. But that's not all. In addition, it turns out your sister, Ursula; younger brother, Leicester; and your granddaughter, Margaux, all committed the same mortal sin. So many of your clan did it they started calling suicide the 'Hemingway Curse.'

"First off, I'm sorry for all of you guys. Things have to be pretty rotten to not be able to take it anymore. I know exactly how you felt. I'm one of you and I'll be joining you shortly. We can have a party. Reminisce about old times. Commiserate, you know. Who knows? Maybe talking to each other will bring us some valor.

"And here's the irony: The fisherman you modeled your old man and the sea story on, well, he lived to be 104 years old. You didn't even make it to 62. You were just nineteen days short, Ernie. Should have held on just a little longer to make that milestone, you know, for the record books.

"I can't help but wonder what you would have accomplished if you had lived to 104, Ernie. More books and stories for sure. More wives? Maybe. More fishing and hunting? Probably. And I like to think that at some point you would have had an epiphany, maybe when you turned 70. Seven is a special number, you know. So when you turned 70, you would realize that hunting just for fun wasn't fun, especially for the animals. So instead, you would buy a farm and raise animals for a purpose instead of just shooting them. That would have helped your soul too. And maybe you would have realized that being a devoted husband was better than messing around. I know it's hard, and you shouldn't try to force something too much if you're sure it's not the right fit—but in the long run, it would show valor. Maybe next time, give it a go. It may help ameliorate some bad vibes.

"But I'm holding onto my fantasy that you really didn't kill yourself. For one, you're an *aficionado*, for Christ's sake; and two, I don't believe anything in the news anymore. You're probably still alive, like Elvis. Maybe we'll see an Elvis and Ernie sighting one of these days. You could sing a duet at La Closerie des Lilas karaoke night.

"But seriously Ernie, I love you and appreciate you, and I've read many of your books several times and short stories once or twice and tried to learn from them. Declarative sentences and your Iceberg Theory and writing truly and working hard so you can feel good when you're done. Good stuff.

"And you would have been proud of me because I swam across the English Channel. Did you know that fewer people have done that than climbed Mt. Everest? Truly, Ernie, it's a fact. So we're best buds, right? Best buds forever.

"Here I am talking crazy again. I'm mentally loopy, physically battered, and willfully negligent. But hey, I deserve to be loopy. In fact, I deserve to be anything I am. I even deserve to die here in the sea. The sea that drives you to sin and the sea that washes them all away. The sea—the water—has been my luck my whole life. And now, dying in water will be my ultimate good fortune."

Large cumulus, moisture-laden, clouds had gathered overhead this late afternoon as they often do in the subtropics, and suddenly the wind picked up and it started to rain. Not gentle, misty rain, but large, hard pellets of rain that fell sideways on the not-so-old man.

"AGAIN?" the not-so-old man shouted in his mind. "Haven't you abused me enough? What is it? I learned my lesson. I've let some of the grief and guilt go. What more do you want?"

In a defiant and simmering rage, he snatched the swim cap off his head, and holding it in his uncramped hand, swatted at the sky as if to slap it across its face.

"Who cares about lessons?" he ranted in his mind. "It's not

about lessons, you moron. It's about seeing how much crap you can endure."

He took the swim cap and half-tucked it under his Speedo swimsuit so a flap of it hung and floated in the water in front of his crotch. He was mindful, though, of making sure the photo of Ray Ray was still secure under the waistband of the swimsuit.

"I thought you understood that, you moron. I'll be damned if I give in. I don't care about how long anymore. It's not a record worth having anyway."

With the swim cap off his head, his scalp felt better—relieved of the constrictions of the cap. He felt free in a way and more powerful in thinking he'd be able to face the sea without that protection, that barrier. He felt more flexible, less constrained, less limited, but at the same time—keeping with his contradictory nature—more vulnerable.

"Now all I care about is how much, you stupid ocean. So bring it on, you pitiless sea. Bring it on!"

This time, the sea listened. The waves crashed into him, and the rain beat down on him.

Chapter X

*T*here are those who have said they achieved a higher state of consciousness by taking certain drugs. For the not-so-old man, this day, his weariness in the uncompromising sea was his drug. The waves and rain beat on him and beat memories—not of his choosing or himself—onto him and then through his skin and unshielded skull, down through the layers of unsuspecting, tired, and receptive cells to the neurons of his peripheral nervous system and brain; and once a few of them were touched with these memories they acted like dominos—one falling and touching the next to fall and touch on the next and so on—until his mind and body *were* the memories and reacted as if it were so.

Each memory was like a molecule of silver or gold—yes, gold—that was gold and is gold and no matter how it gets separated from other gold it will always be gold still.

With buckshot through the brain, there was no need for rhyme or reason; but there was a pattern—a sequence of golden memories each pellet pushed or grabbed and escorted out of the once-living but now dying man's skull. Each morsel of gray and dura matter, along with its imprinted memory, was pushed and pulled along and out, and as they left, each memory rose to awareness. They flew... flew out of him up into the air. Some to the ceiling, some against the walls, some floated down onto the floor—each one distinct and sure and true as they had been before.

So many memories—so many sights, sounds, sensations, flavors, textures, and aromas—bombarded him he could not and need not track them or try to remember. It was as if they were there, now, making themselves known and had been there always, always there before and after and always there. They were past and future and now and now and now and always now, eternally now, that was now and is now and will be now and now.

The not-so-old man's eyes flickered.

Now he felt for the first time that transformation and his face flushed, and his palms moistened with sweat. An angel was standing before him; a gift from the Gods, he thought—no, knew—introduced to him by his friend as his friend's sister's friend whose skin was fair and hair not closely but loosely cropped and reddish and naturally alive and just messy enough to give her some spunk. He shook her hand—so soft, tender, warm, loving, childish, forgiving, encouraging, nurturing, wanting, needing, sacrificing, excitedly alive with anticipation, and hope. It was the hope in her eyes—those somber, shy, and cloistered eyes—that were waiting, pining for the chance he was going to give her—the chance to break free of the Victorian, the manners, the cautions, the deaths of the life she was living. At that moment, when their hands touched and their eyes lingered in each other's—the freedom. Yes, the freedom! The freedom that would, above all, make inconvenience tolerable.

"Ernest, I'd like you to meet my sister's friend... Elizabeth Hadley Richardson, this is my roommate, Ernest Miller Hemingway."

"Nice to meet you Elizabeth."

"Hadley."

"What's that?"

"Hadley. Everyone calls me Hadley."

"Of course. Of course. Hadley..."

Her hand. Her eyes.

"Kate tells me you're from St. Louis."

"That's right."

"But she never told me how lovely you are."

Hadley's eyes rolled, but their corners wrinkled.

"I'm sorry. I shouldn't say that. But I shouldn't say a lot of things."

She laughed a shy, quiet laugh as she held her fingers over her lips and flashed a smile that couldn't hide behind her suddenly full and rosy-pink cheeks. Her eyes finally broke away and glanced at the floor.

He couldn't let go of her hand. She gently, reluctantly, took it back.

"But, Hadley... you are... no... you are more than that... you are..." he paused, deliberately, he paused. He wanted to entice her, to coax her, to tease her, to have her ask him for more.

"Okay. I'll bite. What am I?"

"You are springtime."

She blushed and looked as if she needed to steady herself.

The not-so-old man channeling Ernest knew what to say next: "Can I get you another drink? Another glass of Chablis?"

"Okay."

"I'll be right back," the not-so-old man channeling Ernest said. "Better yet, here," he took her hand again. "Come with me."

He led her through the crowd to a table with hors d'oeuvres of cheeses and fruits, bottles of wine, and some bootleg liquor. Prohibition had started earlier that year and although it was a bit harder to come by, and you had to be careful who you dealt with, getting some 'giggle water' wasn't impossible, and a friend of Kate's had smuggled several bottles of wine in from France where production and consumption were still legit.

The not-so-old man channeling Ernest took Hadley's empty glass and poured the white wine into it as he talked, "Chablis is from France, you know—the Burgundy district up north, where it's cooler. That makes it less sweet and more acidic than the

Chardonnays they make in the south. I prefer Chablis too. We have so much in common."

Hadley quietly laughed. "You're funny," she mumbled.

"What's that?"

"I said you're funny."

"Merci! Merci beaucoup mon ami!" The not-so-old man channeling Ernest raised his hand to his forehead and tipped the cap that wasn't there, nodding his head and bowing slightly as he swept his hand with the invisible hat down in front of his body.

Hadley laughed again, a little louder this time.

"So what do you think of this prohibition thing? We've gone almost a whole year with it. Me? I think it's applesauce."

"I suppose so."

"They don't have it in France, you know. Everything's berries in France. Have you ever been to Europe?" the not-so-old man channeling Ernest asked.

Hadley shook her head. "I'm lucky to be here in Chicago and out of St. Louis."

"Oh, but you'd like it. Maybe even love it. I was there not long ago and..."

"I know. Kate told me. When did you..."

Suddenly, Kate was beside Hadley, tugging on her arm. "Hadley, you've got to see this! This fellow's amazing! And there's someone else I want you to meet. Come on!"

Kate pulled Hadley away and took her through the loud, smoky room to a small group of people watching a man pull coins out of people's ears.

The not-so-old man channeling Ernest watched her walk: graceful, poised, unhurried even though she was being pulled by her friend. "Class. Pure class," he thought. "But still a hotsy-totsy. A choice bit of calico with bubs!"

Suddenly, in this room packed with friends and acquaintances, he felt lonely.

Now and now and now and always now, eternally now, that was now and is now and will be now and now.

The not-so-old man bobbed in the rolling sea, but he no longer fought it, no longer resisted, the corners of his lips no longer troubled.

"Who's that guy she's talking to now?" the not-so-old man channeling Ernest thought. "Oh yeah, I've seen him before. Yeah, that's Pauly or Potsy or Poopsy or whatever they call him. I don't like him. Never did. Just a dewdropper... lollygagger. His dad's an egg. I have no respect for eggs. No discipline. Poopsy couldn't get into the Army because of bad eyesight, same as me, but used it as an excuse. I found a way to get to the war anyway, even if it was just with the Red Cross, and used it as discipline. Damn dewdropper. I hate dewdroppers."

The not-so-old man channeling Ernest felt his anger rise. "Ain't no dewdropper gonna take my girl!"

He wouldn't admit it yet, but he knew what his next steps would lead to. With determination and zeal, he picked his way through the crowd and touched Hadley on her shoulder. As she turned towards him, his expression effortlessly changed from blatant tenacity to calm certainty with a touch of innocence.

"Hadley. Hi. Hey there Poopsy..."

"That's *Potsy*."

"Poooopsy?"

"No, you cad. *POTSY!*"

"Oh, yeah. Potsy. Excuse us for a moment, would you, Plotski? I have to ask Miss Hadley here..."

He gently took hold of Hadley's arm, but he didn't have to tug on it to get her to move. She almost fell into him as she backed away from Poopsy. At that instant—he could admit it now—he knew he was going to marry her.

"Go chase yourself, Hemingway," Poopsy called out as the not-so-old man channeling Ernest and Hadley picked their way through the crowd away from him.

"You read my mind," Hadley whispered to him over her shoulder as they made their way to the front of the parlor.

"I know," he replied. "And you thought pulling coins out of somebody's ear was amazing."

Hadley smiled.

"What'd'ya say we go for a walk? I need some air."

"Sure," she said as she looked up into his sparkling clear blue eyes gently set on his handsome face with his head topping out at just over six feet. "You really can read minds, can't you?"

He chuckled as he grabbed their coats off the coat rack and helped Hadley put her arms in the sleeves. He threw on his own jacket, then gently placed his hand on the small of Hadley's back and gracefully guided her to the front door. Without another word, he opened the door and followed her out into the cold December air. Vapor fog came out of their mouths as they walked and talked along the Chicago street in the fading evening light.

The not-so-old man channeling Ernest wanted to say something, but he stopped himself. He didn't want to appear uncomfortable with the silence. He knew that silence can often establish dominance, and he didn't want to appear needy. A few steps more, and Hadley said,

"Are you sure you want to walk?"

"Yeah. Why do you ask."

"They said your legs were all shot up in the War."

The not-so-old man channeling Ernest stopped in his tracks. He didn't like talking about all that. But when he looked at Hadley standing in front of him with such a profound, serious, and truthful expression on her face, he started walking again and said, "Yeah, they were. But I'm better now. Much better. I can even do the foxtrot on just one leg."

"Oh, stop it, Ernest. You're too funny."

"Well, it's true... Well, maybe a leg and a half."

Hadley looked down at the snow-covered sidewalk as they strolled. "I see you're put off by me talking about it, but I want to say just one thing. I heard you saved some Italian soldiers even after you got injured. What kind of man does such a thing? *What kind,* Ernest? I'll tell you what kind... A brave man. A fine man. A man who is truly a man."

The not-so-old man channeling Ernest's eyes blinked hard. He'd never heard such straight-forward candor from a woman before.

"A man," Hadley continued, "who has grace. Not just when things are going well, but when they are not. Grace when he's under pressure."

The not-so old man channeling Ernest mumbled under his breath, "Grace. Grace under pressure."

They walked down the street past Victorian-style houses—just like the ones in the neighborhood Ernie grew up in—with ample yards and expansive front porches: where in the spring, summer, fall, and even winter sometimes, people lounged and drank lemonade—or in the winter, hot chocolate—and played cards with neighbors, or you'd see wives in their house dress mending socks or patching the worn knees of overalls or peeling potatoes for dinner, or you'd see young'uns scooting around on the stained hardwood floor planks chasing a ball or bottle-top filled with wax or shooting marbles on a rug and screaming when the other team's Tolley was killed. You'd hear babies crying and horses snorting and neighing or an occasional automobile back-firing and mothers yelling their children's names out the front door when dinner was on the table or when they had to come in from playing tag or hide and seek or kick the can because the sun had gone down.

You might smell—and often did, as you walked along the street—pies baking or cooling on the windowsill or roasts basting or fresh manure below the hindquarter of a horse standing at a hitching post. On a sunny, breezy day, you might see a kite being held by a string up in the air with a kid below it trying to make it do tricks or a bunch of boys playing stickball in the street or girls jumping rope on the sidewalk. Many yards had rope swings hanging off the big, old, oak tree in the front or side yard, and in one yard, the not-so-old man channeling Ernest noticed a *Red Flyer* sled leaning against the porch handrail. In another yard sat an abandoned, rusty, child's pedal car. And on another porch, he saw a Teddy bear sitting on a rocking chair with a scarf around his neck.

A light dusting of snow had fallen earlier in the day, and the air was crisp and cold and invigorating. Ribbons of smoke came out of the chimneys and rose effortlessly into the motionless, cold air, and the not-so-old man channeling Ernest noticed the wandering star Venus shining in the gray above the last glow of the sunset. He dug his hand into Hadley's coat pocket, where her hand rested, and took hold of it. Warm, soft, pulsating. She didn't push his hand away but tightened her fingers around it. The not-so-old man channeling Ernest felt a tingle shoot up the back of his spine and across his scalp. They walked into the darkening evening together.

The not-so-old man no longer noticed the raging sea.

"But I'm so much older," Hadley wrote in a letter to Ernest a few months later. "Eight years. That's a long time."

"In spring, there is no such thing as time," he wrote back.

Five visits and nine months later, Ernie and Hadley married.

The sea kept crashing. The rain kept falling. The sea and rain kept beating things into him, and then, the sea and rain beat those same things out of him.

Bits and pieces of Ernie's brain kept flying up and out...

"You really think this'll work?" the not-so-old man channeling Ernest asked, looking down between his legs at the two cold metal electrodes. "This seems very unorthodox, doc."

The doctor stood up from his kneeling position and walked over to the counter where the machine stood. "The research papers say it works," he said. "You've got nothing to lose."

The not-so-old man channeling Ernest said, "Well, okay, doc. I've tried everything else—Spanish fly, Chinese herbal potions, oysters, powdered deer antlers and rhinoceros horns, and medicines. Nothing's worked. Pauline says it's her fault, being so busy and distracted getting our wedding together. I don't want her to think that, doc. I want to keep her happy. I've already disappointed the first love of my life. I don't want to disappoint the second."

The doctor was making adjustments to the machine and was hardly listening, but the not-so-old man channeling Ernest kept talking anyway, "Maybe it's just stress, doc. I'm still numb from Hadley. I still love her and always will, doc. When I was carting her things over to her new apartment after the divorce was finalized, I cried like a baby the whole way. It's all over, doc. I can't believe it. I'm such an idiot. What have I done? I should have listened to Scott. He said if I chose Pauline, it'll just fill me with remorse, and remorse will break your goddamn heart. And it may have broken something else, too. Doc, is it possible to love two women at the same time?"

"What's that?" the doctor said, not looking up.

"I said... is it possible to love... oh, the hell with it doc," the not-so-old man channeling Ernest mumbled. "Let's just get this over with... "

"Well, sweetie," she purred as she flung herself into the not-so-old man channeling Ernest's arms, "how did it go? Are you okay?

Did it hurt?"

"It was like getting stuck in an electric socket. My hair stood on end and every cell in my body burned."

"Oh, dear! My dear, sweet Papa!"

"Pauline... Pilar..."

"Oh, Papa. Don't be ashamed, dear. We tried, didn't we? And you've tried everything. So now there's only one thing left. Will you do that for me?"

"You don't mean..."

"Yes, I do."

"You know how I feel about that."

"Yes, but you've tried everything else. Just try, dear. Just once. Please? For me?"

On his way to the church, the not-so-old man channeling Ernest thought of Pauline and Hadley and how he loved them both and how he hated hurting Hadley and leaving Bumby but how he was mesmerized by glamour and affluence and promises and rivalry. He loved Hadley for being the best mother to his son and supportive and kind and daring in her own way and yet a soft and compliant follower who gently and lovingly melted into his arms at just the right time and who didn't care about money or showing off or having to wear old clothes because they were poor, but just loved him and told him she loved him and loved him.

He loved Pauline for being smart and cunning and always getting what she wanted, expectantly getting what she wanted and almost demanding what she wanted and who would do just about anything to get what she wanted and it turned out it was he who she wanted, and it was she who would take charge and be King of the Hill when she wanted and would explode into his arms at the time that was just right for her and for what she wanted. He loved her for not being poor but rich and showing it off in her mink coat and emerald earrings swinging from her ear lobes under her modern bob haircut with sleek bangs that framed her face like a frame might frame a Picasso and her looking so modern and chic in her designer clothes that she wore and wrote about and paid homage to.

She was so used to money—conceived from in, born in it, fed it, drank it, raised in it, dressed in it, smoothed her face with it, gargled with it, and slept within it so it was part of her and you could sometimes see the gold or silver coins spill out of her eyes as she laughed her knowing laugh because she knew the important people that made the Right Bank the Knowing Bank and the Left Bank the Wanting Bank and she made sure all the important people remembered her because she laughed at their jokes and smiled and batted her eyes at the men who could help her get what she wanted as they tried to impress such a new and cute little thing such as her. She was smart, witty, stylish, and yet self-deprecating, which endeared her even more to the people who mattered to her the most.

The not-so-old man channeling Ernest had spent enough time on the Wanting Bank, and now it was time for him to be on the Knowing Bank and get the recognition he deserved as it would come now with his first novel and he wanted, no needed, his partner to be part of that scene—the scene of knowing people who knew how to get things done. He liked getting things done. He knew that if he stayed with Hadley, yes, he would never stop loving her, but she would never fit into the world of the Knowing Bank simply because she was too good for them. She was better than all of them put together, he thought, but he himself was worse than some of them by themselves, and he knew this and couldn't help it as much as he could help the color of his eyes.

The not-so-old man channeling Ernest walked along the sidewalk, not noticing the trees or buildings or parks that he passed on the way to the church, but remembering the first parts of

Paris and then Austria and back to Chicago where he met Hadley and then forward again to their wedding in Horton Bay, Michigan, and the reception in the Pinehurst Inn owned by a blacksmith named Jim Dilworth and run by his wife Elizabeth. The church was Methodist and right across the street from the Inn so they simply walked across the street to the Inn where the party would be after their union was official in the eyes of the state, and the Lord, he figured, and they had their reception with friends and family. Then back further, his mind drifted to all the summers he spent at the Walloon Lake family cottage named Windemere where his mother let him dress like a normal boy and actually encouraged him in his hunting and fishing.

He remembered his dad showing him how to handle and shoot a rifle—an old .22 caliber that his dad gave him as a gift when he was a boy. He heard his dad say, "Now Ernest, you must always keep a gun pointed away from other people. If you don't, I'll take it away. And you only get three cartridges a day. Then you'll pay attention and make every bullet count. Okay. Now put your cheek on the stock so you can look through the sight with your right eye. Close the left. That's right. Look down the barrel. Put your finger on the trigger like this..." The not-so-old man channeling Ernest as a young boy felt his father's hand guide him to the trigger and help him wrap his right forefinger around it. "Now, when you pull the trigger, squeeze it, don't pull it. Do you have the bottle in your sight?" "Yeah." "Okay, squeeze it." The not-so-old man channeling Ernest as a young boy squeezed the trigger. Pow! He missed the bottle. "That's okay, Ernest. Try again."

Later, in his teens, he would row across the lake and then walk four miles across fields and through forests to get to Horton Bay village to have some summer fun with his buddies. He remembered getting married and having the reception at the Pinehurst Inn and then getting into a Model T Ford and driving to the shore of Walloon Lake and rowing his new bride across the lake to Windemere like he had rowed himself so many times before alone while hoping to find the right girl to marry. Then they spent their honeymoon in the cottage his father built the year after he was born.

How long ago that seemed now and how odd it seemed that he was who he was before he met the girl who was older than a girl but was still much of a girl because she had never had a chance to be a girl which was something he really liked. And now he wished he had realized back then at that time and times like that just how precious those times would end up being to him and how he had wanted both those times and the times to come that would show the world who he truly was and he wanted them both to never be gone, and be with him alive always and how painful it had been when he had wanted them both and thought he could have them both and as he waited for the hundred-day probation to end he had wanted to kill himself and complained to his friends ad nauseam about it before Hadley was kind enough to lift the hundred-day probation on its seventy-first day and let him go to Pauline.

He pulled the large, heavy church door open and stepped inside. It was quiet and still with outside light illuminating the stained glass windows, so they glowed and almost vibrated. A few Catholics were sitting or kneeling in other pews, and one was lighting a candle in front at the altar.

The church smelled of old and recently burned incense that he was afraid would stick to his clothes and make him smell like a priest. The not-so-old man channeling Ernest kneeled down in the first pew he came to just in front of, ironically, a statue of the Virgin Mary, and put his interlaced fingers on the pew in front and bowed his head. He started to pray,

"Dear Lord..."

He felt like a hypocrite. But he had promised Pauline, so he pushed himself to continue.

"Dear Lord, you know why I'm here. Or do I need to tell you? I don't know... I've never done this before. I'm going to go with you knowing. Okay. So you know. But I'll tell you anyway just to be sure. Dear Lord, I'm here to make my wife happy. Yeah, that's it. I want to make my soon-to-be wife happy. I know I've already sinned. I figure you know all that too. Sinned in more ways than one and hurt more women than one. So I ask forgiveness. No, I shouldn't be forgiven. I'm too far gone for that. But please, let Hadley be happy and let Pauline be happy, so we're all happy even though we're no longer together like we were before and will never be again. You don't need to forgive me, just help them."

The not-so-old man channeling Ernest felt a strange sense of pride come to him for being so pious. "How am I doing, God? Am I doing okay? First time for everything, so I'm a little unsure of myself. But wait a minute. Maybe I shouldn't be asking you, you know. Maybe I'm supposed to ask Jesus! Jeez, I don't know. This is confusing. Maybe you're too busy with other things and I should talk to your son. That makes sense. Okay. I'll talk to your son."

The not-so-old man channeling Ernest paused, heavy in thought. "How do I put this, God... errr... Jesus. It's a big one. Or should I say, it should be a big one." The not-so-old man channeling Ernest bit his lip until it hurt because he knew that when he put into words what he was thinking he might just laugh out loud, and that wouldn't be good for his first time praying, especially since he was in a church kneeling in front of a holy statue of a very holy person. Then he said, "Please, Jesus, I'm asking you... would you please... give me... an... erection?"

He couldn't help it. He jumped up from the pew as if it was on fire and rushed out the door onto the stone steps outside the church and let out a howling laugh that could be heard a block away.

"You just asked God for an erection, you bum!" he laughed.

"There are no atheists in foxholes... or with spaghetti between their legs!"

He stumbled back to their apartment, shaking his head and thinking this was the funniest thing he had ever done. But when he opened the door, he felt something. And when he saw her already in bed waiting, he really felt it. Once again, she was King of the Hill and he was her loyal follower, and this made her and him together again. "Maybe there's something to that praying thing," the not-so-old man channeling Ernest thought before he drifted into a gentle, victorious sleep.

Pauline wasn't just cute and sassy; she had a generous, childless uncle—Uncle Gus. He and Pauline's dad virtually owned the town and all the businesses of Piggott, Arkansas, and probably most of the state, too. Gus bought them a house on Key West—at 907 Whitehead Street—and financed the couple's African safari extravaganza to the tune of $25,000. Not to leave any luxury unpurchased, Generous Gus paid for their car and fishing boat, *Pilar,* too. Pauline was generous in a different way—she gave the not-so-old man channeling Ernest two sons while they lived on *Cayo Hueso* (Island of Bones, aka Key West—named for being the native islander's dumping grounds for dead, native islanders back in the day), both after grueling pregnancies requiring cesarean deliveries. Soon after they moved there, the hardware store owner, Charlie Thompson, introduced the not-so-old man channeling Ernest to deep-sea fishing. He was immediately hooked...

"Carlos, my good man," he said as he sat down in the fighting chair. "It's a great day to fish and the weather'll be fine all day. We're gonna catch a record today. I can feel it. Hand me a skipjack so I can set him on the hook, and let's get started."

Carlos gave the not-so-old man channeling Ernest the fish, climbed the ladder to the main bridge, and started the main engine—a 75 horsepower Chrysler—of Hemingway's 38 foot, fully equipped fishing boat, *Pilar*. They sailed west out of the Navy Yard harbor, past Sunset Key on the right.

"No Marquesas Keys today," the not-so-old man channeling Ernest called up to Carlos. "Let's go further south. I have a feeling." Carlos turned the wheel—from a Ford Model T car—and turned the boat to port towards Cuba and the Gulf Stream. The not-so-old man channeling Ernest said to his friend Joe standing next to him, "In the meantime, how about a daiquiri?"

An hour and a half and several daiquiris later, Carlos shut down the main engine and started the 4 Cylinder Lycoming trolling engine. Forty minutes later, the fishing line went taut.

"Not too hard," Joe said. "Don't lock it down too hard, you'll snap the line."

"I know that!" the not-so-old man channeling Ernest muttered back as he pulled up on the rod. "It's only linen line, but I put a piece of lignum vitae on the reel to slow it down and increase the drag gradually." He felt the tension on the line between his thumb and forefinger and, deciding it was okay, settled back into the fighting chair.

He held the rod firmly in his large and strong hands, keeping it steady and the drag constant. "Get me another drink," the not-so-old man channeling Ernest said. "We're gonna be here a while."

Four hours later, the crew of five watched as the fish finally jumped. Totally out of the water he came, his blue shimmering belly clearly visible as sparks of water droplets sprayed all around in the bright late afternoon sun.

"That's a big-un," Charlie exclaimed. "Look at the size of him!"

"Could feed a whole village," Joe said.

"He's beat," the not-so-old man channeling Ernest said quietly. "He's lost it. But he's majestic, isn't he?"

"Keep pulling," Joe said. "Easy and slow. He's losing strength with every pass."

Everyone watched in awe as the fish got closer and closer to the boat and appeared larger and more beautiful even as it died. Joe and Charlie stood fast against the gunwale, as the marlin came around touching the boat for the first time. They readied the hook and net, but they wouldn't need a net—they would need a crane. But it wasn't just a marlin coming closer to *Pilar*. Several sharks had caught the scent and were charging towards the floating corpse.

"Charlie, take the rod," The not-so-old man channeling Ernest shouted. "Joe, hand me my rifle. Look who's trying to steal their next meal."

Joe grabbed the rifle from the gun rack on the bridge and, stumbling once as he climbed down in his haste, handed it to the not-so-old man channeling Ernest, who was straddling the gunwale on the starboard side where the fish floated. The not-so-old man channeling Ernest pulled the bolt of the semi-automatic Remington and served notice:

"Damn *galanos!*" he called out in a hearty and exuberant rant. "You spawn of the devil. You think you're going to get away with this?"

He lowered the rifle and got the first shark charging with wide-open jaws in his sights.

"No scum of the sea is going to take my prize!" He pulled the trigger.

POW!

"Take that you damn parasite!"

POW!

"That's right, spout your wretched blood!"

POW!

"Here's another! Show me your mouth, you're insatiable

mouth."

POW!

"Have some lead for lunch, you blood-sucking scum!"

POW!

"And another..."

POW!

"Keep coming, you spineless parasites!"

POW!

"Here's a present, right into the top of your hard-headed skull!"

POW!

"That's right. Die, you bum. Sink back into hell!"

"You got 'em all, Hem." Joe pulled the not-so-old man channeling Ernest's shoulder to get him fully back on deck. "You emptied the whole magazine, and got 'em all!"

The not-so-old man channeling Ernest's heart was racing. He was high as a kite: nervous and proud and guilty and elated, all at the same time. *This is what real combat must be like,* he thought. *But I was too unlucky.* "I showed 'em, didn't I, Joe? I let them know who's boss. Ain't nobody gonna take my blood and sweat, especially damn *galanos*!"

As the marlin floated up along the side of the boat on its side, the one visible eye was dark, lifeless, powerless, and blank. It was a record: a 468-pounder—the largest marlin ever caught with a rod and reel.

The not-so-old man channeling Ernest said as he admired his catch, "Not a bad day's work."

Once the fish had been pulled onboard and hung from the boom, all hands except Carlos' had celebratory drinks. The not-so-old man channeling Ernest looked up at Carlos, who was way up on the flying bridge watching the sky with concern. "Don't worry, Carlos. We'll make it back all right. We won't get marooned like we did at Fort Jefferson on Dry Tortugas." Then, turning to

Charlie, he said, "That was one hell-of-a storm and seventeen days, wasn't it Charles? Almost starved to death. Good thing we know how to fish. Almost ran out of rum, too."

After the celebration as the sun was going down and as they motored full speed back to Key West, the not-so-old man channeling Ernest's eyes closed. Just before his jaw dropped onto his chest, he recalled an article he wrote in the *Toronto Star* back in 1922:

"It is a back-sickening, sinew-straining, man-sized job even with a rod that looks like a hoe handle. But if you land a big tuna after a six-hour fight, fight him man against fish until your muscles are nauseated with the unceasing strain, and finally bring him up alongside the boat, green-blue and silver in the lazy ocean, you will be purified and will be able to enter unabashed into the presence of the very elder gods, and they will make you welcome."

Once asleep, he dreamed of himself aboard the *Pilar* hunting German U-boats in the Gulf Stream. The war had not started yet— it was still years away—but he was itching for action. Later, in 1942 and 1943, his dream would come true, and he joined the Hooligan Navy—volunteers who patrolled the waters of the Atlantic and Gulf of Mexico coasts looking for German U-boats. He outfitted *Pilar* for action with government-supplied hand grenades, two 50-caliber machine guns, bazookas, short-wave radios, and the services of a Marines Master Sergeant. The *Pilar* patrolled the waters near Cuba—Ernie sometimes taking his three young sons along. Although he never encountered a U-boat, he did spend a lot of time looking for them. Martha—his wife at the time after Pauline—thought it was all just an excuse to fish and drink. However, Ernie's patrolling (which he tagged *Operation Friendless* after one of his cats) was more than just fishing and drinking; it was truly serious business. By mid-June, 1942, 360 ships had been sunk off the eastern coast of the United States; and by the end of November, 263 boats had been sunk by German U-boats off the coast of Cuba. Army Chief of Staff George Marshall stated, "losses by submarines off our Atlantic seaboard and in the Caribbean now threaten our entire war effort."

"Will this battering never end?" the not-so-old man thought when his eyes stopped flickering. The sea raged and the rain continued. He was too tired to argue and, reluctantly—but with a perverse feeling he didn't want it to end—he realized there was still a lot more to come.

His eyes flickered again as the bits and pieces kept flying...

Another rival. This time, a real and present rival. The not-so-old man channeling Ernest didn't realize it yet: It would take a while for him to realize it but would take no time at all for him to hate it.

That while was over. It was now he hated it. She came to him and told him she wanted out; that she didn't want to be a footnote in anyone else's life. She wanted to go to another war on another continent and report for another magazine what she would see from another perspective. She wrote about injustice from the downtrodden's view, inciting understanding and then pity, demanding change. She was oh so cute and cunning, so exact in her desire to be the best, to rule over other journalists, including him, in a way that he thought was just not womanly.

Years ago, after he had just met her, he couldn't get her out of his mind. The contrast was like pearls on a bucking bronco—what they had and how they got it—borne out of clever repartee and booze in Sloppy Joe's bar down the street in Key West around Christmas time in 1936. Sharp and witty, confident and pretty—all of her shaken and stirred, served with two green olives skewered on a toothpick—she teased him with the priggish defiance of competition and the denial of roles.

By the next Christmas, they were in Madrid after traveling to Spain together to report on the Spanish Civil War. War and confrontation always got the not-so-old man channeling Ernest's juices flowing, as it did Martha's, so they couldn't help falling in love.

Both lived in the *Hotel Florida* in Madrid (Hemingway wrote his only play, *The Fifth Column,* there) a mile from one of the fronts that Franco's artillery frequently shelled. Their relationship was consummated and steeled to Chopin's Mazurka in C Major playing on the phonograph while the windows and ceiling shook from a shelling:

"Hem! Hold me!"

"I'll hold you. Be brave, dear."

"I'm shaking. I'm a mess." She reached to turn off the phonograph...

"Leave it on. It's a good piece. Listen to it and forget the artillery."

"I can't!"

"Yes, you can. You're the bravest woman I've ever met. Listen to the music. Focus on the music instead of the crashing. Listen and dive into it and let it move you."

"I'm trying. I'm trying."

"Here," the not-so-old man channeling Ernest said. "Feel my arms wrapped around you. They will keep you safe. Feel my arms. Feel my arms."

"Oh, Hem!"

"Get lost in my arms, dear. They're all that matters now. The music and my arms holding you, protecting you, loving you."

The ceiling shook again. The windows rattled again. The music kept playing. They melted together.

"Oh, Hem!"

After the bombing, they kept it up, and later, kept it up still, even with Pauline insisting she was married to Ernie and pretending not to see it or care.

Martha Gellhorn was born in St. Louis, the same as Hadley and Pauline, to a gynecologist father and an activist mother. She lived with Hemingway on and off from their time in Spain until 1940 when he divorced Pauline. Sixteen days after the divorce, she married Hemingway. Hem and Martha went from Key West to an apartment in Havana to a country estate Martha discovered for sale in a local paper, fifteen miles east of the city with views of downtown from the upstairs veranda. The house was named *Finca Vigia*, which in English means The Lookout Farm. She wanted it, in part, because it was in the country and away from bars and other temptations her husband couldn't resist when living in a city.

Martha had reported from Spain and then Germany as Hitler came into power. To Czechoslovakia, she went in 1938 to report on the Munich Agreement. Later, in April 1945, she went to Dachau to report on the concentration camp. As WWII escalated, she was sent to London as a correspondent for *Collier's Magazine*, and Hemingway didn't like it one bit.

"Where does she get off doing such things?" the not-so-old man channeling Ernest thought. "She's a woman, for Christ's sake. I don't care if she's friends with the Roosevelt's—she can't cover a story like me. Nobody can. I'm the best, and she knows it. Besides, I taught her everything she knows about journalism—how to find her own style and all that. I won't stand for it. I won't.

"And now another assignment? Does she want to go to another war or be a wife in my bed? That's what I'd like to know."

The not-so-old man channeling Ernest wondered, "I wonder what Hadley's doing at this very instant. Hadley wouldn't have done it. Hadley would have been in my bed on her back. Good old Hadley."

As Ernie was wont to do, he didn't let moss gather. He went to Great Britain and joined the Royal Air Force and even flew on bombing missions.

The breaking point in the War was near. In 1944, *Collier's* needed someone to go as a war correspondent in the one spot they could offer. They wanted Martha.

"I'll show her," The not-so-old man channeling Ernest thought. "I'll use my connections, call in a few chips, offer my byline to *Collier's* and take her spot. That'll show her who's boss."

But that didn't stop her.

The night was cold and wet. Martha walked along the dock, hoping for a chance to be part of the invasion.

"Oh my God," she thought. "Here they come."

"Papers, Ma'am."

She flashed the MPs her expired Press Pass—her thumb over the date—and talked fast: "My name is Martha Gellhorn. I'm a war correspondent for *Collier's Magazine.* I'm here to interview nurses—the brave women on that hospital barge right over there." She snatched the Press Pass back and waved her hand that held it at the white barge with three red crosses painted across its hull. "The folks back home in the States need to know what these women go through. They need to know, gentlemen, and I'm here to tell them!"

The MPs looked at the barge, then back at Martha, measuring her up and down. "You can't sail with them, you know," one of them said. "The ship's set to shove off at midnight so you'd better be sure to get your little fanny off it before then."

Little fanny my ass! Martha thought but held her tongue. "Of course, officer. Of course. I'll only be an hour, two tops. The last thing I want to do is go to war."

"All right then," the other MP said. "Have a pleasant evening then, Ma'am."

"You too, gentleman. And thank you for your service."

She climbed the gangplank and hurried into the first door she saw. Down a narrow hallway, she found a head, went in, and locked the door. She muttered to herself, "If anyone finds you, you're toast. They'll put you in prison as a spy for sure. What the hell are you doing, Gellhorn? You must be nuts."

She found the flask in her satchel and opened it. A few sips later, her nerves calmed down. "See what you got me into, Hemingway? If you hadn't been such an ass, I'd have been doing my job the way I should have, with permission from the brass and accolades from the troops. But noooo. You had to mess it all up, didn't you?"

She took another couple of sips of liquid courage. And as much as she scorned her husband then, she found it terribly exciting to be in such a dangerous spot. She felt the walls and floor tremble with a low, hollow growl as the engine of the barge started up. A few minutes later, the ship started moving. Operation Neptune—the code name for Operation Overlord and commonly known as D-Day—had begun. "No turning back now," she thought. She took another couple of sips.

By morning she was seasick and drunk as a skunk. But that wouldn't stop her. Somehow she cleared her head, climbed out of the head, found a nurse's aide uniform, and went up on deck. There she saw it—Normandy France—the fifty-mile long beach where the largest seaborne invasion in history was occurring.

She was on the first hospital ship to make it there. The initial landing had already occurred. There were Allied bombers dropping bombs inland where the enemy was entrenched. The air above the water and beach was dotted with barrage balloons to stop air attacks by the Luftwaffe and the water was sprinkled with crippled landing craft, half-floating bodies of soldiers, scraps of uniforms, and pieces of junk that wouldn't sink. She helped load food, water, bandages, coffee, and anything else needed onto landing craft when they pulled alongside the barge.

As night was falling, male doctors and medics were going ashore. She jumped into the chest-high, bone-chilling water right behind them and followed—right behind a mine-sweeper—to the shore of Omaha Beach. The doctors and medics might have noticed, but they didn't ask Martha for anything but help. Death and dying were everywhere—Omaha beach suffered the most casualties of the five beaches (Utah, Omaha, Gold, Juno, and Sword) stormed that day. All night she toiled—helping, moving, carrying, encouraging, mending, crying, hugging, holding, caring, loving—turning her hands into red and blistered mush. Of the 160,000 who stormed the beaches that day, June 6, 1944, only one was a woman. It was Martha Gellhorn.

There were hundreds of other journalists there, but they were all on ships floating in the sea in the English Channel watching from afar. One of them was Ernest Hemingway, looking through binoculars, oblivious to what Martha was doing. Later that day he followed the 4th Infantry Division onto the beach hoping for action.

Both Martha's and Ernie's stories ran in *Collier's* side-by-side.

Ernie didn't stop his wartime meanderings. He once threw a grenade into a cellar where Nazi SS troops were supposedly hiding and boasted about killing them. Another time he ripped off his war correspondence insignia, said he was a colonel, and led a group of French resistance fighters. He was there when Paris was liberated and even claimed to be the one to liberate it, but other accounts said the only place he liberated was the bar at the Ritz Hotel. Ernie tended to exaggerate sometimes. Makes for good stories, though. But the brass didn't like all his shenanigans and charged him with violating the rules for non-combat war correspondents. But, his friend, Colonel Buck Lanham, came to Hemingway's defense, saying, "He is without question, one of the most courageous men I have ever known." The charges against Ernie were dropped, and he later received the Bronze Star for his bravery.

The war ended September 2, 1945, six years from its start on September 1, 1939.

The war between Gellhorn and Hemingway ended soon thereafter too. They divorced on December 21, 1945.

The not-so-old man came out of his trance. He was weary of having no control over his mind going where he didn't want it to go, but he felt the worst was over. He floated mindlessly and effortlessly for several minutes.

His eyes started flickering again as the bits and pieces kept flying...

Yet again, another rival. But his time, not a real one. She knew her place and embraced being a supporter instead of an instigator. The not-so-old man channeling Ernest liked that and needed it too. For as tough a man as he was, he was getting a little tired.

Once again, Ernie was a tree-swinging monkey when it came to women. He wouldn't let go of the vine he had in one hand until he had another vine in the other. This time, while still married to Gellhorn, he reached out soon after D-Day, and another journalist was there—a smile on her lips and a compliant heart beating in her chest. The not-so-old man channeling Ernest grabbed that vine and pulled his new heart-throb, the twice-divorced and presently married daughter of a lumberman, to him. Her name was Mrs. Noel Monks; aka, Mary Welsh.

Thirty-two years old, blond hair, blue eyes, stocky build, a wartime stringer for *Time* magazine, she radiated confidence. A journalist too, she promised to divorce Monks to be with the not-so-old man channeling Ernest. But he had his doubts...

He slammed the door to their Ritz Paris suite door and turned his ruddy face toward her.

"I don't believe it, Mary!" he shouted. "You tell me one thing, and then you turn right around and do what I told you to never do again!"

"I didn't do it, sweetheart! *He* called *me!* *He* called *me!* I was just telling him to leave us alone!"

"That's not all you said."

"I had to be civil, dear! This is hard for him, you know."

"I don't care about him!" the not-so-old man channeling Ernest shouted. "To hell with Noel! I don't want you talking to him at all, ever again, you hear me?"

"But dear! I'm just telling him goodbye. Doesn't he deserve at least that?"

"NO!"

"But Ernest... "

"Don't call me Ernest! You know I hate that name! Call me Papa!"

"Ok, sweetheart. I'm sorry..."

The not-so-old man channeling Ernest was bare-chested and wore only boxer shorts. He looked around the living room of the suite. He didn't see it.

"... It was a slip-up, dear... "

He went into the bedroom and reached under the bed.

" ... I know you don't like that name, Papa."

He marched back into the living room, muzzle pointing down at the floor. He opened the break-action shotgun. It was loaded, just as he had left it.

"I'll show you what I think of that clown," the not-so-old man channeling Ernest yelled as he snapped the shotgun closed and raised the barrel.

"Oh, sweetie! What are you doing? Put it down! *Put it down!*"

He marched past Mary, into the bathroom holding the gun in

front of himself, pointed it at the toilet from just a few feet away, and pulled the trigger...

KA-POW!

A flash, then smoke, came out of the end of one of the barrels.

KA-POW!

The walls and windows shook both times in quick succession. Water and pieces of porcelain exploded up to the ceiling, putting pock-marks in the plaster and causing it to drip. Water exploded onto the not-so-old man channeling Ernest too, but he never felt a thing. The toilet had been shot to smithereens.

Mary lowered her head onto the sofa she was sitting on and sobbed. She didn't look up to see the not-so-old man channeling Ernest walk back into the bedroom and replace the shotgun under the bed. "That'll show him!" he muttered under his breath.

He walked back into the room and saw Mary sobbing into the sofa. He studied her for several seconds and then sat beside her. He started stroking her hair.

"You know I love you," she said.

"Yes, I know. I just hate it when there's someone else."

"There is no one else. You must believe me. There is no one else."

"I'll try. Sometimes it's hard to control my anger."

"But you can, dear. You can. Just think of me and how I love you."

The not-so-old man channeling Ernest got up from the sofa and stood over her. He bent down and wedged his hands and arms under her torso. He picked her up and carried her—as if he were carrying her as his bride—across the threshold into the suite's bedroom.

"We will be married," he said.

"Yes, I know."

He set her down on the bed and turned to the armoire next to the window. He poured two whiskey sodas as she unbuttoned her blouse. He sat beside her on the bed and gave her one of the glasses.

"Thank you, dear," Mary said. "Here's to us."

They clicked their glasses together, gulped down their drinks, and turned to each other.

Welsh divorced Monks, Hemingway divorced Gelhorn, and they married each other in Cuba in March of 1946. In August that year, while living in *Finca Vigía,* Mary had a miscarriage due to ectopic pregnancy. Ernie is believed by many to have penned the shortest short story ever written—just six words: "For Sale. Baby shoes. Never worn."

In 1958, Mary and the not-so-old man channeling Ernest still called *Finca Vigía* their home, traveling frequently between his writing and fishing on *Pilar.* He even fished with Fidel Castro once.

"Do we really have to leave?" Mary asked.

"Yes. The revolution is here. Castro will take our home. We have no choice."

"Where will we go?"

"Idaho."

"Ketchum?"

"Ketchum or Sun Valley, six of one, half dozen of another."

"Yes, dear. That will be fine. Have you heard from Mr. Williams?"

"Mr. Williams!" the not-so-old man channeling Ernest laughed. "Why must you insist on calling him mister? His first name is Taylor. Can't you remember that?"

"Of course, I remember that. I just feel funny calling him by his first name because he's so much older than me."

"He's only seventy-one! That's just thirteen years older than I am!"

"Are you really that old, sweetheart?" Mary smiled. "I guess so. With that beard, you look old."

"I thought you liked the beard."

"I do, dear." I'm just joking, you know."

"Sure. I didn't tell you, but I bought a cemetery plot for Taylor in Ketchum Cemetery. That's where I'll be buried too. Under the pine trees with a view of the mountains."

"Oh dear, don't be morbid."

"I don't want a gravestone. Just a simple granite slab with my name, birthday, and death day on it."

"Oh, sweetie! Stop. You have a long way to go."

"Then you'll be free, dear Mary."

"Stop it. Stop it."

"You'll see."

"Stop it. Stop it."

"I've arranged for us to rent a house in Sun Valley until December. Then we'll see what the wind wants to do with us."

"Anywhere in Sun Valley is fine, dear."

"I'm thinking we can buy a house. Near a river. Facing the mountains."

"That sounds lovely, Papa."

In 1959 the Hemingway's bought a house near Ketchum overlooking the Big Wood River and Sawtooth Mountains that Hemingway once called "the loveliest mountains that I know." Taylor Williams, one of many dear Idaho friends and hunting companions, died in February that year. The not-so-old man channeling Ernest was one of the pallbearers at his funeral. They buried him in the cemetery plot the not-so-old man channeling Ernest had bought.

In the winter of 1960, the not-so-old man channeling Ernest picked up the phone.

"Hadley."

"Hi, Tatie."

"I'm a goner."

"How so."

"They want to zap me."

"What do you mean?"

"They want to electroshock me—send me into convulsions with a wooden bit between my teeth. They say it'll help with my depression."

"Oh, Tatie. I don't know..."

"They've done it once already. Makes me feel like hell."

"I'm sorry. Are things really that bad?"

"Worse. I can't stop thinking about our first apartment at 74 rue Cardinal Lemoine. That stinking little place we had to climb four flights of stairs to get to that had nothing but a bucket for a toilet... and the times we had laughing about it."

"We did have some times."

"I miss you like hell sometimes."

"I know Tatie. I miss those times too."

"What should I do? I don't know what to do anymore."

"I don't know, Tatie. You always said writing about things that bothered you made them go away."

"They don't go away anymore. I can't get the thoughts out on paper anymore. Kennedy asked me to write something for his inaugural address, and I just couldn't do it. I spent days at it, and all I had was crinkled up pages of junk. There's something inside of me I can't see that's making me a bum."

"You're not a bum. You're just worn out."

"It's like I'm rusting from the inside out. The rust has crept into my brain."

"Your brain is fine. It's always been your strength. It will come back."

"No, it won't."

"Then just remember those times and remember those feelings."

"Sometimes I can do that. You know I've always loved you."

"And I you. But life messed up and we just couldn't stop it."

"You know that's not true. It was me who messed up."

"Yes."

"And I'm sorry."

"Yes."

"I've always loved you."

"I know."

"That's the best I can do now."

"That's enough."

"Is it enough? It will never be enough. I just want the rust to go away. I want it all to end."

"We will never end, Tatie."

"I know. That's all I have now. I'm sorry. You deserved better and I'm glad you found it."

"Thank you."

"I'm going now, Hadley."

"Okay. Goodbye, Tatie."

"Goodbye, my love."

The not-so-old man channeling Ernest hung up the phone. He knew it would be the last time he talked to her. He felt more empty than he ever had. He knew the emptiness would be gone soon, one way or another. He thought of his dad. He thought of the cottage on the lake his dad built, and the fish in the clear water and the pheasants flying up out of the autumn fields when the air just turned cold and the tracking to shoot only what they were hunting, and the long walks into town.

He thought of rowing Hadley across the lake to the cottage when it was dark and quiet and the stars shone and the water was like a black mirror with the new moon just leaving and the peace he felt holding her in his arms. He thought about all the questions they had about their future: Should they move to Italy or Paris? Should they go to the horse races or go for a walk in the park? Should they save their money to go skiing or have nice dinners at nice restaurants? Should he stay a journalist or try to be a novelist? Then his own decision: Should he catch the first train back to her or miss it for Pauline?

He went downstairs and saw the gun rack in the foyer. His hand reached out for one of the rifles, but he caught himself and turned away. Not yet. Maybe there's hope. "Hadley always gives me hope. Just write about it. Just one true sentence. Start with one true sentence, the rest will come." He found a piece of paper and pencil and stood at the bookshelf. He started to write...

I... feel... like... hell.

That's as far as he got. He knew it was as truthful a sentence he could write. It made him feel like everything he had done since the moment he decided to miss that first train back to her was a mistake. "You had it, Hem. You had it. The most important thing."

Someone else might have taken it for granted, but he had never realized it before: "Maybe that's why I fight. All that confrontation... I don't have to think about other things. Other things that bring me...

"...bring me... Not excitement. Not accolades. Not pain. Lord knows I've had enough pain, and I can handle that just fine. Remember when you broke your arm in that car accident and had it operated on without anesthesia? So I know pain well. It's other things I can't seem to handle... Other things that bring me... bring me..."

His mind stalled. He couldn't find the word to describe it. It was getting close—on the tip of his tongue—but it was still foreign enough he couldn't put a name to it.

Although he felt physically rotten now, he felt a queer sort of satisfaction that at least now, also, he realized it, and now, also, he saw a ray of understanding poke its little head through the fog in his mind.

He shuffled over to the desk. He pulled open a drawer and took out a photo album of the good old days in Paris. He turned the pages slowly, fumbling due to the nerve damage, noticing but not dwelling on the photos of Sylvia Beach, Gertrude Stein, and Erza Pound; James Joyce and Ford Maddox Ford; Zelda and F. Scott Fitzgerald; Lady Duff Twysden (Lady Brett Ashley) and Harold Loeb (Robert Cohn); John Dos Passos (the pilot fish); and Gerald and Sara Murphy (the rich) until he came to his all-time favorite—him and Hadley standing there, her face in profile looking into his eyes with a questioning yet confident look on her face. He closed his eyes—remembering the image that had been burned into his brain. A tear rolled down his cheek.

"Contentment," the not-so-old man channeling Ernest mumbled, his chin hanging down, so the words spilled out of his mouth onto his chest. "That's the word. That's what she gave me I couldn't handle. Contentment. Hadley. Contentment."

The not-so-old man channeling Ernest—who looked as old and battered as a very old man—closed the photo album and walked slowly over to the large picture window. He sat down in the easy chair and gazed out the window at the river, the trees, and the mountains. He sat there and thought—sat there and let himself feel content—for a very long time.

Later in the day, after trying to write one more simple, true sentence and failing, he asked himself what his biggest fear would be if he were to carry out the act. It was not the fear of dying. It was not a fear of pain. He was not afraid of surviving as a cripple or realizing an afterlife. It was the fear that he would never hold that woman in his arms again.

The bits of Ernest Miller Hemingway's brain dried on the

surfaces they stuck to and were wiped and swept into dustpans and then put into garbage bags to be driven to a dump a few miles out of town where they'd become food for the bacteria and worms. They were no longer now, but then, then, and only then, forever then, irrevocably then and then and no longer now but then.

The not-so-old man's eyes stopped flickering for the last time. They opened and stayed open.

CHAPTER *XI*

*T*he sea was calm, and the sun was just a foot above the horizon, and the not-so-old man turned onto his back and did a few elementary backstroke strokes straight at the setting sun.

He noticed with a start his swim cap wasn't on his head. He immediately felt like he would when he suddenly remembered he forgot his car keys or wallet or didn't know where they were. "Oh no! Not that!" shot through his mind. After a few seconds, he noticed the suit flapping against his crotch, let out a sigh of relief, and put it back on his head. He felt the tension and constraint of the cap, but that now felt reassuring.

Comfortable again, he floated with his eyes closed. His hand was still cramped, and his body was tired and sore, but he still had some strength. He was loopy, in part due to his trip of becoming Ernie, in part due to his catharsis, and in part knowing—as Ernie had—his suffering would soon be over.

He heard a fin break the surface. "There he is again," he thought. "He's following you. He can smell you getting weaker... They can always smell your weakness... Just like a woman."

The not-so-old man heard a second fin break the surface. He opened his eyes and righted himself in the water.

"Bring it on," he whispered. "I will fight you with everything I have left, even though it is nothing. So bring it on." He weakly clenched his left hand into a fist. His right hand was still cramped into one.

He heard the fins—one to the left of him, one to the right—but he still didn't see them. By the time he turned his head toward either of them, they had disappeared.

"Now I will die," he thought. "I will fight them both with my bare hands and feet and teeth if I can. I will fight them with everything I have. I will fight them with all my might, all my will. If I am to die, so be it. But I will die with dignity."

He didn't hear or see fins for several minutes. He floated on his back again, eyes closed.

He heard the fins again, and then he heard something else. He heard a breath that was deep and loud and not his own. "Can it be...?" he thought. He turned his head, righted himself, and treaded water looking in the direction of the sound. But he didn't see a fin. And he didn't hear another breath.

Suddenly, all his attention went to his body and how it ached. He could no longer think about Ernie and his wives or his own ex-wife or his dad or even Ray Ray and the boy who never was. In a heartbeat, he was on the edge of a knife, and one small push from a wayward swell would knock him off that edge and send him sinking down to Davy Jones' locker. He realized how bad off he was for the briefest of moments, and then he was beyond that.

Instinct. It was all instinct now: The base response after everything else is stripped away or exhausted. The mindlessness of survival. Panic set in. But he had no energy left to act on it except to hear his brain taunt him, "Oops... I should have thought this through a little more."

He half floated, half treaded water, with his chin barely above the surface and his feet four feet under, almost gulping for air as an asthmatic would. His breaths were not chaotic, however, and had a certain timing and depth to them: Quick inhale, pause, slow exhale, pause. Quick inhale, pause, slow exhale, pause.

Those breaths, as desperate as they were, established a new rhythm—a rhythm that was unlike any rhythm he had ever felt before. A rhythm that wasn't helping him to swim faster or think clearer or relax. Rather, a rhythm that was crushing his ego, maiming his pride, and butchering his prejudice. A rhythm that wasn't serving to save his life, but to save his soul.

Hidden in this new rhythm was a certain and palpable nonchalance: A nonchalance of everything that has come before it and everything that will arise from it. It was a nonchalance toward life that had the nerve to admit to itself, "Ho-hum. Another life? No big deal. It has happened before—it will happen again. Let's just get on with it."

When he felt that lack of caring and un-obsessiveness emanating from the very fabric of existence itself, he felt the release of a smothering tension he had held all his life. And as paradoxical as it was, this release of caring about living gave him the energy to live a little longer.

"Living is nothing," he thought.

The panic left him. His breathing returned to normal. He could think again. He thought that it was certain he was going to die, either by drowning in the sea or getting eaten by sharks. He realized that the bad luck he had all his life had not left him, but been transformed. It was no longer the *saloa* he had hoped and prayed would somehow, magically, change to good luck and deliver him from his misery. No. Now his luck had no element of chance at all—it had simply become the certainty of death. He let out a sigh.

But life wasn't over. Not yet. Sharks didn't attack him. Instead, from behind him, he heard it again: a snort... two snorts. He wasn't sure if the sound was real or imaginary, but it didn't matter; he was past the point of caring.

Then they surfaced. He saw one fin and then the other and heard a blow that was more like a sigh and then a blow that was more like a whale's. But this was no whale. That was no shark. They were dorsal fins of two dolphins. The sigh was from the female, the loud snort was from the male.

"A couple of dolphins," he feebly thought. "A couple."

The fins dove and he waited for them to surface. They didn't surface. The not-so-old man waited several minutes as he treaded water with his chin just above the waterline. And he noticed something strange. He noticed that for the first time, the sea felt lonely.

He had thought for a moment that he had found new friends who understood his love of the sea and water and swimming. Mammals like himself who were smart but didn't mess up their lives with egos that have to find ways to fight each other and their own compulsions because their only compulsions were simply to eat and be happy and make love and care for their babies. "Maybe that's why they're always smiling," he thought. "Come back, little dolphins. Come back! I want to say goodbye."

Panic didn't return. Instead, he bordered on delirium. He kept his chin above water for a few more seconds, wanting not to leave, to wait for his new friends. He heard a song. The words were, as usual, a little messed up…

> *Would you like to come over for tea?*
> *With my Mrs. and me?*
> *It's a lovely way to spend a day in Dayton Ohio*
> *On this lazy Sunday afternoon in nineteen hundred and*
> *three*

Then he heard something else. Something different than the swish of fins or the snorts from blowholes. He slowed his breathing. He stayed as still as possible and listened closely. It was undeniable:

"They're having an argument!"

The dolphins were a hundred yards away from him. One was talking loudly, "EH, EH, EH, EH!"

The other replied in a softer tone, "Eh, eh, eh, eh."
Back and forth several times:
"EH, EH, EH, EH!"
"Eh, eh, eh, eh."
The not-so-old man thought in his delirium that this was the funniest thing he ever heard. He heard a song...

I say yes
You say no
You say stop
And I say go, go, go

Again, "EH, EH, EH, EH!"
And the reply: "Eh, eh, eh, eh."
The not-so-old man thought, "At least they don't interrupt each other."
Again: "EH, EH, EH, EH!"
And the reply: "Eh, eh, eh, eh."
Then silence.
He was about to go under...

Turn out the light
This party's over

A few seconds later, he heard a fin break the surface and the sigh of the female as she exhaled just a few feet away.

The not-so-old man turned his head slowly and feebly and righted himself in the water. He was no more than an arms-length from the dolphin who was looking him right in the eye.

They gazed into each other's eyes for less than a minute, but to the not-so-old man, it felt much longer. He saw her eyes as big as billiard balls glisten in the fading light. They were inspecting him, questioning him, yet at the same time confidently consoling him. Those two eyes—one on each side of her slender curving skull and above her tapering snout and perpetually smiling lips—made him feel something he had not felt in a very long time: he felt justified.

The not-so-old man felt a tingle across his back up across his shoulders. A small spark of electricity coursed through his nervous system. The same kind of spark he had felt when he proposed to his wife, and she said yes.

"Valerie, will you marry me?"

"Yes, Daniel. Of course I'll marry you!"

It lasted only fifteen seconds—it was almost as if the memory of her acceptance was all there all at once: complete and whole, without a sequence, just every thought and feeling all at once. They hugged, and he felt the warm, soft, feminine body he had always craved press hard against him.

"She said yes! She said yes!" exploded in his mind. "She wants me! She wants me! For the rest of my life!" His face flushed and his heart beat even faster than when he was building up the courage to ask her. "She wants me! Now I can show her off to all my friends. Now I'll be able to drive around with a beautiful woman beside me. Now I'll have a partner to share everything with. And kids. We'll have kids. I like kids. I want kids. I'll have kids with her. I'll toss them up in the air and play with them in the backyard. I bet we'll have beautiful, smart kids." Then they drew back and kissed. He was excited, giddy with approval, and felt a thousand butterflies flapping their wings in his stomach. "This is it. This is true and everlasting love. Yes, this is what love is," the not-so-old man as a new fiancé thought. He lowered her to the couch and they sat there turned towards each other, still holding each other and kissing. Long and slow kisses. Kisses that made the hair on the back of his neck stand up. "Yes, this is it," he thought. "This is finally it. This is why songs are written. This is what I've been missing. This is what life's all about," he thought. More kissing. Then some groping. "What should I do now?" he wondered. "Does she want more? Should I do more? Yes, this is love. This is it. We'll go on vacations and fix up our house just the way we want, maybe with a pool in the backyard. And we'll go out to dinner and play charades with our friends and have a glass of wine every now and then," he thought. "Stop thinking! You're ruining it with your thinking. You're tarnishing this moment with your thinking. You shouldn't think. Just do. Don't think. Just do. This is it. This is love." He lowered her onto the couch so he was above her, their feet still on the floor, but he was above her still, kissing her, now, her neck. She purred like a kitten. "Yes, this is it. This has to be it." The butterflies, the heart-pounding, the sweat on his brow. "Yes, this is it. This must be it. These emotions are too strong for it not to be love. But there's something missing. No, not that. That feels too good. But there's something missing..."

"Oh!"

"Yes, dear, that feels amazing."

"Oh!"

"Yes, that's it, my love! Valerie loves that! Yes, that's it! *THAT'S IT!*"

"But do you feel the earth moving? Do you feel it shake and shutter? Yes... well, yes... well, maybe... that must have been it. I shook. I shuddered. But did the earth move? Did it tremble and try to shake me off? Or did *I* shake *it?* I think too much. Now, she's in my arms. I should feel the earth moving below us. But... Where are her eyes? They're away... away. Turned away as she lays here nestled in my sweaty arms. Turned away so my face is in her hair and I smell her shampoo—like flowers—like flowers after a thunderstorm smell—flowers. And where are her eyes as I hold her, here in my arms, her hair in my face? My eyes seeing only the back of her head as she purrs like a kitten, contented, I imagine, but did the earth move for her? Did it? *Where are her eyes?* Is this love? It is. It has to be. Or is it the closest I'll ever come? No! No it will not be! I won't let it be. This is it! Damn it, this is it! This is love!"

Those fifteen seconds were up.

She blinked. He blinked.

"But these new eyes, as big as billiard balls, staring into my pupils, deep into me, past the iron gates that are suddenly wide open, into a well—a deep, deep unfamiliar well. Can this be? But she's not even like me. And yet, the water is shaking. The water is shuttering around me. Like somebody's rocking the boat and I might fall out of it. Does it make a difference? It is—she is—a soul. Does it matter what form? Does it? Her vibration is palpable—bright, warm, peaceful, welcoming, prideless. Yes! Prideless…!

No! Not pride*less!* Pride is okay. Not the smug and condescending kind of pride, but a joy in being kind. Yes! That kind of pride! It's ego that's the problem—not being able to admit when you're wrong. She's egoless. Yes. Egoless. Self-effacing and gentle as a woman. Prideful as a female as I am prideful as a man. But egoless as a soul. Her soul. The soul. It matters. It matters. The soul."

The not-so-old man wanted to say something—say hello or ask how she was doing—but he was too weak. All he could muster was a hoarse and feeble grunt, "Uhuughhh."

The dolphin kept smiling, "Eh, eh, eh, eh."

"Her laugh—all-encompassing and penetrating—in harmony with all that is, all that was, all that will be. As if the whole of all that is is laughing with her, playing from her, and giving her back what she is giving and she's passing that along to me, unselfishly passing that along to me, wanting to do something for, seeing my distress and wanting to do something for; as I would in kind want to her to do something for.

"Yes, the laugh. And her eyes—directly in front of me, facing me, looking at me, into me, unafraid of what they're seeing. Even enjoying what they're seeing. Enjoying and laughing not in my face, but to my face, and wanting, hoping, to do something for."

The not-so-old man somehow found the strength to raise his cramped right hand. He heard a song...

Hello, I don't even know your name
But I'm hoping all the same
This is more than just a passing hello

Hello, should I smile and look away?
No I think I'll smile and stay
To see where it might go

For the last time I felt like this
I was falling in love
Falling and thinking I'd never fall in love again
Oh the last time I felt like this
Was long before I knew
What I'm feeling now for you

The water kept shaking, shuttering, trying to knock him over. He had no notion to define or justify it. Now, he knew. He just knew.

"Eh, eh, eh, eh."

A few yards away the other fin circled around the two. He came up for air and snorted loudly, "EH, EH, EH, EH!"

The water stopped shaking, shuttering. It didn't stop out of anger, resentment, or fear. It stopped because the moment was over. That moment ended, and it will never come again, and yet, that moment will never go away.

The female spun around and replied in a louder voice this time as if telling the male, "I heard you. Now enough!"

The male stopped circling and stood up in the water, showing his chest to the not-so-old man.

The not-so-old man raised his hand again and waved and finally croaked, "I hear you, brother."

The female dove again and resurfaced near the male, and they swam around each other and back and forth beside each other several times. But they no longer spoke.

The not-so-old man watched. He noticed the sun behind the dolphins and the golden light from the new sunset. The clouds were gone, and he could see the true sun as a vibrating circle of light just above the horizon.

Just witnessing her and her mate and seeing the sun shedding its last light on the couple would have brought tears to his eyes, but he had no energy to make them. But the thought occurred to him, "It's been worth it. To witness this, this purity of life playing, *playing* out in front of me. It makes it almost worth it. And her soul. Her soul. I felt her soul. And if Freddy is right—if there is such a thing as the eternal recurrence—I hope this reoccurs for me."

His body finally gave out. He went underwater for the first time. He thought to struggle to come back up, but his right hand was still cramped, his left arm and shoulder extremely sore, and he finally, without effort, resigned himself to his fate. He had one last weak thought as he sank,

"Living is nothing..."

The not-so-old man heard the dolphins underwater. This time, both dolphins wailed together, "Eh, Eh, Eh, Eh!" "EH, EH, EH, EH!"

Their voices were muffled and melded together into a humming that, if he had the energy to realize it, would have reminded him of the Ommm he would hear in a room full of meditators Omming out loud and to themselves all at once and in harmony. The sound and all that vibration in the air all around him, would comfort him and yet at the same time enliven him and make self-evident the fact that there was more to life than what we can know.

His eyes were open in the saltwater and all he saw was darkness. No conscious thoughts were in his head, but his primitive mind had remembered to take a deep gulp of air before he had gone under.

The dolphins stopped wailing. Everything was quiet, there, in the water as he sank little by little further into the sea. A bubble or two escaped his nose.

Then suddenly it was as if he was watching a movie against the blackness of the sea. On the screen in front of him, he saw Ray Ray stuck in her safety seat with the edge of the car door crashed in on her.

"Daddy, it hurts."

Behind her, he saw not the shattered and twisted inside of the car, but a ghost—the ghost of a toddler boy wearing a ball cap and holding a plastic toy baseball bat in his hands. The boy was so small the bat was larger than he was.

"It hurts, Daddy."

The not-so-old man looked his little girl in the eye. He reached out to grab the safety seat as he had in real life, and he pulled and pushed to move the seat and undo the straps that pinned her as he watched her in the movie in front of him. His hands and arms flailed at the twisted car seat and belts—pushing, pulling, twisting, and prying at them to relieve the pressure from the dagger pointing into Ray Ray's back.

He saw the fear in her eyes and yet the confidence that her daddy would save her. Those eyes. Oh my God, those eyes!

"Daddy. Daddy. It hurts, Daddy."

He heard the snap of the metal that would plunge into his little girl's lung.

His legs kicked. His arms kept flailing, but now at the water.

His head broke the surface and bobbed up out of the sea. He gulped for air.

He saw the dolphins. There was no confusion in his eyes. No anger or hostility—only a wide-eyed stare filled with horror. The not-so-old man had no idea what he was doing now. He went under again. The dolphins wailed again.

Again, he saw the darkness of the sea. Again, a movie appeared before him, but this time, his little girl didn't appear, nor the ghost of a boy. Rather, there was a grown young woman with auburn hair pulled back into a ponytail leaning over him and smiling. On her right temple was a golden freckle—not large and not prominent, but noticeable. The young woman looked directly into the not-so-old man's eyes, smiled, and said,

"Daddy, I'm okay."

The not-so-old man floated six feet underwater, watching.

"I'm okay, Daddy."

The young woman smiled and stretched her cupped palm out to the not-so-old man's face.

"Daddy. Daddy. I'm okay, Daddy."

Behind her was a healthy teenage boy wearing a little league uniform and ball cap, holding a baseball bat. The young woman kept smiling,

"We're okay, daddy."

The not-so-old man floated underwater without moving a muscle—his arms hanging in front of himself like a floating corpse—watching the movie in the dark seawater in front of his eyes. The teenage boy swung the bat as if he were taking a cut at a fastball. The young woman spoke again,

"Daddy, Daddy. We're okay, Daddy. We're okay."

The not-so-old man's legs kicked hard, and his arms flailed at the water, desperate to get to the surface. He felt a push upwards from behind from the nose of one of the dolphins.

As his head broke the surface of the sea, a new thought broke through and surfaced into his consciousness:

"I don't want to die," he thought. "My God, *I don't want to die!*"

He took a deep breath and started treading water.

Both dolphins were no longer screaming or wailing, but quietly chattering, almost purring. The not-so-old man felt light in the water—his arms, hands, and legs almost unneeded to keep himself afloat. He kept treading water.

"Eh, eh, eh, eh."

"EH, EH, EH, EH."

Suddenly, the female sprinted away and turned in a tight circle around him. She swam gently to the not-so-old man so she came up from behind him. She let out a sigh, and a gentle "eh, eh, eh, eh," and rubbed her left flank against the not-so-old man's right side. She was offering him her back.

The male dolphin talked again, his tone no longer loud and aggressive, but encouraging: "EH, EH, EH, EH!"

The not-so-old man watched his left hand go to his right hand and open it from its cramp. His left hand placed his open right hand on the female dolphin's dorsal fin and then squeezed it shut so that his cramped hand clamped onto the fin like a vice. He watched his left arm wrap around the dolphin's midsection just below the blowhole and clamp itself tightly there. He watched as he lowered his head onto the back of the female dolphin and then coughed once involuntarily. Two seconds later, they were off.

As the female dolphin turned to head east, the not-so-old man saw the golden horizon turn before him. The sun had set completely, but the golden glow was still in the sky.

The not-so-old man looked behind and saw the male dolphin following. The male dolphin gained on the pair quickly and quietly, surfacing for each breath and showing his belly. With drooping eyelids, the not-so-old man watched as the male swam past him and the female until he was ahead of them.

The not-so-old man hung on with his cramped right hand and sore left arm. He felt the water rush past him, and the spray from the female's exhales showered down on him like gentle drops of rain.

"Each stroke better than the last. Each stroke more true to itself."

"Eh, Eh, Eh, Eh!"

The not-so-old man felt his left hand pat the dolphin's side.

The not-so-old man's arm held fast across the dolphin's back, and his hand remained clamped to the dolphin's dorsal fin. His legs trailed like limp strands of spaghetti beside the dolphin's flank. She swam not fast and not slow, but sure and true, with grace, humility, purpose, and strength.

The male dolphin forged ahead chirping, alerting other fish and birds to stay out of his partner's way. Every now and then he let out a menacing snort.

The not-so-old man let himself relax. His mind slowed. The waves—not of the sea, but of his mind—went from choppy, to smoother and slower, to smoother and slower still; then all the way down to the deepest, most restful sleep with the slowest, most powerful waves which gently rocked him as he heard his mother slowly, tenderly sing:

> *There, there, my precious*
> *There, there, my darling*
> *I am here*
> *You are safe*
> *Mama gives you*
> *All her loving*

The not-so-old man's mind stayed and listened to her unaware, but listened and stayed and reveled in the sound of his mother's voice, resonating with the notes, comforted with the soothing tone of her voice as she pressed his little infant body firmly against her bosom making his little instinctive mind believe that the words she was singing were true. They were the slowest truth he would ever experience—until now—when they were now and again now and always now.

He woke up with the side of his face pressed against the side of the dolphin's back. It took him a few seconds to remember he was being carried along on the back of a dolphin. He found it hard to believe, but as the cobwebs cleared from his mind, he knew it was so, and he knew this dolphin and her mate were there to help him.

"How am I to think of you two since we're now friends?" he thought as he pressed his forehead against the dolphin's back. "Friends call each other by their names. My name is Daniel. You can call me that or just plain old Dan. But what are your names? Since I don't speak Dolphin, I'll give you names in English. Good old-fashioned English."

The not-so-old man thought for several moments. "Okay. I think I've got it. I'll call you Gracie because that's what you are. And your boyfriend? I had a friend years ago named George. He was a good guy, sometimes a little loud, but honest and true. So I'm going to name your boyfriend George. So you two will be the George and Gracie Show. They were a comedy team back in the day, you know. I think that's fitting since you two are always smiling."

The not-so-old man remembered something… "George was my friend's English name. His real name was Jorge since he was born in Puerto Rico. So I'm going to name your boyfriend Jorge. I know I said I'd use English, but what the heck. Jorge is fine, and that's who he'll be. Is that okay with you, Gracie?"

Gracie replied, "Eh, Eh, Eh, Eh."

"I'll take that as a yes," the not-so-old man thought.

"And Ernie, I'm not naming my new friend after your mom. I know her name was Grace. It's just a coincidence. Just an ironic coincidence."

A few seconds later, the not-so-old man fell asleep.

Chapter XII

*T*his evening, as the not-so-old man clung to Gracie's back, and as he slipped in and out of consciousness, he dreamt a dream within a dream that felt more real than waking life. He was a middle-aged man visiting his parents and was asleep in bed in his boyhood room. This not-so-old man as a middle-aged man dreamed he was all packed up and ready to leave in the morning. When he woke he went into his parent's bedroom and saw his dad was in bed alone, sleeping, completely wrapped in a white blanket from head to toe, so he looked like he was in a cocoon. The not-so-old man as a middle-aged man dreamed he peeled back the blanket to reveal his father lying on his side—his old, weathered skin yellow and blotchy—sucking his thumb. He turned his father to face him and woke his father up. He gazed down at his father— his dad—and noticed the old man's sunken cheeks from not having his dentures in and his gray eyes wide open in quizzical wonder, perhaps wondering who was waking him up and was now standing over him.

The not-so-old man as a middle-aged man kept looking at him, then leaned over and kissed his old father on his forehead and told him, "Dad, I miss you. I love you so much."

His father kept looking at him and didn't change the expression on his face or utter a word, but his eyes said something. What that was, the not-so-old man as a middle-aged man couldn't figure out exactly, but he felt it was profound and meant for him alone. It gave him some hope.

In this dream, the not-so-old man as a middle-aged man knew

he had to leave and go home to his own house. But as he looked at his father now, so old and weathered and vulnerable, he thought, "What on earth is so important you have to leave him for?" Then the not-so-old man as a middle-aged man woke up.

And so did the not-so-old man.

Gracie was still swimming, and the not-so-old man was still clinging to her back. It was now dark, but the sky was clear and the stars shined and shined their light on the sea. He felt the water rushing over his back and along his arms and legs. The dolphin's skin was smooth and firm, but no longer slippery. And the not-so-old man felt his heart beating against the dolphin's back.

He wondered what it would have been like having Ernie as his father considering his drinking and explosive and unpredictable temper. "It would have been hard," he concluded, "to put up with his mood swings, perfectionism, wandering eye. But that's just part of it. Fame and fortune don't favor even the bold."

The not-so-old man recalled how, when Ernie ran into Scotty in Paris one time after one of his safaris, Scotty was about as down as a man could be. Scotty told Hem that ten years ago, he and Zelda were the genius writer/Debonair Husband and Golden Girl wife, and now, she was in a sanitarian and he was a fall-down drunk. He told Hem that Hem had been right—that a rummy married to a crazy person was not a winning combination.

And Ernie told Scotty that he was right too when Scotty had warned him about fame. "You told me that struggle is a heck of a lot better," Hem said. "My quick and easy fame and Pauline's money ruined everything."

They were both quite miserable. That's when Ernie gave Scotty his rabbit's foot. When Scotty asked him what lucky piece he would have, Hem told him he didn't need any, that he had had all the luck he could handle.

The not-so-old man thought about Ernie's depression and

Ernie's father's depression and all the suicides in the family and how he found out that Ernie had a little known hereditary blood disorder that could have caused it. (†) And depression could, of course, lead to drinking and suicidal thoughts. The disorder was probably passed on to Ernie from his father and his father before that and onto his children and so on.

"Ernie, you had one hell of a ride—six concussions causing headaches, mental fogginess, and ringing in your ears. One was from mistakenly pulling a cord in a bathroom in Paris, thinking it would flush the toilet, but instead, it pulled a skylight down on your head that split it open so badly it required multiple stitches and left a permanent scar across your forehead. Another was from flying through a windshield in a car accident that required fifty-seven stitches in your scalp. You were in two airplane crashes just two days apart that ruptured your liver, spleen, and kidneys, sprained several limbs, dislocated your shoulder, crushed your vertebra, left first-degree burns over much of your body, and cracked your skull. The first plane crash was in Nairobi, in 1954 when your plane went down into a thorn thicket and you sprained your shoulder. The next one happened when the rescue plane you were in two days later burst into flames on the runway. Your wife and the pilot escaped, but you were in the rear of the plane and trapped. This is when, after all the close calls you had had with death during your life, you thought for the first time for sure, you were going to die. But you mustered the moxie and strength to twice head-butt the door and escape, emerging with your clothes smoking, skin singed, and the hair on your head burned off. Months later, you told a friend you heard the pops of exploding bottles of booze as the plane burned to the ground. Any one of these injuries would be hard to handle. But all of them? Give me a break.

"You suffered through malaria, dysentery, skin cancer, high

blood pressure, and high cholesterol. It's amazing you lasted as long as you did. And although some say you were weak to kill yourself and your family was loony-tunes, I say they're the ones who are nuts. Put any other man in your shoes, and they would have tried to walk into a spinning airplane propeller blade just like you had. Heck, if God had to go through all that, he'd probably want to kill himself too.

"And your mom—she dressed you like a girl and raised you as a twin to your elder sister Marcelline until you were six when she finally allowed you to cut off your long locks for good. She called you her 'Dutch Dolly' and later forced you to take cello lessons, which you hated but later said helped you consider rhythm in your writing. And your dad, Clarence, would beat you with a razor strop. I read that you'd hide in the shed out back fantasizing about shooting him as a youngster, but you ended up loving him. You resented and hated your mom because of her dominating personality, and quipped that it "would make a pack-mule shoot himself let alone poor bloody father." In any event, it sounds like your childhood was messed up. And I'm sorry that toward the end they gave you electroconvulsive therapy about fifteen times in December 1960, and was 'released in ruins' in January 1961. Then in April, more electroconvulsive therapy. Maybe they were out to kill you, Ernie, just not so suddenly or obvious-like.

"They didn't kill you outright by shooting you, stabbing you, injecting you, or by creating an 'accident.' They zapped your memory, your creativity, and will until they were mush. Either knowingly or unknowingly, they used that technology to turn you into a shell of the human being you once were. I don't care if they say it's useful, somewhat successful, and safe. How can sending up to 120 volts through a person's brain for up to six seconds to induce a seizure be good for anyone? Let's use some common sense! It's applesauce, I tell you. And it turned your brain into applesauce. So, you see, Ernie, you really didn't commit suicide. You were murdered, at least in my mind, and hopefully in God's mind too. It was suicide*—with an asterisk.

"Just you watch, Ernie. I bet you get that free pass out of hell I talked about. Like you said, '...the hard times will pass, everything will get better and the sun will shine brighter than ever.'

"You were a victim, Ernie, just like me and Ray Ray were when we got hit by that garbage truck. You did an amazing job creating all you did, given all that happened to you. Some of it was self-inflicted, I know. But some of it was *salao*, too.

"And Ernie, I have to thank you. You made me realize something important: As grand as they may first appear, even great men have their weaknesses."

The not-so-old man paused. Then he thought, "Which sometimes makes that great man even greater."

The not-so-old man fell asleep again. The not-so-old man dreamed again...

"Let's show them what you're made of," the not-so-old man as a champion swimmer thought. "I may have slipped in the final turn trying to qualify for the Olympics, but I can show them now in the Nationals what they'll be missing."

The starter barked, "Take your mark. Ready. Set..." *Bang!*

The not-so-old man as a champion swimmer sprang from the starting block and sliced into the water cleanly. He kicked as he glided underwater and surfaced for his first breath. Nine other champion swimmers flanked his left and right, but he didn't think of that. Once his fingertips touched the water, he was all alone. He was alone in his swimming and he disappeared into it and there was nothing else. No competitors, no grand-stand, no audience, no family, no friends, no stopwatch, no swimming pool, no water. Just him and his strokes.

"Each stroke better than the last. More true to itself."

He wasn't raising his arms and pulling through the water with cupped hands. He was no longer making freestyle strokes. He had simply become the strokes.

He flipped into the first turn. He didn't wake from his trance. The next wall came. Another perfect flip and turn. He was ahead by a head at the second turn. By the fifth turn, his lead was a full body's length. He kept swimming. Three more walls. Three more perfect flips and turns.

"Each stroke better than the last. More true to itself."

By the fifteenth turn, he was five body lengths ahead. There were swimmers from Virginia, Hawaii, Florida, Texas, Southern California, and South Carolina. Some had qualified for the Olympics. All were past national champions in one style or another. The audience sensed something great was happening. A murmur spread throughout the stands.

Twenty laps. Twenty perfect turns. He had lapped two of the other swimmers and was ahead by nine lengths on the others. Ten more 50-meter lengths to go.

The murmurs continued. People in the audience had seen other swimmers bolt out ahead in these long races only to tire and fade down the stretch. Could the not-so-old man as a champion swimmer keep it up?

By the twenty-third lap, the crowd started applauding. He heard nothing.

"Each stroke better than the last. More true to itself."

The not-so-old man kept dreaming, remembering, and feeling what he had already experienced in real life. This dream was more vivid, felt more real and more true now than when it had actually happened.

Still faster. The next wall. A perfect flip and turn. Perfect contact with the wall. Strong push against the wall. Short glide underwater. Perfect stroke. Faster.

Next wall. Flip. Turn. Push. Glide. Stroke.

Faster.

The not-so-old man as a champion swimmer swam like he had just been released from bondage. He swam. He just swam...

The not-so-old man's eyes opened. Gracie was still swimming and he was still clinging to her back.

He felt his stomach and chest against her body. He felt the air brushing through his nostrils. He heard his inhales and exhales whisper as they sailed onto the sea. He slowed his breathing down. His neck and shoulders relaxed, his chest expanded, his stomach released, and his spine inched straighter.

"Each breath better than the last. More true to itself."

His brainwaves slowed with each breath he truncated and hindered, and a physical mushiness spread through every muscle. His heart, still beating against Gracie's back, slowed but strengthened. Gracie slowed to a stop, raised her head, and said, "Ehhhh, ehhhh, ehhhh, ehhhh." Her tone—like organ music in a cathedral—reverberated in him as if he was a tuning fork. He grunted, "Uhhhh, Uhhhh, Uhhhh, Uhhhh."

Gracie resumed swimming. The not-so-old man glanced up at the canopy of the night sky and found the Big Dipper. He traced The Pointers to the North Star. He saw it was on Gracie's port side. She was carrying him due east.

"Maybe it's not about lessons," he thought, "or even seeing how much crap you can handle. Maybe the pain is pushing you towards more. It's shouting at you, 'Get busy! Make something! Make *yourself* something!' It takes time, but that's not so important.

"Ernie knew this, although maybe only intuitively. He would take a whole afternoon to write just one true paragraph. He tried forty-seven times before getting the ending to *A Farwell to Arms* just right. He didn't care how long it took."

The not-so-old man opened his eyes briefly. He saw the dark water below and the starry sky above. He felt the air pass by him, and the spray on his face.

He let his eyes close...

The not-so-old man saw his father under the canopy of maple trees in their backyard. His dad raised his right hand and threw the not-so-old man as a boy a baseball. The not-so-old man as a boy loved baseball and played in the Little League. He played second base, third base sometimes, and pitcher, and played in the street when there was no Little League.

He was playing catch with his dad, as he often did, and today, he was practicing his pitching. His dad squatted down like a catcher and the not-so-old man as a boy wound up and threw the baseball to him hard. His dad caught the ball and called out like an umpire, "Strike two!"

The not-so-old man as a boy called out to his dad, "Was that good? Was that a good one, Dad?"

His father threw the ball back to him and held up his right hand in front of him, pointing at this son and wiggling his hand at the wrist like a fish wiggles as it swims.

"Yeah, that was a good one, son. It had good movement on it." He wiggled his hand again. "That's gonna be a tough pitch to hit!"

"Thanks, Dad."

"That makes the count two-and-two," his dad called back.

"Okay!" the not-so-old man as a boy replied. "Now I'm Tom Seaver, and it's the bottom of the ninth in game seven of the World Series. The Mets are ahead by only one run, bases loaded, and the count's two balls and two strikes. If I don't strike this guy out, we lose the game and the Series!"

The not-so-old man as a boy was excited, imagining he was really in the World Series. In his haste, he took hold of the baseball haphazardly, wound up as his father was just starting to squat down into a catcher's stance, and threw the ball. It sailed off to the right and crashed into an overhanging limb way off target.

"Daniel," his dad said. "See what happens when you rush into things? I know you're excited, and that's okay, but you have to control it. You need to learn how to take your time. We've got all the time in the world. Slow it down, son. Slow it down."

The not-so-old man as a boy frowned and hung his head. "Yeah," he mumbled. "I know. I know."

"Okay, Danny. Try again."

His dad played announcer: "The count is full and the bases are jammed. Danny Marino on the mound in this final game of the most exciting World Series in history. It all comes down to this final pitch. It's now or never for this talented young buck. Can he do it? The fans are going wild here in Shea! I bet people can hear 'em all the way to Coney Island! Marino takes the sign. Here's the wind-up. Here's the pitch..."

The not-so-old man as a boy wound up slower this time—and with a smile on his lips—threw his father the ball. The ball zipped through the air faster and right on target. It slapped into his dad's glove.

"Strike three!" his dad yelled. "You're outta here!"

The not-so-old man as a boy jumped up, raised his arms in the air, hollered, and bounced around like he had just won the World Series! Both he and his father laughed.

"Okay, Danny boy. Now try throwing a changeup. Remember to hold the ball in your fingers the way I showed you."

"Sure thing, Dad."

The not-so-old man opened his eyes, expecting to see his dad, but his dad wasn't there. "What's happening?" he wondered. He felt the water push against him and the spray on his face. "Oh yeah. I'm on the back of a dolphin."

He let himself bask in the memory of that time under the maple trees with his dad. He realized then, just weakly, perhaps, that he had had some good times in his life. But that feeling wasn't going to last very long.

CHAPTER *XIII*

*T*he no-so-old man opened his eyes. It was still dark. This time, he heard trouble.

Jorge was behind him and Gracie now and was snorting and yelling loudly. The not-so-old man heard churning in the sea beyond Jorge. Jorge rose up, showed his chest, and yelled, "EH, EH, EH, EH!" Gracie turned around.

Gracie squirmed and shook to get the not-so-old man off her back. The not-so-old man understood and let go. His right hand was no longer cramped, and it opened and slipped off her fin easily. He started treading water.

Gracie sprinted to Jorge, picked up her head, and rubbed it against the side of Jorge's head. They both started screaming. "EH, EH, EH, EH!" "Eh, Eh, Eh, Eh!"

In the sea beyond them were thirteen first dorsal fins of sharks circling each other churning up the water. The not-so-old man could see them now in the starlight and the light from a sliver of a new moon. "Those ain't no dolphins," he thought. "Damn *galanos.*"

One fin stopped circling and sprinted straight for the not-so-old man and the dolphins. Jorge and Gracie split up—one swam left, the other right. The shark kept coming straight… straight for the not-so-old man.

The shark was just thirty yards away from the not-so-old man and charging fast when he saw the fins of the two dolphins surface—one to the left of the shark, one to the right. Two seconds later, both dolphins slammed into the shark—one at its midsection and one at its head.

All three fins stopped dead in the water.

One of the dolphin's fins moved away quickly as the shark fin remained still. It was Jorge circling and sprinting straight at the shark's front, right at his head. Gracie moved away too and circled just as Jorge had, next in line to attack the shark.

Jorge head-butted the shark. Gracie head-butted the shark. The shark fin sank below the surface. It didn't resurface.

Jorge and Gracie started screaming again. Another fin was fast approaching. This time, the dolphins didn't split up, but Jorge sprinted directly at the shark, and Gracie was fast behind him. Jorge hit the shark directly in the head. Gracie hit the shark directly in the head.

The shark fin sank.

Two more sharks came. Each dolphin chose one and sprinted directly at it. Jorge hit his mark. Gracie hit hers too, but not squarely enough. That shark paused and then started swimming directly at the not-so-old man.

The not-so-old man had watched the action in a detached sort of horror. Now, he wasn't detached. Now he saw the fin twenty yards away from him coming straight at him. Jorge was too far away to intercept. Gracie was recovering from her collision. The not-so-old man was all alone to face the shark.

He thought, "Okay *galanos*. I don't have a tiller handle and I don't have a broken oar. All I have are my hands and feet. And I will fight you to the death."

Funny what a man might do when he's under pressure.

The not-so-old man raised his arms as if unfurling his wings—his hands above his head, arms like a 'Y', wrists limp. He bent his left knee, so his thigh was horizontal and extended his right leg straight down like he was balancing himself on a stump. He looked like a crane spreading his wings in defiance. He heard a voice close to his ear say, "If do right, no can defense."

He heard another voice behind the sharks yell, "Finish him!"

The not-so-old man pushed off the water with his right leg as his left foot shot straight down. His right leg kicked up hard and straight and right at the shark that was now upon him.

The not-so-old man grunted, "Eeee Ahaaaa!"

The heel of his foot smashed into the shark's skull right between its eyes. The shark recoiled backward and downwards deeper into the sea, causing his dorsal fin to disappear.

Mr. Miyagi smiled.

The impact pushed the not-so-old man up and backward and briefly almost totally out of the water. Once he splashed down, he started swimming slowly to the dolphins. Jorge swam toward the not-so-old man. He sprinted past him. The shark had been dazed, but not out, and when his fin reappeared, Jorge met him head-on and finished the job.

Gracie moved slowly. Jorge went to her side. The water beyond them was still churning with fins just fifty yards away. The fight wasn't over.

This time, they came slowly. Nine fins weaved back and forth in front of the dolphins and the not-so-old man. Jorge rose up and bellowed. He splashed and swam back and forth between Gracie and the sharks, trying to shield her, but the sharks kept coming.

The not-so-old man knew what he had to do. Gracie had sacrificed for him: she had carried him on her back for miles as she and her mate tried to save his life. They knew and understood him. They could feel him through the water—his brain waves, his thoughts, his intentions, his past. They could sense what he had endured and that he was good. And they wanted good to survive, to triumph.

Now, it was his turn. He took what little strength he had and crawled past Jorge and Gracie directly at the swarming sharks creeping their way. He was meat to them, and that would distract them from his new friends and give them time to get away. "I may be destroyed, but I won't be defeated," he thought. This was his chance to shine. It was his chance to do something for.

It was his chance to do some things he wished he could have done long ago. He wished that the garbage truck had hit *his* side of the car and smashed in *his* door so it would have pressed and then punctured *his* lung. He wished he could have been strong enough to yank that safety seat from around his little girl and pull that dagger off of her back so she would still be here today.

He wished he could have scooped his son out of his wife's womb and untied that umbilical cord from around his neck and breathed life into him so his heart would still be beating today.

This was his sacrifice, not just to save Gracie and Jorge, but in an obtuse but honest way—to his children. And nothing, nothing was going to stop him.

Jorge chattered at him. The not-so-old man kept swimming.

The sharks were just fifty feet from him now, circling closer. The not-so-old man stopped dead in the water. He treaded water and waited.

The fins weaved back and forth, swishing through the water. Closer they came. Like some sick, twisted villain in some sick, twisted horror movie, they kept coming... and coming... and coming.

"Pain is nothing. Dying is nothing..."

The not-so-old man took two more freestyle strokes towards the sharks. Then he stopped, clenched his fists, and readied his legs for a sidekick. He saw one of the shark fins break out of the pack and race directly at him. The not-so-old man's eyes involuntarily glanced up at the stars for a second, then immediately back to the fin now just a few yards away.

"Living is nothing," he muttered out loud.

He heard the swish of the shark's fin slicing through the water. His left thigh came up beside his belly with his leg horizontal and about to push out at the muzzle of the shark, when…

…out of nowhere, he felt a current in the water brush his side—like a puff of wind heralding a coming storm—and then, TH-WHAP! The thud of nose to head sounded above the swishing.

The charging shark's fin went under, and in its wake, a screaming dolphin burst through the surface, showing his chest.

Then three... five... thirteen... nineteen... twenty-three dolphin fins swam past him straight for the pack of sharks. They barged into their circle, and each one or two dolphins singled out a shark and attacked. The water churned like it was a piranha feeding frenzy:

Smashing, crashing, crushing, cracking.

Pounding, wounding, maiming, killing.

Sinking.

"Lee! There's one off your port bow!"

"I see it!" Leeward said charging. "Thwap! Got him!"

"Finney has the one to your starboard, but look astern!"

"Yeah. I see it! I'll lead him out and then Tack can catch him coming back 'round."

"You got that Tack?"

"Copy that! I'm on it!"

"Look left, Lippy! Dive Lippy! Dive!"

"No problem, Sardi! You get so hysterical!"

"I'll get him when you come back up, Lippy!"

"I know, dear. That's why I love you."

"Yarn-spinner! Go around! No, the other way!"

"Yeah, that was close. Thanks, Windjammer. I owe you one."

"Where's West-Indies?"

"She chased a couple of 'em south. Muddy Waters went with

her. Here… They're coming back now—no sharks to be seen."

The battle lasted only ten minutes. No blood was shed. Just broken bones and crushed skulls. Some of the sharks limped away. Some sank to never rise again. Jorge and Gracie watched from the sidelines, knowing their help wasn't needed.

The fight over, the dolphins swam past the not-so-old man to Jorge and Gracie. They were greeted warmly, but quietly. "Like something you'd see in the Amish," the not-so-old man found himself thinking. "Like a barn raising or funeral or birth." The new dolphins chatted to Jorge and Gracie and amongst themselves, congratulating each other on their victory.

But it was far from over, at least for the not-so-old man. As he watched the group of dolphins chattering and swimming around each other, Jorge rose above them back-peddling on his tail, and screamed louder than the not-so-old man had ever heard him scream before,

"EEEHHHHH, EEEHHHHH!"

The not-so-old man thought perhaps Gracie was hurt or in trouble, so he turned to go to her. But that wasn't it. He first turned his head to the right towards them and raised his arm to start swimming, but Jorge called out again,

"EEEHHHHH, EEEHHHHH!"

The not-so-old man quickly turned his head to the left, and there it was—just a few yards away and coming right at him with jaws open wide, its head rising out of the water to take its first bite. Its teeth—three rows deep into its cavernous mouth— glistened in the starlight; and its eyes—beady and wide open, oval-shaped with large, purely black pupils in the middle of their ghostly white sclerae and positioned on the sides of its head to see forward, sideways, and backward—had a vacuous, soulless stare that was staring single-mindedly directly at the not-so-old man's face.

The shark's jaws started to close.

Then. . .

Nothing but reflex.

Without a moment's delay—as he had been trained through hours of practice in the dojo by his sensei—his hand, with his fingers curled up hard and his thumb folded over his clenched fingers, shot out to block the attack...

"EEEE AAAHHH!"

His fist hit the shark right on the tip of its snout as its jaws were closing and stuck there for a full second as the momentum of the shark pushed forward still, pushing the not-so-old man a yard sideways and up, and as his hand stayed on the shark's nose, it acted like a pivot point around which the not-so-old man flipped up and over the shark, over its head, and onto its back right next to the shark's first dorsal fin.

The not-so-old man didn't think—there wasn't time to think. When he felt the dorsal fin below him, he grabbed it with both hands. The shark didn't stop swimming but bucked like a wild stallion would buck refusing to be broken: up and down, side to side, any which way to get the not-so-old man off his back. The not-so-old man held on.

They were moving away from all of the dolphins, and the not-so-old man realized his new friends wouldn't be able to save him. It was him against the shark now. Him against the shark. The last shark, the final shark. One-on-one. One-on-one. One-on-one.

Now he tried to think. He forced himself to think. If he let go, the shark would turn on him, and that would be the end because kill is what sharks do. If he kept holding on, one of them would eventually tire, and he knew it wouldn't be the shark. The result would be the same.

"So this is it," he thought. "You've said over and over you'd fight them with your hands and feet and teeth if you had to, with everything you had, so you would die with dignity. Here's your chance." He took a deep breath.

The shark ducked its head underwater and dove. The not-so-old man held on. Three feet down. Five feet down. Ten feet down. The not-so-old man felt the pressure build on his head. He remembered one fighting technique that could instantly kill someone. But he had to get to the shark's head to do it.

He took his right hand and let go of the dorsal fin, curled his fingers as if he was going to grab a ledge as a rock climber would and thrust them into the gills on the shark's side. He felt them slide into the gills and break through some membranes, and he grabbed onto the tissues like he'd grab a ledge, and he pulled his body forward. He took his left hand and did the same thing—plunging his fingers into the shark's gills on its left side, grabbing whatever he could, holding on, and pulling himself forward.

The shark dove deeper... fifteen feet... twenty feet...

The not-so-old man's stomach was against the back of the shark, his legs straddled its first dorsal fin, and his face was just behind the shark's forehead.

"Now," he thought. "Now."

But nothing happened. His hands and arms didn't move. He stayed there on the shark's back for several more seconds.

"Twenty-five feet... thirty feet..."

The pressure in his head was building to the point of pain.

"Now," he thought again. "Now!"

Still, his arms didn't move.

"Forty feet down... fifty feet..."

"It's either you or him," he thought. "You have no choice. You or him. Us or them. You or him. Us or them. You or him..."

He pulled the fingers of his right hand out of the shark's gills and held on tighter with his left hand.

"Do it! Do it now!"

He ignored his queasiness—no time for queasiness. He straightened the fore and middle fingers of his right hand and held them tightly together as he thrust his hand forward in front of the shark's face. He bent his wrist back towards himself, and finding the shark's right eye with his straightened and hard fingers, plunged them as hard as he could into that eye. He plunged them in hard and fast and deep and didn't pull them out but kept pushing them as hard as he could through the shark's eye, through the bony eye socket, and into the shark's brain.

The shark shuddered and shook violently, violently, violently, as the not-so-old man held on with his fingers and hand in one eye and the other hand's fingers and hand in the gills of the shark.

But still deeper. Sixty feet... seventy feet...

The not-so-old man's head ached from the pressure but he took his left hand and put the two fingers together and pushed his hand in front of the shark's face as he held fast with his right hand deep in the shark's eye socket and found the shark's left eye and plunged his fingers and hand into that eye too.

The shark stopped swimming and threw his head back hard. The not-so-old man was thrown off the shark's back, and his left hand fingers came out of the shark's left eye, but the fingers of his right hand stayed in the shark's right eye as he kept pushing and jabbing them in and into the brain of the shark.

He was beside the head of the shark now, and the shark opened his jaws wide and snapped them shut and opened them and snapped them shut and he couldn't see anything because it was totally dark, but he heard the three rows of dagger-like teeth clamp together and grind on each other over and over and over again as the shark withered and thrashed.

Steady at seventy feet...

He felt something rigid and taut like a stretched rope inside the eye socket—a nerve or artery, perhaps. He hooked his two fingers around it and pulled as hard as he could, trying to pull it through and out of the eye socket.

His fingers slipped. He felt around inside the shark's brain again and found the fiber and hooked his fingers around it and pulled.

Again it slipped off. The shark was shaking its head from side to side in convulsions of denial and the not-so-old man thrust his left hand into the shark's other eye again and held on as the fingers of his right hand searched again for the fiber.

Finally, he found it, and hooked all of his fingers around it clamping his opposable thumb down on it, and pulled it hard right through the eye socket. He felt it stretch and stretch and resist, and then suddenly, it snapped. The shark stopped moving.

The not-so-old man pulled his fingers out of the eyes of the shark, let go of the fiber that was still held firmly in his right fist, and pushed himself away from the corpse. He'd been holding his breath for over five minutes. His lungs were about to burst. He wasn't sure which way was up. He had to pause and feel which way his body would rise. Then he kicked and pulled with his arms, making the most important strokes of his life...

"Each stroke better than the last, more true to itself."

Sixty feet... fifty feet... thirty feet...

He wanted, needed, desperately to breathe.

"No! You can't breathe yet! You'll die if you breathe! Just a little farther. Just a little longer. Hold it. Hold your breath, damn it!"

His mind was fading. He felt like he was going to pass out. He saw deep colors of purple and blue and one spark of light, then many sparks of light—like shooting stars that danced around but were all going to the same place—and he felt something buoyant leave him and float up faster than he was, and he felt heavier—like dead weight—but he could still think too and he hazily, almost drunkenly, thought,

"Five more seconds. Hold it. Just five more seconds."

Twenty feet...

The sparks oscillated back and forth quickly—full of energy and unbridled desire as if they were anxious to get somewhere—as they migrated slowly towards one intensely bright, large, star three thousand miles away, that seemed to be within arm's reach. He felt a push up on his rear end from underneath.

Ten feet...

He was about to inhale. He couldn't hold it any longer. That single star expanded and spread out with its perimeter curling towards him, reaching out as if to envelop him and make him part of itself and he felt a presence, a knowing, a welcoming.

His final thought was, *"Please God, just two more seconds!"* Simultaneous to that thought came another push up, harder this time.

He felt the surface break as his head and then chest and then stomach shot out of the water—like a dolphin jumping and proudly showing his belly. He shot out of the water and up into the air and just before he started to come down to earth, to the sea, he felt that lightness return into him right through the top of his head. That lightness lingered in his skull and he felt for just an instant he'd never come down and he didn't want to come down and he could float up into that singular star along with all the other sparks and let it envelop him and become one with it and never regret a thing.

Then the lightness shot down his spinal cord and took a turn into his gut and settled right behind his belly button, back into his center it came, and it too lingered there.

He opened his mouth and gasped as he fell, not onto the water, but onto the back of a dolphin that was there beside him. He wrapped his arms around Jorge, his face right up against his dorsal fin, and panted like a dog on a hot summer's day. Jorge stayed still in the water, waiting.

The not-so-old man panted. He breathed. He lived. He stared straight ahead over the dark blue-green, very dark blue-green water of the ocean, to the straight line of its horizon, then past the horizon, his eyes continued up until he saw Polaris shining and he saw for the first time in his life a tube of light rising up from the middle, the middle of the earth, straight up from where the North Pole would be to the North Star—an amorphous tube of light of neon purple and blue with streaks of silver and yellow this light flowed and it flowed to the star and when it got there, it hit it like a freight train hitting a car stuck on the tracks and the light exploded into a million pieces and rained down in all directions like fireworks sparkling down and he held onto Jorge and loved Jorge and loved Gracie and loved his dolphin friends and loved Ray-Ray and loved the boy who never was and loved Valerie and his mother and father and sister. He didn't think about himself, but instead, he loved his friends and his enemies, health, and sickness and poverty and wealth. He loved the sea and the earth, the air and the stars, the moon, and the sun. He loved. He just loved.

Gracie swam to them. The other dolphins also came and swam around them in a circle, like a wagon train rounding up. It was quiet. No one was talking or chattering. It was the calm after the storm, and they were all somber and reflective about what they had just done, but it had been necessary. And each of them felt justified in his and her actions.

Gracie floated closer to the not-so-old man and Jorge. She nuzzled her nose against Jorge's snout and nodded her head as she whispered, "eh, eh, eh, eh," into his ear. She paused in front of the not-so-old man, nodded her head to him too, and then inched her way forward, so he was even with her dorsal fin. She was offering him her back.

The not-so-old man grasped her fin as before, wrapped his arm around her as before, felt her warm slippery skin as before, lowered his head onto her back as before, and felt his heart beat against her back as before. He felt the water shutter and shake.

Two seconds later, they were off.

Chapter XIV

*T*he not-so-old man looked around and saw Jorge out in front, leading the armada of dolphins that had formed around him and Gracie. Like a fleet of destroyers protecting the aircraft carrier, together, they moved through the sea toward the lightening eastern sky.

The not-so-old man pressed his forehead against Gracie's back. He was exhausted. He held fast to Gracie's back as he had before with his right hand grasping her dorsal fin and his left arm wrapped around her midsection. His left arm and shoulder and all the way down the left side of his body ached miserably. He fought to keep his eyes open, and they did not close, but instead, rolled back into his head so only the whites of his eyes were visible. He entered into a deep altered state. He heard a voice echo in his head, and his mind, as much as it didn't like what it heard, had no choice but to listen...

Shark Prophesy

There were nine sharks in a line with the center one a half-body ahead leading the pack. Their first dorsal fins were painted white and on their tips were blue electric bulbs like you'd see on a Christmas tree. The sharks weren't in water but flew together through the air, below or above the clouds and below or above the sun and moon. They each had a gold coin stuck on their heads right between their beady black eyes. As they flew, each shark left a white streak in the sky that was a thin ribbon that spread out over time to give the blue sky a milky haze. The sharks flew in a pack in a line all together and yet they seemed to be everywhere at once.

Below the flying sharks, there was land—that was once before green and lush, flourishing and flat. And on this land lived a population of cute little cuddly creatures called Snamuh. The Snamuh were peaceful and liked to have fun, much like the fish-like creatures called Snihplod that inhabited the sea that encompassed the land. These Snamuh were of all sizes and colors and liked apples, and each Snamuh always had at least a little slice of apple with them at all times, and they would look down at their slices of apple and admire it and pet it with the tips of their fingers and talk to it and listen to it. The Snamuh loved their slices of apple. But the Snamuh had not always had apple slices. Apple slices were a recent discovery for these Snamuh, and once the news spread about the new discovery, every Snamuh across all the lands wanted a slice and eventually got one and never let it go. Now and then, fresh slices of apple would arrive, and the Snamuh would discard the old slices and scramble for a new one.

As the sharks flew overhead, the Snamuh stopped noticing them as much if at all, and this pleased the sharks because the sharks didn't like the Snamuh. In fact, the sharks hated the Snamuh because they thought they were weak and inferior and didn't look like them or smell like them. So the sharks set out to destroy as many Snamuh as they could. They flew back and forth over the land turning the sky from blue to hazy to gray, blocking the health-giving sun and causing great storms across the lands of the Snamuh. The Snamuh were admiring and petting and talking to their apple slices, so they didn't notice, and if they did notice, the apple slices told them it was normal, and the Snamuh heard this over and over and over again so much that they eventually believed it.

Then the sharks used their electric bulbs to shoot beams of blue light that looked like lightning down on the land of the Snamuh, causing great harm and many fires. The apple slices told the Snamuh that this was all natural and said they would help them put out the fires and save the Snamuh who were hurt. Since the skies were always cloudy, heavy rains came and caused floods and hurricanes, and in the winter, great blizzards and many Snamuh suffered and died. But the sharks told the apple slices to tell the Snamuh that these were all natural too, and they would send help and supplies to all the Snamuh who were hurt by the floods and hurricanes and blizzards. And the Snamuh thanked the apple slices and didn't notice the sharks flying overhead.

And the sharks put things in the water that made the Snamuh forget. So many Snamuh forgot, and other Snamuh who didn't forget had to care for the Snamuh who did forget. There were so many bad things in all the water everywhere that many Snihplod died, as did other creatures and trees and grasses that were both in the seas and on the land.

The sharks told the apple slices to tell the Snamuh that great diseases would spread across the land of the Snamuh and amongst the children of the Snamuh unless they protected themselves with Wings of Mercury. And since all of the Snamuh were taught from birth to believe in fairy tales, ghosts, and magic, many Snamuh took their baby Snamuh to get these wings. But some Snamuh didn't, so it became law that every Snamuh child had to take the Wings of Mercury. But the wings didn't help the children or even the older Snamuh but instead made them sick and dull and sometimes angry and unable to learn, so these young Snamuh never got to know what it was like to truly be a Snamuh.

The sharks had the gold coins between their eyes and would never give them away or pay the Snamuh with the gold coins, but instead, they made fake gold coins that they said were real but were not and controlled how many got made and how they got used and who would get them. And since the Snamuh believed the apple slices, they would work hard to acquire the coins they thought were real but, were in fact, fake. Since the sharks could make the fake coins very easily and cheaply, they could pay a Namuh (a singular Snamuh) as much as they wanted to in order to get the Namuh to do whatever they wanted them to do. And Snamuh that were desperate or greedy or stupid or very gullible would try hard to impress the sharks so they could get a lot of fake gold coins. So the sharks had these desperate Snamuh pretend that everything was fine and there was nothing to worry about except for what the sharks wanted the Snamuh to worry about, which would make the Snamuh afraid, and ask the sharks for help.

Sometimes the sharks would pay a certain kind of Snamuh (called srotca*) to pretend that there was a riot or a bomb had gone off or some Snamuh got killed or even children Snamuh got killed and it would be shown on the apple slices so all the Snamuh would see it and believe it to be true when really, it was all just a play like you'd see on a stage in a playhouse. But the Snamuh believed their slices of apple and would worry and get mad at each other and complain and call for justice. And the sharks would tell the Snamuh by way of the apple slices that they would fix the problems and make new laws to stop those problems from happening again. Each time the sharks made a new law, the Snamuh could do less and less without getting in trouble with the* ecilop *(the Snamuh who were supposed to protect and serve the Snamuh). The ecilop were paid well and didn't want to get fired for not doing their job even though many of the laws didn't make sense or even if they caused hardship and pain for other Snamuh. So more and more laws were made, and more and more Snamuh became ecilop to enforce those laws, and more and more*

Snamuh could do less and less without getting in trouble.

And the sharks flying in the air above the Snamuh laughed and laughed at the gullibility of the Snamuh and thought that if the Snamuh were so dumb to believe the lies they were told without trying to see if they were lies or not, then all these Snamuh and all their children deserved to die.

But some Snamuh found out the sharks were lying to everyone because they did more than only pay attention to their slice of apple, and some tried to warn the other Snamuh. But the sharks would curse the Snamuh who saw the shark's lies and called them evil and stupid and told the Snamuh by way of the apple slices to do the same, even if the wise Snamuh who saw the lies were close friends or family. So some Snamuh were spited and denounced, which made them unable to help the Snamuh who refused to understand the lies.

The sharks did things using srotca to make it look like one color Snamuh hated another color Snamuh, or the women Snamuh didn't like the men Snamuh, or one land of Snamuh didn't get along with another land of Snamuh, or parent Snamuh didn't know what was best for their baby Snamuh, or even that some men Snamuh wanted to be women Snamuh, and vice versa. So all these things eventually looked normal to the Snamuh, and they accepted all of the things they never used to accept because if they didn't, they would be considered mean.

The sharks would show all these conflicts on the apple slices and tell the Snamuh that only they could fix them because only the sharks were smart enough to be able to tell what good sense really was. And the sharks took over the schools, too, to tell the children Snamuh their lies from an early age so they would not doubt the sharks, ever, and encouraged them to keep watching their apple slices and to believe what they told them no matter what.

Then the apple slices told all the Snamuh that a great plague was upon them from a thing they called a SURIV which nobody could see or feel but the apple slices told everyone it would kill them and since everyone everywhere had a slice of apple they all believed them and told all their friends about the great danger of the SURIV and they all felt like they were one, all across the land, and they were smug in their believing they were each part of all the Snamuh who were pulling together all as one to fight the SURIV and deliver the whole world from this plague—a plague unlike anything the earth had ever seen before—that would kill them if they didn't obey the law that made them stay in their houses and not touch other Snamuh or even breathe on them.

There were so many things that did not make sense: The Snamuh weren't allowed to shop at small businesses, yet the biggest stores stayed open; the Snamuh were told they must stay several feet away from others (they could no longer hug, kiss, or even shake hands), but they were encouraged to donate blood without being tested for the SURIV; they could not assemble in churches, but they could assemble for riots in the streets; they were supposed to cover their faces, yet the leaders never seemed to cover theirs, and soon there were robots warning Snamuh to put on their masks; the hospitals were not crowded, and many nurses and doctors stopped working, but the apple slices showed hospitals overwhelmed with sick and dying; although the SURIV was lifeless ('non-living' and dead), Snamuh were instructed to kill the SURIV with toxic chemicals that were slowly poisoning them. Many Snamuh didn't realize the incongruity of these nonsensical things, and the ones that did just told themselves, "Well, there must be a good reason for it."

And the Snamuh were distracted and bombarded with facts and figures shown on the slices of apple, so they began to forget what their elders had told them and written in the scrolls they used to believe. Instead, they believed all the facts and figures and these became their new religion, and these facts and figures were invented by the Sharks and were often not true. And some wise Snamuh who hadn't been mesmerized by the complexity of the facts and figures told other Snamuh that this SURIV was nothing special, that it was no worse than other sicknesses of its kind, and that there was nothing out of the ordinary to fear. They tried to help the other Snamuh remember something written in the scrolls—

What has been is what will be,
and what has been done is what will be done,
and there is nothing new under the sun.

But many Snamuh would not listen and believed that the SURIV was different and new and special, and they felt special themselves and took great pride in thinking they knew all about the SURIV and what it was and how it worked and why all the things the apple slices were telling them were true. And these Snamuh, although thinking they were doing good, were really helping the sharks in their efforts to frighten and enslave all the Snamuh. And the sharks sat back and laughed, knowing these Snamuh were doing the work for them.

The Snamuh were encouraged, at first, to get silver put into their hands that made them a kind of machine so they could get permission to go places easier and pay for their food and everything else easier, and to show they didn't have the SURIV and many Snamuh thought it was okay and even better. Then it became law, and all the Snamuh were told that if they did not take the silver in their hand they could no longer buy food or anything else or go anywhere other than their own little house. Some Snamuh thought it wrong and against their God's wishes for man to never become part machine and to bow down to a shark, so these Snamuh suffered greatly and died.

The sharks loved to watch the Snamuh from cameras on the ground and other things flying in the air and wouldn't let the Snamuh do all sorts of things and, if they did, when they got seen—which was wherever they went since there was a sort of net over the whole earth that saw everything by way of rays nobody could see—they would get marks against them, and, other Snamuh who always listened to their apple slice and never stopped to think about anything else, would ridicule the Snamuh who got these marks and they would no longer be friends with them. So the Snamuh were no longer happy and peaceful, but instead, very, very peaceful and obedient and unaware of what happiness was.

Year after year more Snamuh got sick and died from the fires and floods and snowstorms and Wings of Mercury and the hardships imposed upon them due to the lie of the SURIV and not taking silver in their hand. Many of the Snamuh thought it was strange, but the apple slices had told them it was just the way it is—that it was now the lamron wen, *they called it, and that the land the Snamuh lived on was getting* rettoh *all the time even though there were more snowstorms than ever and the sun hardly shined anymore. But the Snamuh didn't question the apple slices, and they kept praying for help, but their prayers didn't seem to work anymore, and more Snamuh died each year until millions had died, and they kept dying until there were hardly any Snamuh across all the lands at all.*

And all the trees and all the grasses in the fields and all the birds and animals and fishes died too, except for a very few, because the sharks loved to kill and they kept killing everything they could in any way possible without being discovered for carrying out the killing.

And the earth was no longer the earth it was created to be, and the Snamuh were no longer who they were created to be.

The delight in destruction the sharks feel is an inversion—a reversal—of the sorrow they should feel. So they twist everything into its reverse: pain is pleasure, right is wrong, up is down, high is low, left is right, black is white, winning is losing, flat is round, near is far, darkness is light, cold is hot, weakness is strength, sickness is health, slavery is security, tolerance for perversity is noble, and purity is servile, following orders is democracy, and rebelling against tyranny is injustice, male becomes female, female becomes male, young becomes old enough. They shout that they love you and will protect you but will put you in chains and abuse you. But isn't that the way of evil? Isn't that what evil would have to do to succeed? Is there a Namuh anywhere across their lands that believes evil ones are going to come right out and admit they're evil and are trying to rule and then destroy him?

Some people live to sing. Some live to play an instrument. Others live to play a game or write a book or take care of others or work at a job to provide for their family. Some others, who may not be people at all, live to deceive. They delight in causing Snamuh to believe in lies and fairy tales and ghosts and that this world is all there is. And often these lies end up causing division amongst the Snamuh and harm and suffering and death.

Sharks are ruthless and pitiless and delight in the pain of others. But the Snamuh, being much more righteous, tend to see in others what they are themselves, so they could not fathom how treacherous, dishonest, and deadly a shark could really be.

Then, when the sharks see that enough Snamuh have died or were beat and would obey them without rebellion, and all the young Snamuh believed them, and all the cameras were working, and all the things flying in the air were watching, they cast the final all-encompassing net across the sky and all the Snamuh got trapped. It had happened gradually at first. So gradually... as the Snamuh who were hired to make and install the apparatuses and electronic things that would imprison them in their own homes, and those who passed the laws the sharks wanted them to pass, and those who injected the Snamuh, and those who put the silver in other Snamuh's hands were all 'just doing my job.'

Then suddenly, like a thief in the night, a new law was passed and all the Snamuh across all the lands became slaves of the sharks. And the sharks rejoiced. They rejoiced in knowing they had done what so many others before them had tried and failed to do—they had taken over the whole earth, and the whole earth and seas were theirs. They were now, in their own eyes, God.

And the Snamuh who took the silver and injections were really Snamuh no longer—they were Stobmuh: They had become part robot and part Namuh. And the God who created the Snamuh long ago was sad and angry when the sharks took the Stobmuh's babies away without a whisper of resistance from the parents because these parents were no longer Snamuh at all.

The sharks may throw the Stobmuh some food every now and then to keep them alive. They may even let them keep their slices of apple so they stay occupied and distracted enough not to rebel. But the Stobmuh won't be able to go anywhere. And if the sharks want them to work on something, they will be forced to work on it; and if the sharks want to inject the Stobmuh with something, the Stobmuh will not be able to stop them; and if the sharks want to put a new interface on the Stobmuh, they will be happy to get it. And since the sharks already took away his and her children, the Stobmuh won't have a family anymore.

Once the sharks have conquered, enslaved, and transformed the Snamuh, they are happy. But that happiness doesn't last long because sharks have to conquer and they have to kill. So they will turn on each other and kill each other and then themselves—a snake eating its own tail with a smile on its lips. That is the nature of evil. In the end, it cannot succeed simply because it is rooted in death.

Death has nowhere else to go. Death dies.

Life journeys into the unknown. Life struggles. Life triumphs. Life lives.

All along, the earth sits and waits. The earth is very patient. It sits and waits for this latest pestilence to pass, and watches the sharks kill themselves, and waits and wonders what life will come next. For the earth abideth forever...

> *One generation passeth away,*
> *and another generation cometh:*
> *but the earth abideth forever.*
> *The sun also ariseth,*
> *and the sun goeth down,*
> *and hasteth to his place where he arose.*

The not-so-old man's eyes rolled back down, and his eyelids closed, so the whites were no longer visible. He slept, but his mind was not finished.

He heard a prayer he was taught as a boy, "Our Father, who art in heaven, hallowed be thy name..."

His dad was in bed, wrapped in a white blanket like a cocoon. The not-so-old man as-not-yet a man sat on a chair next to the bed with his elbows on his knees, then reached over with his right hand and peeled a corner of the blanket away to reveal his father's face. It was no longer yellow and blotchy with sunken cheeks, but full and fair and smooth. His father wasn't sucking his thumb in this dream, but simply had his open palm resting on his neck just over his Adam's apple.

The not-so-old man as-not-yet a man shook his father's shoulder. When his father opened his eyes, they were not old and tired and hazy. They were alive and strong and true. He turned his head a little away from the pillow to look the not-so-old man as-not-yet a man squarely in the eyes, slowly opened his mouth, and said one word:

"Son."

With that, the not-so-old man's father stretched his right arm and hand with pointed index finger toward the not-so-old man as-not-yet a man's limp left hand that dangled there in front of him.

"My son. My son. You're okay, my son. You're okay."

His father's finger touched his as he looked him right in the eyes and said, "My son. My son. I love you, my son. I love you."

The not-so-old man as his child took a breath. The father dropped his hand back to the bed and smiled.

The not-so-old man as his child's lips quivered. A tear ran down his cheek. He had known his father felt that way about him and always had. But hearing his father say that to him, as he looked him directly in the eyes, touched a chord in him he never knew existed. Suddenly his heart felt new. He said to his father, "So are you, Dad. You're okay too. You're okay, Dad. You're okay."

The not-so-old man as his son reached down and pinched the white blanket between his thumb and forefinger and gently peeled it further away from his father. As the blanket fell away, it revealed his father floating as if in a cloud surrounded by twelve naked angels nestled in a red half-shell the shape of a cross-section of the right side of the human brain. His father's expression was relaxed, yet determined. The not-so-old man as a man saw but did not see. He opened his eyes. Night was over. The sun was about to rise.

Chapter XV

The young woman reset the timer on her phone and left it on the driver's seat. She closed the door to her SUV and raised her arms above her head and stretched them upwards toward the sky. She reached down and touched her toes, then did a few jumping jacks. She bounced up and down in place while punching the air in front of her chest like a boxer would.

"Let me at 'em! Let me at 'em," she laughed under her breath.

The young woman's auburn shoulder-length hair was pulled back into a ponytail and tucked through the back of her blue ball cap with her favorite team's logo on its front. She wore beige calf-length yoga pants and a beige leotard tank top divided at her waist by a black-belted fanny-pack that held her sports drink in a rubberized glass sports-drink bottle. She wore a sturdy sports bra underneath and had dark blue running sneakers with silver racing stripes along their sides on her feet.

The young woman jogged slowly across the parking lot, through an opening in the gray and weathered post and rail fence, and onto the beach. She noticed the tide was out, and the sand was smooth and clean close to the water-line.

"No rocks," the young woman thought. "It's my lucky day."

She returned to her SUV, threw her sneakers onto the back seat, and gingerly walked back to the beach. Once there, she began jogging north.

The beach was deserted. Every Sunday morning, she came to this state park and ran the two-and-a-half miles to its northernmost point. She would stop, sit on the sand, have a few sips of her sports drink, and then run back. She was usually the first one to enter the park on days like this, and she loved the peace and quiet she could experience so close to the hub-bub of where she lived and worked just five miles away.

Barefoot, she ran. She ran slowly at first, then faster, and faster. Then she slowed to a walk and looked out over the ripples of the Gulf as the sun rose behind the palm and palmetto trees and beach grasses inland.

She started running again. Slowly... then faster... and faster. Then she walked. "The best way to run," she thought. "It may be weird, but it's the best."

By the time she had gotten to the northern point, the sun was completely up. She sat and had a few sips of her sports drink while she admired the clear blue sky and reveled in the perfect 75-degree temperature. Her feet felt good on the warm, dry sand, and she dug her toes into it and wiggled them.

A few minutes later, she was running again, this time, back the way she had come.

CHAPTER XVI

*T*he not-so-old man clung to Gracie's back as she swam east. He thought about the dream he just had, and it stuck in his mind because all his dreams about his dad stuck in his mind. But what the dream could have meant didn't come to him then. That would take some time and reflection. But the meaning was there then and always had been there, and now the sea had washed away some of the dirt and grime that had accumulated over his lifetime to cover up those truths. And when the time was right for him, he would realize that Mikey was trying to tell us something. He wrote:

Look up at Michelangelo's painting. Tilt your head back and look at it—high up there on the chapel's ceiling. The right side. Michelangelo had the old man with the white beard and the angels on the right side—the side that knows this is all temporary and at the same time timeless. The side that encompasses all the acceptance, understanding, love, and peace. It revels in the quiet artistry you can't explain in words or track with a stopwatch or count on your fingers, but which comes through your fingers—the thumb and forefinger mostly—that are linked with more of the gray matter of the brain than any other parts. The fingers that touch, that are smart enough to use a pencil or paintbrush, play a musical instrument or throw a baseball, feel the tension on a fishing line or the trigger of a rifle—but more importantly, the fingers that feel what's happening—feel what's happening—so it can tell the left side what to do to make what you want to create happen. The fingers that can feel—when the dirt and grime of living are washed away—what's truly in your heart and can understand it and express it flowingly, gently, gradually; or abruptly, forcefully, quickly if needed.

Then, there's the other side—the left side. The side where all the thinking, all the ego is: All the plotting, planning, worry, and noise; all the right, wrong, structure, and constraints. All the numbers you can put in a calculator, seconds that tick off a clock, and sentences that seek to explain. All these things life's dirt and grime reinforce, and that dirt and grime need to be washed away in order to discover that the left side can never understand what the right side knows and lives for.

But there's a bridge: a highway between the two where sparks of information let the two sides communicate—for as pesky and greedy as one side can be, to deny it wouldn't be in the other side's nature, and to acquiesce to the other side is not in the thinking side's nature either. So there's this bridge—and one side shouts and the other side whispers and they don't agree to disagree, but coexist because each knows they wouldn't exist without the other. The tension must be there. The peace must be there. But when one dominates, that's when things get lopsided. And something lopsided is out of balance.

Balance. Like balancing on a stump on one foot while the other is up in the air waiting for the next move.

Ernest Hemingway knew this. He expressed it by writing a novel about a burning-with-passion love affair while there was a war going on. He didn't write just deep philosophical treatises; he would sprinkle a seedy scandal or some trivial debauchery in amongst the heavy thoughts.

High isn't high without low being low. He called it his high/low strategy. He said he did it to appeal to a larger audience—both the high-brow and the low-brow. That may be, but that strategy also appeals to the high-brow and low-brow that's present in everyone; because truly, it isn't so much as a high/low strategy, but a right/left strategy. The low lights up the left side, the high lights up the right. And the bridge is busy futilely trying to keep each informed and happy. And if the bridge gets blown? Well, then love, and everything that goes along with it is lost. Goodbye Maria. Goodbye Robert Jordan. Goodbye Ernest Hemingway.

Hemingway knew how to tap into the artistry. It's simple. It's simply to be quiet and sit in that quiet and let the art come to you. Hadley said that on days her husband wrote, he would insist on silence in the mornings: No conversation over coffee or breakfast; no reading newspapers; no music or other distractions. Silence. His son Greg told of him shouting down from his writing studio at their house on Key West, "Would you PLEASE stop making that noise! I'm trying to write!"

Hemingway was in the silence—he was in the silence when he wrote. But he could also create the silence—in the Parisian cafés when he disappeared into his stories, and the outside world became quiet to him, because to him, then, it didn't exist. And as you quiet the complaining side, the artistic side can tune into the ethers that hold the messages you want to express and can only express through your fingers. Just like what that old man on the chapel's ceiling was doing by using his finger to bring to life a son.

The not-so-old man noticed the sky getting lighter and changing from gray to yellow. He was weak. Every cell in his body throbbed in pain. He was still loopy in the head and very thirsty, and he felt his hunger sharply. "Other than that, Mrs. Lincoln, how was the play?"

The not-so-old man thought, "I must not be that far gone."

As the not-so-old man looked east toward the lightening sky, he wondered if Gracie could make it. He had never felt her waiver during the whole time he was on her back. But it was probably over eleven hours she had carried him, and that had to take a toll. She never stopped to eat, never complained, never slowed.

"Amazing," he thought. "All on one tank of gas."

Jorge was still leading the way, and there were still several fins around him and Gracie. The armada had lost a few members but remained generally intact.

Then he saw it: The first sliver of the sun rose over the horizon, and in front of it were the tops of high-rise buildings. Soon after that, the not-so-old man saw land. He was going home.

He closed his eyes, but he didn't sleep. He closed his eyes and gave thanks.

He heard a song. It was John Denver singing one of his favorite songs. But it wasn't about taking country roads to get back to West Virginia, it was about Daniel coming home in a different way...

Sandy roads, take me home
To the place I belong
West coast Florida, sunshine Mamma
Take me home, sandy roads

I hear her voice in the mornin' light she calls me
A radio reminds me of my home not far away
Coming back to land I get a feeling
That I should have come home yesterday, yesterday

Take me home, sandy roads

The not-so-old man opened his eyes. He started counting. He counted time: "One Gulf of Mexico, two Gulf of Mexicos, three Gulf of Mexicos..."

He got up to sixty Gulf of Mexicos. The not-so-old man as a boy, young man, middle-aged man, and not-so-old man had always been good with time, and he had always, as his wife had noted, been obsessed with it. He could tell to the second how fast he had raced. Now he was timing how many minutes it would take him and his friends to get to dry land.

And it was odd, because just then—when he had gotten to sixty Gulf of Mexicos—it suddenly dawned on that him he just didn't care. Let it take all day—it no longer mattered. The sea had taken him, swallowed him, and spit him out. The sea had taunted him, threatened him, confronted him, and abused him. The sea had tried, either knowingly or just by chance or fate, to destroy him.

But he still found a friend. He still found help. And he still found at least a few rays of truth.

"So Ernie," he thought, "I won't be seeing you any time soon, my friend. Somehow, I got lucky—*suerte*—in a way that finally meant something. Maybe you were watching and sent me some help, Papa. So give my regards to the gang and hang in there. I'm sure things are gonna get better. Just you watch."

The not-so-old man was exhausted but didn't want to sleep. His head was spinning. Was he really going to make it home? His eyes closed for a couple of seconds. He caught himself and forced them open. He blinked his eyes hard and shook his head. His eyes stayed open as he watched land get closer and closer.

"Each stroke better than the last. Each stroke more true to itself."

His eyes fluttered...

"Now the final turn," the not-so-old man as a champion swimmer thought. The slip he made in the Olympics qualifier didn't enter his mind.

"Go for it," the not-so-old man as a champion swimmer thought. "Finish it. Finish strong. Finish true. Finish... with dignity."

He sensed the wall. He ducked his head down and brought his feet up over himself and hit the wall more perfectly than he had ever hit it before. He knew it the moment his toes touched it and his full foot flattened against it. His coiled and hungry legs pushed his fully extended torso forward through the water. Fifty meters to go. Short glide. Stroke. *No problemo.*

Fast...

His body became super-charged from added adrenaline.

Faster...

He had lengthened his lead to a dozen body lengths.

Fastest.

He swam the last fifty meters more powerfully than he had ever swum before. It was the fastest lap of any freestyle race ever recorded. He touched the final wall with his left hand and didn't come up, but just stayed there floating in the water, knowing. The audience had been giving him a standing ovation for the final three laps. He finally heard it. He picked his head up out of the water. The PA announcer's declaration was drowned out by the screaming and applauding crowd, "And the winner—smashing the previous record and setting a new World's Record for the 1500 meter freestyle—from Long Island New York—Daniel Marino."

The not-so-old man as a champion swimmer looked up into the stands and saw his father and mother and sister waving at him. Everything else was a blur. He waved back and then saluted them.

The not-so-old man's eyes stopped fluttering. He saw the beach ahead.

As the armada of dolphins and Daniel approached the beach, the extra dolphins split away and turned back to the open sea. A couple of them rose up and said goodbye, "Eh, eh, eh, eh." "EH, EH, EH, EH."

The not-so-old man raised his hand and waved.

Jorge swam aside to give Gracie an open lane to the beach. She slowed as she got in more shallow water. The not-so-old man's head was still spinning. The skin all over his body was tingling.

Gracie stopped swimming and said, "Eh, eh, eh, eh."

The not-so-old man let go of her fin and slid his left arm off her back. His legs dropped down five feet, and his feet landed on the sandy bottom. Immediately his knees buckled, and his whole body went underwater. His feet fumbled around on the bottom of the sea for a few seconds as he spread his arms out for balance, and once he found his footing, he straightened his legs, and his head and shoulders popped out of the water.

He swayed back and forth a few times while keeping his arms out to steady himself. Gracie stayed by his side, floating, making sure he could stand on his own. He noticed deep impressions on Gracie's dorsal fin from where his fingers had clamped onto it. He wanted to hug her, even though he'd been hugging her for dear life for over eleven hours. The not-so-old man stretched his arms out and wrapped them around her midsection just ahead of her dorsal fin and the spot he had clung to while she carried him through the sea. He didn't want to let go. Gracie raised her head and sighed, "ehhhhhh."

Jorge sauntered up to them. The not-so-old man let go of Gracie and took hold of one of his flippers and shook it. A tear ran down his cheek. Then he bent down and reached under Jorge with his other arm and feebly gave him a bear hug. Jorge nodded his head up and down, snorted, and then floated away.

The not-so-old man turned back to Gracie and patted her on the back, bent his head down, and kissed her on the forehead. She raised her head and looked him in the eye.

He would never forget. And neither would she.

The not-so-old man watched her eyes and then fin disappear underwater as she smoothly and quietly pulled away. Then he saw two fins surface about thirty yards westward, out where they had just been. Both dolphins rose up and back-peddled on their tails and called out one last time,

"Eh, eh, eh, eh!" "EH, EH, EH, EH!"

They splashed down, showing their smiles, then they were gone.

But the not-so-old man didn't want them gone. He wanted them to be there, to stay, stay with him now and forever. He wanted to shrink them down into tiny little dolphins so he could put them in his pocket like a rabbit's foot and keep them with him all the time.

He realized the time he had spent with Gracie and Jorge were some of the most important, emotional, and rewarding times anyone could experience, and he knew those times were over. He knew that time does not lie, and it hadn't lied to him before and wouldn't lie to him now as much as he wanted it to or thought he deserved.

But then he remembered, "No one you love is ever truly lost."

"Farewell, my friends," he thought as he turned towards the beach. "Farewell."

The not-so-old man stumbled to shore—swaying back and forth and forward and backward—like a toddler learning to walk—as he tried to remember his land legs. A few feet from shore, he stumbled and fell on his hands and knees, but his face stayed out of the water. Finally, he crawled out of the water and onto the beach. He glanced back once over his shoulder and collapsed.

CHAPTER XVII

*T*he young woman was running. She sprinted, then slowed, then walked. It was a glorious day, and she was enjoying herself immensely. But halfway back to her car, she started feeling uneasy. Something had happened. Something wasn't right. Someone was in trouble. She had learned not to doubt her intuition. She broke into a gallop.

A few minutes later, she saw him. At first, he was just a dark mass on the beach just beside the waterline. Her first thought was that someone had left a beach chair or towel there the night before. But she would've noticed it when she had passed on her way out.

"A piece of driftwood? A beached dolphin?" She squinted and ran faster. Her ponytail bobbed furiously up and down on her back. She felt her heart beating faster, and her breaths getting quicker and deeper.

"Good Lord!" the young woman exclaimed. "It's a man! It's a man washed up on the beach!" She was nervous. She was worried. She ran toward him.

Quickly she was beside him. His legs were curled up, his face was pressed into the sand, and his arms lay limply by his side.

The young woman felt his forehead and then his neck. She felt for a pulse. It was weak, but it was there. She dropped to her knees and examined him. She noticed his racer's swim cap still on, slightly twisted on his head. She noticed a gaunt look on his face and puffy cheeks that had wrinkles in them—like fingers that were too long in the water. She saw his Speedo swimsuit. And then she saw the corner of the photograph of Ray Ray.

"Maybe it's some form of ID," the young woman thought. She did not hesitate. She gently pulled up the elastic band and pulled out the photo. It was soaked and slightly faded, but the image was clearly visible. As she looked at it, she saw the smooth, happy face of the toddler girl with a dark brown birthmark over one of her temples. A strange tingle shot up her spine, and she thought for a moment that she might faint.

She pulled her fanny pack around her waist and unzipped it. She took out her sports-drink and put the photo in the pack. She touched the not-so-old man's shoulder and shook him gently. The not-so-old man mumbled but didn't open his eyes. She shook him again. He mumbled again. One more time. Same result.

She took a step toward the water and cupped some in her palms and threw it on the not-so-old man's face. He opened his eyes.

"Hey there," the young woman said. "Hey there."

The not-so-old man tried to open his mouth, but couldn't.

"My name's Christina. You made it to the beach. You're going to be alright. I'm going to go get help. You'll be okay."

The not-so-old man grunted but didn't move.

"Can we get you up a little?" the young woman said. "You need to drink. You must be really dehydrated. Here. Let's roll you onto your back. That's it. Now I'm going to get behind you and put my arms under your armpits. Okay. I'll lift you up. There. Balance on my leg. There you go." She grabbed her water bottle, unscrewed its top, and put it to the not-so-old man's lips.

"Here you go. Can you swallow some? It's good stuff. Made it myself from my own secret recipe. The best sports drink you'll ever love. That's even my motto." She was babbling now, and she knew it, but she wanted to keep him awake.

The not-so-old man opened his mouth a crack, and she put the bottle to his lips and tilted it up.

"That's it. Swallow. Now, wait a second. Here, have another

one. That's it. Now we'll wait a few more seconds. Yeah, my name's Christina. My dad liked it, and my mom liked it, so they named me Christina. Who woulda thunk it? Okay, there you go. Here's another sip. You feeling better? Feeling any better?"

The not-so-old man saw her face above her upside down since she was leaning over him from behind. So when she frowned down on him all concerned, it looked to him like she was smiling. He thought of Gracie.

"Good job," the young woman said. "Good job, young man. You drank almost the whole bottle. At least ten ounces. That'll get you going. Before you know it, you'll be running sprints."

The not-so-old man smiled in his mind.

"Here," Christina said. "Let's lower you back down. I don't want you to even try standing yet."

She took a step back with one leg and let the not-so-old man slide down the other. "That's it. Good. There you go."

The not-so-old man laid flat on the sand.

"I'm going for help. It's too far to try and make it walking, and you might be too heavy for me to carry you all that way," she said half-laughing.

The not-so-old man looked up, still seeing her face upside down.

"We're about a mile from the nearest Pavilion. I'll get a ranger out here with a Club Car. We'll load you up and get you to a hospital."

The not-so-old man just watched her upside down as she talked to him.

"So don't sneak off on me," Christina smiled. She took off, running south down the beach.

The not-so-old man turned his head and saw her sideways in his field of vision, running—her ponytail bobbing up and down as she got smaller and smaller. He turned his head back and saw the sky above and felt the earth below.

He closed his eyes but did not sleep. He thought he would but didn't. Instead, his attention went to his body, and he felt his aching muscles. But they didn't feel that bad. Nowhere near as bad as they felt after fighting the sharks. And as the minutes passed, his muscles felt better and better. It surprised him because he knew how long it usually took for his body to recover from a hard swim. "That must be one amazing sports-drink," he thought.

A few people walking the beach passed him but didn't say anything. He felt them staring at him as they went by as he lay on his back right near the waterline; no towel underneath him or anywhere to be seen, a racing cap slightly askew on his head, hardly any sign of life in his body. But he didn't care. Instead, he thought about Ernie again and what he might have done if he was in this situation. "He probably would have jumped up and challenged them to a boxing match," he thought. "Oh yeah? What's your problem, buddy? You want a piece of me? Well, let's step outside and settle it!"

Ernie would have had the energy to do it, too, the not-so-old man reasoned. "Besides taking the time to do all the things he did in his life, he also had the energy to do them. All those parties, wives, expeditions. All his books, stories, letters. Where did all that energy come from?" he wondered. "It certainly wasn't from living a chaste lifestyle."

The not-so-old man pondered, "Ernie always knew he wanted to be a writer since excelling in English in high school. Then he knew he wanted to reinvent prose. He had no plan B. He worked hard, sacrificed, and let nothing stand in his way. He did not doubt."

The not-so-old man knew what doubt was. He had lived it most of his life in just about every aspect except for swimming. He knew being unsure of oneself is a grind, and that takes effort. Self-assuredness, on the other hand, is direction without the static. It's smooth sailing. It's freedom. It not only preserves energy, it also focuses it like a laser.

Behind Ernie's self-assuredness, there was unwavering direction—not scattered by guilt or shame. He hated his mom and hated his dad and even wanted to shoot him at one point. But he ended up loving him and admitting as much. But he didn't judge himself for feeling these ways. He didn't blame himself. He didn't waste energy by denying and covering up his feelings. This was part of his power: a Dionysian celebration of himself with no taking it back.

Was he cocky sometimes? Overbearing? Spiteful? Yes, yes, and yes. But always self-assured in his vision and understanding. "He didn't doubt. He hardly ever got bogged down in which way? What now? Who with? Why? When? His inner belief took care of all those details. He could feel his destiny, and he let himself believe in it. Could Ernie's superhuman drive have been a result of his super self-assuredness?"

Now, as the not-so-old man lay on the sand waiting, he thought of himself and what he could have been so sure of. Although he was good at it, he never had a passion to crunch numbers and plot profits. Swimming was a passion, yes, but it was also, as he had just discovered, a distraction. But hearing the music? Now that was something else.

For a special assignment in high school, he wrote a symphony. He only had a piano, so it was just a skeleton, but he would hear it in his head, especially in the mornings, while in that dream-like state between slumber and life. He would hear the piano intro, gentle and slow and simple; then the strings—first, *adagio,* then *andante*, then *allegretto viva,* and finally *allegro,* and then back to *adagio*—supporting and coaxing the melody to sparkle. He would watch the violinists pull their bows across the strings all together as if they were one—each instrument making its own full, rich, entraining, and mesmerizing sound—their wrists and fingers wiggling just so as they peered down at their sheet music illuminated by little lights above their music stands. He'd hear the oboes and French horns complementing the rhythm and the snare drums, cymbals, and trumpets, punctuating the first crescendo— with a single little tinkle of a triangle at just the right time.

He would lie in bed with closed eyes and see the dimly lit orchestra in front of him set against the backdrop of the dark brown back wall of the stage and feel the warmth of the audience sitting in the sold-out concert hall behind him as the musicians responded to his direction—his right hand holding the baton and setting the beat and his left hand directing each section of instruments. He would lose himself as the notes washed over him, into him, and through him, and feel the endorphins sing from the sounds, sights, and feelings, as they sent him skyward as if he was a dove making a mad dash for heaven. Then he would drop back down—like a hawk plunging out of the sky straight for its prey— back down into the lower notes: the baritone and bass of the minor scale of the music that would cause his skin and then every cell in his body to vibrate in sympathy with it. He would feel himself shoot headlong into the sound, the deepening sound.

And then, the woman's voice—clear and full and proud— luring the mind, begging the body to come, to throw caution to the wind, to relax, to give in, to relinquish oneself on the jagged rocks below the cliffs with foam crashing at their feet. That voice, up and down it goes, so robust in its need and wantonness, exact in its pitch and roll of indecency and pleasures of unfathomable delight. She sings, then another joins her and sings, the harmony almost unbearable. The woman's song. The woman's song. The woman's heart opens before you like a blossoming flower of kaleidoscopic intensity as her voice descends into you—and you resist, you resist, and finally succumb.

Then silence.

The lights come back on. The music has ended but is never complete.

His music teacher gave his little symphony a thumbs-up and told him he had talent. The not-so-old man as a high school student liked hearing that, but he scoffed at it too. "Pipe dream," he thought in his teenage smugness. So he wandered around for several years until he settled on business. He kept playing the piano and guitar for years, but life kept distracting him, and he gave it up completely after the accident. Now, he thought, maybe...

He heard a motor approach. He noticed the Club Car in his peripheral vision pull up beside him and stop. Christina and two park rangers hopped down from the Club Car. Christina approached the not-so-old man from his front with a determined look on her face. The not-so-old man saw her right side up.

"Hey there, stranger," she said, her voice betraying her expression. "Come here often?"

The not-so-old man's throat tried to laugh but got caught. But he nodded his head up and down, and the corners of his lips curled up. Christina's expression instantly softened.

"How about," she said to the rangers, "you pick him up by the shoulders, and I'll get his legs, and we swing him onto the bed of the car?"

"Sounds good," Chuck, one of the rangers, said.

"Just a second," Christina said. She went to the Club Car and unfolded a beach towel over the flatbed of the car. She brought another beach towel over to the not-so-old man and said, "Here, guys. Get him up, and I'll wrap him with the towel."

Chuck and the other ranger pulled Daniel up off the sand, so he stood. Christina took the towel and draped it over his shoulders and around his body, so the ends of the towel met in front of his chest.

"You guys take him up there first, so his head is at the front. His feet can dangle off the end of the bed."

Once the not-so-old man was on the flatbed, Christina climbed in and lay on her side next to him. He felt her body.

"I don't want you rolling off, you know," she said. She wrapped her arm across his chest and held this shoulder down with her hand.

The Club Car started moving. "This'll only take ten minutes or so," Christina said. "They already called 911, and an ambulance is on its way."

The not-so-old man felt better, and he knew he wouldn't need an ambulance or a hospital. He hated hospitals. He forced himself to open his mouth and murmured, "No... No hospital." His voice was scratchy and weak.

"What's that?" Christina asked, craning her ear over his lips.

"No hospital. No ambulance."

"You sure?"

"Yeah."

"Okay, young man," Christina said. She wanted to believe her sports drink was as revitalizing as she thought it was.

The not-so-old man mumbled, "Thanks." He found it pleasant not to have to insist.

Christina called to the ranger driving, "Hey Chuck. We won't be needing an ambulance. Better call Mary on the walkie and tell her to cancel."

Chuck turned around, "You sure?"

"Yeah. He had a dose of my sports drink. You know it can raise anyone from the dead."

Chuck smiled and shook his head. "That woman!" he thought.

"So what am I going to do with you?" Christina asked

playfully. "What's your name? Do you live around here? Do you have someone to help you? Are you feeling any better?" She didn't pause for him to answer; "Just paw the ground once for yes and twice for no," she chuckled softly. "I'm just kidding. Just kidding."

"Dan... iel," the not-so-old man croaked.

"Da... what?"

"Daniel," the not-so-old man said. "My name... is... Daniel."

"Oh!" Christina replied. "Good to know! Nice to meet you, Daniel." Christina reached through the towel wrapped around the not-so-old man, took hold of his hand, and shook it. "Nice to meet you, Daniel-son."

The not-so-old man's ears pricked up.

"I'm just kidding again, Daniel. It's just that whenever I hear that name, I hear in my head Daniel-son, you know, from the *The Karate Kid*. You ever see that movie?"

The not-so-old man pawed his leg once. Christina laughed hard.

"Yeah," she said, "you don't need a hospital. Anyway, that movie is one of my favorites. Remember the scene at the end when Daniel-son was in the finals, and he held up his arms like a crane and jumped up and kicked the guy in the head and leveled him? That was so cool!"

A thought occurred to Christina. She took her hand away from Daniel's shoulder and clapped her hands together hard and loud, rubbed them together vigorously, and said, "Remember this? I learned it first-hand from Mr. Miyagi."

She lowered her warm palms onto Daniel's chest, just left of center and below the clavicle, and held them there for a minute. "Who knows? Maybe this will help," she said.

The not-so-old man let his eyes close. It had been so long since someone had touched him.

The Club Car drove past Pavilion #3, then past Pavilion #2.

"We're almost there," Christina said. "See?"

She touched his chin and pushed it lightly so it would turn toward land and away from the sea. Everything was sideways again in the not-so-old man's vision: a couple putting up an umbrella; some people already lying on towels; beach grass behind them and behind that a washed-out post and rail fence. He heard a radio playing. He knew where he was. The not-so-old man moved to push himself up.

"Hold on there, cowboy," Christina said. "We're almost there."

The not-so-old man struggled to raise his torso as he turned to look. Christina pushed him up a little to help him. He couldn't believe his eyes. There it was—just in front of the beach grass where he had spread it out a lifetime ago—his blue and white striped beach towel.

"Stop," the not-so-old man croaked.

"What?"

"Stop the car," he said a little louder.

"Hey, Chuck," Christina called. "Hold on. Stop here for a second."

Chuck stopped the Club Car.

"What is it?" Christina asked.

The not-so-old man's voice was returning. "That," he pointed. "That towel. That's my towel."

He moved to climb down, but Christina caught his shoulder and held him back.

"That's yours?"

"Yeah."

"Okay. I'll get it." She stepped down off the back of the Club Car. The not-so-old man touched her arm. She looked at him.

"My wallet and keys are tucked under it."

"Okay. I'll get them."

Christina picked up the towel as the not-so-old man looked on. She shook the towel to knock off the sand as she scanned the sand underneath.

"Daniel," Christina called back, "I don't see them." She dropped the towel and got down on her hands and knees and hunted around, turning up the sand all around. "There's nothing else here."

Daniel saw she was right. The keys could easily be replaced, but his wallet—his wallet held his life: his ID/driver's license, credit cards, picture of his ex-wife, YMCA membership card, ATM cards. He knew it was going to be a hassle replacing all those, but he really didn't care. He glanced over the beach grass and saw that his car was no longer in the parking lot. "They took everything," he thought.

And his phone. His phone was in his car. But the only things he cared about in his phone were some photos he had scanned into it that he still had at home, so that was no big deal. All of this didn't really bother him. It was almost a relief.

"Living is nothing," he thought.

Then he remembered: The only copy he had was in his phone, which was in his car, and his car was gone.

He put his hand on his hip and didn't feel it. He felt the other hip. It wasn't there either. He started to panic as he sat up and felt around and around his waist-band, hunting for the photo, then looking around the bed of the Club Car. "No! It can't be! Where is it? Where is it? Where did it go? Where did she go?" He felt his hip again, then ran his fingers around the elastic band again. "It has to be here somewhere. It *has* to be. It *has* to be!" He looked around the bed of the Car again, his face flushed and worried, and his heart racing as he felt his hip once more and then even felt around his swim cap in panic-driven desperation. "She has to be here somewhere!"

"It's in my fanny-pack," Christina called out to him as she approached the Club Car holding his towel out in front of her. "It's all right. I have it right here," she pointed to the fanny-pack strapped to her belt as she handed the towel to the not-so-old man.

"Sorry about losing all that other stuff," she said.

Daniel sighed and settled back down into the Club Car. His heart rate returned to normal. He looked back at the area of sand where his towel had been. And it dawned on him just then that all the sand had run through the hourglass of the life he had when he stepped away from that sandy spot on the beach and dove into the sea for the final time. He wasn't sad about it, or angry; but he did feel unsettled, a little lost, and even, you could say, naked.

He had bundled the emotions of loss, guilt, and shame into a big fiery ball of suppressed rage, and that rage had been the filter he perceived everything through and the cornerstone of every decision he made. So what was he going to do now? What was he going to hold onto—identify himself by—now? He didn't know. What he did know, however, was that whatever that new thing might be, he was going to dive into it headfirst.

He reached up and peeled his latex racing swim cap off his head. He handed it to Christina and asked her to throw it in the trash.

CHAPTER *XVIII*

*T*he Club Car started moving again. It swung around to the entrance of Pavilion #1.

"What now?" Larry, the other park ranger asked.

"What now?" Christina asked, looking at the not-so-old man who was sitting upright on the back of the car. He felt better but not good, but he thought he could handle it.

"Want me to call someone? Your wife? A friend?"

The not-so-old man replied, "A taxi."

Christina did not hesitate. She turned to Chuck and said, "He's coming home with me. Friend of the family. Long lost friend. Happy to see him, Chuck. Do drive us back to my car. It's in #3's parking lot."

Chuck raised an eyebrow. "You sure, Chrissy?"

"Sure as spit," she replied.

When she said that, for the first time, the not-so-old man noticed her ball cap—blue with an orange logo of the NY Mets. Between the strands of hair hanging below the cap, he thought he saw, over her right temple, a golden freckle. His heart skipped a beat.

"Okay then," Chuck said.

"But before we go," Christina said, "would one of you guys go grab a T-shirt from the gift shop? A large men's would work. Tell Mary I'll pay for it later. Or she can just put it on my tab," she said with a smile.

Larry hopped down from the Club Car and climbed the stairs to the first floor of the Pavilion built on stilts. He returned with a white T-shirt with the name of the state park silk-screened across its front in amusement park-like lettering and a blown-up reproduction of a circa 1950s postcard of the island on its back.

"Now you'll be a walking advertisement," Christina chuckled as she helped Daniel slip on the shirt. She reached up and ruffled and then smoothed over his hair. "You don't look half bad for a shipwrecked sailor," she smiled. "Ok, Chuck. We're all set."

As the Club Car started moving, Christina said softly, "Onward..."

Once inside her SUV, Christina reached into the back seat and pulled a bottle out of a small cooler in the back seat, and handed it to Daniel.

"Try some of this," she said. "It's not my sports drink, just some juice." She started the engine.

Daniel put the bottle to his lips and squinted.

"I know," Christina said. "It tastes funny, but it's loaded with all sorts of good stuff. It'll help you recover faster."

"Wha... What's in it?"

Christina put the SUV in gear.

"Oh, just some celery and cucumber juice." She laughed when she saw Daniel's face pucker.

"I know. I know. I'm a health nut. People think I'm kinda weird. But being a girl, they tend to forgive you."

The drink went down easily. The not-so-old man thought, how ironic—Ernie always talking about how an apéritif or brandy went down, and here he was scrutinizing celery juice.

"It has a nice finish," he said calmly.

Christina burst out laughing. "That's hilarious! Yeah, 2019 was a very good year... for celery!"

Daniel smiled.

Christina took a right turn out of the parking lot onto the park's central road. "So you know all about Honeymoon Island then?"

Daniel nodded his head.

"It's a wonderful place. Sometimes you can even see dolphins out past the jetties. I come here to run every Sunday. Always have a good time."

She glanced at Daniel and smiled, the corners of her eyes all wrinkly. Strands of hair had fallen over her temples.

They drove past the entrance buildings, past the condos overlooking Caladesi Island, across a bridge, and onto the causeway. Daniel looked at it all. He remembered in one of Ernie's books how Jake got knocked out in a fight and how afterward everything looked the same but new—like he was seeing it all for the first time but knew he had seen it before. That's how the not-so-old man felt now. He saw the palm trees and cars parked at the water's edge and the nylon hammocks tied between two palm trees with someone hanging in them, all sunk down in the hammock so you couldn't see them, and the place that rents kayaks with the *High & Dry Grill* covered in palm fronds beside it and people fishing on the other side of the causeway and people jogging on the bike path or riding bikes or rollerblading or walking or walking dogs and some people wading out into the shallow water. He saw people standing on paddleboards paddling and people in kayaks paddling and people racing on jet skis out in the water and the *Caladesi Connection* ferry boat taking passengers across Hurricane Pass to the island. It was like being in an amusement park for him. He had seen all these things many times and remembered that, but now all of it was fresh and new. He wasn't thinking. He didn't hear his mind complaining or planning. He just sat there and saw.

And when he glanced at Christina, he knew he had never met her before, and she was new and yet it was like he had known her before and she was just now becoming new to him just like everything else he was seeing being new as they slowly drove along the causeway.

Neither of them talked for a few minutes until after they got over the drawbridge onto the mainland and stopped at the red light at the intersection of Causeway Boulevard and Bayshore.

"So you're coming home with me until I'm sure you're okay. I was almost a nurse, you know. I know all sorts of First Aid and stuff, so you're in good hands."

"Uh-huh."

She took a right on Bayshore.

"Where do you live, anyway, Daniel?"

He didn't answer right away, not that he couldn't or didn't want to, but because he was still noticing how everything looked new.

"Okay," Christina said. "We can get to that later."

Her phone rang. She pushed a button on the steering wheel and said, "Hey, little brother. What's up?"

"You still coming to my game Tuesday, Sis?"

"Sure. Why?"

"Just wondering."

"You sure?"

"Yeah. I guess I'm a little nervous. Just glad you'll be there."

"Of course. Wouldn't miss it. You're gonna be great. Always are."

"Yeah, thanks. Anything going on?"

"Funny you should ask. Had a nice run this morning. Made a new friend. Come over for dinner tonight and meet him."

"What's up? Some guy try to pick you up on the beach again?"

Christina blushed and laughed. "No. Quite the opposite. Tell you all about it tonight. Seven o'clock."

"Right. Copy that. See ya."

"Love you, Bro."

"Love you back, Sis."

"Wait!" Christina said quickly. "Do me a favor, would you?"

"Of course."

"Bring over a pair of sweatpants or shorts. I'm gonna need them tonight."

"Okaaayyyy... You goin' to an early Halloween party dressed like a dude or something?"

"Like I said, wise guy," Christina smiled, "I'll explain everything tonight. Get your mind out of the gutter, brother!"

"You know guys can't do that," he replied. "But I'll explain all that tonight."

"Oh, brother!"

"Oh, sister!"

"See ya."

"Right."

Christina turned to Daniel grinning. "That smarty pants is my little brother, though he's not little anymore. Besides being a smart aleck, he has a nasty fastball and drop-dead slider. He's got a big traveling team game Tuesday. College scouts are coming to watch him. He's a little shy and a little nervous."

Daniel smiled.

"You like baseball, Daniel?"

"Yeah."

"I knew it! I can always sense a ball fan when I meet him."

"I noticed your cap," Daniel said.

"Yeah, the New York Metropolitans. My brother got me hooked years ago. It's funny—here we are growing up nowhere near New York, and he ends up falling in love with the Mets. Saw them once... *once*... on TV when he was six or seven and declared that they were his team. Made no sense to me. Always buys me a new Mets ball cap every birthday. He's kinda weird, like me, but in a good way. Now he's hoping to get a scholarship to FSU and then maybe even get to the Bigs. He's ranked the number one pitcher in the state, you know, and I'm so proud of him."

Daniel listened. It was all new to him, but also a matter of fact.

They got to downtown Dunedin and stopped at the light. Daniel noticed the wrought iron arch over the street, honoring the military. On the corner to his left were a couple of benches in front of an ice cream store. Christina took a right, then followed the main road as it curved left with a park with a playground on the right in front of the marina with a seafood restaurant overlooking the boats.

"Someday," Daniel said out of nowhere, "I want to go to the beach just south of Clearwater. There's a playground there I want to visit."

Christina saw that his thoughts were far away. It almost sounded like he was asking to take her there. "Sure thing," she replied matter-of-factly. "I like Clearwater Beach too."

They went a few blocks, and Daniel kept watching and saw the bike path beside the road and ocean water beyond that, and over the water, he could see the buildings of Clearwater Beach. Christina turned left.

"I know. It's funny. I live right near a ballpark—Blue Jay's spring training camp. They've got to be the ultimate snowbirds, wouldn't you say?"

She turned into a short driveway to a one-story bungalow.

"Home sweet home," she said. The yard was small but clean and well kept. Once inside, Christina pointed to the couch in the family room that opened to the kitchen.

The not-so-old man eased himself down on the couch and sat. Christina got a couple of pillows and blankets and put them on the couch.

"Next up, I'm gonna make some chicken broth. That fixes everything. Then some beef broth. Chicken for the nerves first, beef for the muscles later, all loaded with good old fashioned animal fat."

Daniel raised an eyebrow.

"Is that okay? Bet you thought I was vegan or something with all that juice and stuff. Let me tell you, Daniel, I don't believe it. All that propaganda about fat being bad. Farmers used to work all day eating bacon and eggs and beef jerky and butter. They did pretty darn good. Built this country up."

Daniel was loving every minute.

"Now, most men can't even father a child, for crying out loud. Need some blue pill or something. Bunch of politically correct sissies eating soy burgers."

Daniel smiled. He saw she had lost herself in it. She reminded him of Pilar, sans the sadness and ugliness. The ugliness replaced by beauty; the sadness now exuberance.

"Anyway," she said as she adjusted the pillows against the arm of the couch. "Here. Lay down. I'm sure you're sleepy. I'll get cooking while you rest."

Daniel lay down, but his eyes wouldn't close, and he didn't feel tired. He sat up and looked around the room. He saw an old fireplace that was closed up, now with a potted plant in it, and flanked on both sides by dark hardwood bookshelves with books and magazines in them. There was a Lazy Boy recliner to the left of him and a compact stereo and a large flat-screen TV, covered over with a beach towel, on the wall to the right. Leaning against the wall behind the stereo, he saw a guitar.

Christina was behind him in the open kitchen, cutting up chicken, pouring spring water out of a bottle into a pot, and cracking eggs. Daniel got up and sat in the recliner so he could watch her. She saw him but didn't say anything. After a few minutes, Daniel's eyes closed, and his chin dropped onto his chest.

Daniel opened his eyes.

Christina was sitting on the couch reading a book. Daniel

smelled chicken soup.

Christina said, "Hey, you awake? Have a nice nap?"

Daniel cleared his throat.

"You must be hungry. Ready for some soup?"

"Sure," Daniel replied. He pushed himself up out of the recliner.

"You can stay there," Christina said. "I'll bring it to you."

"That's alright. I'd rather eat at the table. I feel fine."

Daniel sat at the table as Christina ladled soup into a bowl.

"I feel pretty good," Daniel told her. "What was in that sports drink, anyway?"

"Ohhh... that's my secret recipe. If I told you I'd have to have you arrested," Christina chuckled. "I'll show you how I make it later. For now, have some soup. It does the body good, you know."

Daniel looked down at the steaming bowl of yellow broth. "You made this from scratch?" he asked.

"Yeah. Another secret recipe. It's more like egg-drop soup. It's got egg whites in it. They're good protein, you know. Pumps those muscles up." Christina held up her arm and pulled her sleeve up to her shoulder, made a fist with her hand, and flexed her bicep.

Daniel rolled his eyes. Christina laughed.

He tasted the soup. It was bland but good.

"Doesn't have any salt in it, if that's what you're wondering," Christina said. "I don't believe in salt. Nasty stuff. Kills red blood cells, you know. Any shipwrecked sailor knows if you drink seawater, you die, and..."

She stopped abruptly. Daniel looked up at her.

"What?" he asked.

"Sorry. I'm sorry for babbling."

"Were you babbling?" Daniel asked between spoonfuls.

"I just get carried away talking about it sometimes."

Daniel took another spoonful. "No worries. I'm interested. Go on."

Christina's eyes brightened. "Most people get turned off. It's like talking politics or religion or something."

"No worries. Go on."

"Okay, but then I'll stop. You get plenty of the good kind of sodium from the celery juice. There. I said it."

"Well," Daniel said. "The soup is okay. But if I can't walk on water in fifteen minutes, I want my money back."

Christina chuckled and kissed him on the top of his head. She went to the refrigerator and took out some meat.

Daniel went back to the couch and laid down. He felt relaxed. He closed his eyes and fell asleep. When he woke, he smelled beef stew.

"It's stew without the stew," Christina said as he sat down at the kitchen table. "Good old beef broth now. You can eat the stew tomorrow."

Christina's brother, Tom, came over at seven o'clock and ate stew with Christina as Daniel had more broth. They talked mostly about Tom's life and his love of baseball and about the game he was to play in a couple of days. He was a strong, healthy nineteen-year-old young man, and Daniel was impressed, but he didn't gush about it. He was more matter-of-fact about the boy and his success and dreams. Tom liked that. It seemed to take the pressure off.

Tom left a couple of hours later, and Christina started cleaning up. Daniel insisted he help, telling her he was feeling much better and almost as good as new. Christina insisted he stay the night just to be sure and, "It's getting too late to drive you home anyway."

They sat at the kitchen table and Daniel said, "Tell me. Tell me about yourself."

Christina blushed. "What is there to tell? I'm just a simple gal who likes simple things."

Daniel raised his eyebrows.

"Okay. Well, maybe not that simple. But still..."

Christina started talking, first about simple things, like some of her friends and some of the places she had been. Daniel didn't say much, he just followed along and nodded, and asked a simple question now and then. But as the minutes passed, Christina opened up more about more important things. And as her confidence in her new confidant grew, she shared even more.

Christina's and her brother's parents died in a light airplane crash in Hawaii when she was six-years-old, and Tom was three-and-a-half. They had been left behind because their parents said they needed some time away and were going on their second honeymoon. Of course, the children couldn't understand why mommy and daddy had left them, and later found it hard to understand they would never be coming back.

Their father was a hard, stubborn, and spiteful man who openly admitted he never wanted kids in the first place, and his rancor was always palpable. His wife was weak and exuded a spirit of apology, and patronized him by shunning the children too. So, in the long run, it was probably best they died.

But things didn't get better for the two children for quite some time. They went to a foster home and struggled to fit in, and mostly stayed away from the other kids. They were finally adopted when Christina was eight. The family they went to already had six children, four of them adopted. The wife had a selfish obsession with trying to save people and pets, and the husband was too busy working three jobs just to support the brood and drank when he wasn't working. So Christina and Tom never got the attention they needed and craved and ended up basically raising themselves. "At least they adopted both of us," Christina said.

A few days after Christina's eighteenth birthday, the man got drunk and struck her because she hadn't cleaned a dinner plate well enough. Tom was there and jumped on the man from behind and scratched his face, trying to gouge his eyes out. The man shook Tom off and threw him across the room so hard that Tom's elbow busted a hole in the drywall. The next morning, Christina woke Tom up at four o'clock, packed some clothes and food in a backpack, and they took off. They stayed in a homeless shelter, and both found jobs. Nine months later, they got an apartment with three other runaways.

Christina had discovered that humor helped her cope. She played with her brother and told him jokes and comforted him with her levity. When Tom was seven years old, he, by chance, watched a Mets game on TV. The team came from five runs behind in the eighth inning to win in extra innings. He was smitten. Plus, he said, he thought the team uniforms were cool. He started Little League the following spring and never looked back. Now he was on the cusp of getting a scholarship.

Daniel sat there at the kitchen table while Christina shared all of this. She felt safe telling him the truth and appreciated finally being able to bare her soul. Daniel listened closely, watched her expressions, felt her passion, and nodded his head. He had disappeared into her story and lost himself like he would lose himself in his swimming. Daniel had no inclination to tell Christina what he had been through. "What's done is done," he thought. "I don't need to belabor it anymore." And Christina never asked him to explain himself.

They had found each other.

"Well," Christina said as she wiped away her tears. "Would you look at the time! It's almost midnight."

They rose from their seats. Christina led Daniel to the spare bedroom. Daniel stood at the foot of the bed as Christina pulled down the sheets and fluffed up the pillow. He noticed a mirror hanging on the wall above the dresser in front of the bed and stopped himself from looking up into it, afraid of seeing what he had become. But his eyes were pulled up to look into the glass as if someone else had guided them.

First, he saw his body. It was much the same as he remembered, just a little leaner. Then he saw his face and looked into his eyes. His mind went blank. He felt nothing. It was him, a not-so-old man, standing there, but it wasn't him.

Christina turned and saw him staring. "Daniel," she said softly.

Daniel didn't respond.

"Daniel. Daniel. Is everything alright?"

Her voice snapped him out of his trance.

"Uh... What?"

"Is everything okay?"

"Yes. Sure. I'm okay. I'm okay."

He turned and looked at Christina. He reached out and touched her on her shoulder, and looking her in the eye, asked, "You're okay too, aren't you?"

Christina smiled. "Yes," she replied, "I'm okay too."

Christina stepped aside for Daniel. He took the two small steps to the side of the bed.

"Here you go, Daniel," she said. "Lay those weary bones down and sleep. When you wake up, I'll be here, and we can get some solid food in you. And if you want..." Christina paused, "tomorrow... if you hang around until I come home from work, I'll make you the first supper... after your swim."

"I'd like that," Daniel replied. "Thank you."

"My pleasure, Daniel. Happy to be here for you."

Daniel crawled into bed and lay down his weary bones. She pulled the sheet and blanket over him and light-heartedly tucked him in like a mother would a child. The not-so-old man smiled.

Christina asked him if he needed anything else and pointed to where the bathroom was. Then she leaned over and cupped his cheek in the palm of her hand and told him good night.

As she was walking out the door, Daniel said, "Christina..."

She turned and looked at him. "Yes, Daniel."

"Living is something."

Christina smiled. "Yes, it is, Daniel," she said. "Yes, it is."

In the end, the old fisherman in Ernest Hemingway's story was dreaming of the lions. Hemingway wrote that the old man now only dreamed of places and lions on the beach. The old fisherman was simple—a simple fisherman with a simple life.

The not-so-old man was not simple, and he had not had a simple life. Now, Daniel dreamed not of places or lakes or swimming pools, crashing waves, or setting records. He only dreamed of people.

And the occasional dolphin.

The not-so-old man as a better man closed his eyes and quickly fell asleep. And soon, he was dreaming of his children.

Epilogue

*T*here are some people, Daniel thought, who have the worst kind of luck—*salao*—all their lives. There are others who have bad luck, and then something happens: the final straw is added that breaks their back so they have to change or die, or they simply have it so bad for so long that they use up all the bad luck and things turn good, or an angel comes down from heaven or from up out of the ocean and touches them and keeps the sharks away.

Christina was the third kind of person. Once she and her brother had delivered themselves from the bad luck of their parents and foster parents, their lives turned good. Christina met a good guy who liked her sense of humor and loved the Mets and was just as kinda weird, but in a good way, and they both knew they no longer needed to search. A year after they were married, they had a baby boy. The first article of clothing they bought him was a little baby Mets baseball cap.

Tom made it to the Bigs. He wowed the scouts at that important game and got that scholarship to FSU he wanted, and in his junior year, got drafted by the Yankees in the first round. He told them, no, using the excuse that since they played in the American League, as a pitcher, he wouldn't be able to bat. "Besides," Tom thought, "the National League plays *real* baseball." He then called the Mets and told them it was them or nothing, and they'd have to wait until he finished college. They gave him a multiyear, multimillion-dollar contract once he graduated. Now he's a starter and doing just fine.

The day after his rescue, Daniel stayed at Christina's home, napping, eating stew, drinking her sports drink, reading, and plucking on the guitar. When she returned from work, they had another long talk. She told him she wanted to take him to her doctor for a check-up. He objected. "I feel fine," he told her. "A little more rest, and I'll be back to normal."

But Christina wouldn't take no for an answer. A few days later, she took him to her doctor, Dr. Karin Graves (not a very auspicious name for a doctor, Daniel thought), had his blood drawn, and all the other doctor-patient stuff. It turned out that Daniel had the same blood disorder Ernie had, and Dr. Graves told him, "Your levels are extreme. It's no wonder you've been depressed and have had such a hard time coping. This is what you need to do." Daniel did what she said, and within a few months was feeling kind of strange, but in a good way. Yes, he still had regrets. Yes, he still longed for his former family—those feelings would never go away. But his ability to live and live in the now got better with a lot less effort.

This day, he was reclining on the easy chair in Christina's house as she was cleaning up after dinner. He started daydreaming about what could have happened if...

A few days after Ernie had talked to Hadley for what he thought would be the last time, the phone rang. Ernie shuffled to the phone on the wall and picked it up,

"He... He... Helloooo."

"Hem, it's Marti."

"Huh?"

"I said it's Marti...

Silence.

"MARTI!"

Silence.

"Martha Gellhorn, for crying out loud!"

"Ohhh... Okayss... Whatsss..."

"Listen, Hem. Hadley called me a few days ago. Yes, we talk now and then, mostly about you, of course, but we do, so get over it. Anyway, she told me about you feeling your brain was rusting."

"Uh huhhh."

"Well, I did some digging..."

"Of courssse," Ernie replied sarcastically. "Thasss all you dooo."

"Listen, you idiot. I'm trying to help you."

"Okayss. I'mss sorry."

"So there may be a reason for it... besides your stinking drinking, of course."

"Yous shoould talllk."

"Unbelievable! This isn't about me, you moron—it's about you! So keep your mouth shut while I explain."

"Okayss."

"There may be a reason for the rust, Hem. I remembered your dad, well, don't worry about him. It may be something genetic."

"Whatss may be geneticssss?"

"The rust, Hem! The rust!"

"Ohhhh..."

"For goodness sake, let me talk to Mary."

"Okayss."

Martha explained to Mary about what she found in her research and told her what to do. She was to take Ernie to a different doctor she recommended and get the treatment done, and as soon as possible. She also told her to stop the "damn, insane, electroshock" treatments. Mary agreed. Ernie's doctors didn't. Mary didn't care. She had never seen improvement, so why continue?

That was in December. The first treatment was in January. February came... another treatment. March came... another treatment. April came... another treatment. May came... another treatment. June came... another treatment. July came...

It was the morning of July 2, 1961. Ernie woke up just before dawn. He was thirsty. He let Mary sleep and went downstairs. He walked through the foyer, past the gun rack on the wall, to the kitchen, opened the refrigerator door, and took out a bottle of beer. He looked at it for a full minute, the refrigerator door still open, then put it back and took out a pitcher of orange juice. He poured himself a glass, went to the picture window, sat down in his easy chair, drank his juice, and stared out at the mountains as the sun came up.

He rose from his seat and went over to the bookshelf where a pencil and notebook waited on its top. He thought to himself, "...and all of the Sawtooth Mountains belong to me and I belong to this pencil and this notebook." He picked up the pencil in his right hand and put it to the paper. He wrote in a steady hand,

Love in the Time of Blood-letting
~~*It was a dark and stormy night... (just kidding)*~~
Then there was the nice weather. It would come early in the day when spring began, and Nick Adams opened the windows in the morning to let the sun and the cool, but warmer, fresh air into the room in the house he was renting in the Sawtooth Mountains. The branches of the trees that lined the road to the house had small green buds on them that would open some as the sun rose over the peaks of the mountains and the air smelled clean and crisp and light. The delivery truck parked outside the outdoor café down and around a bend in the road in front of his house brought pastries and fruit and sausages that the people in the town found to be wonderful and they sat in the morning light drinking coffee and eating pastries and talking about which mountain trail they would hike that day or which stream they would fish or what lake they would paddle.

Nick walked to the café with his notepad and pencil and began writing about a similar day in the mountains of Spain and ordered orange juice with rum St. James and told the waitress to hold the rum. He drank the juice missing the rum but drank it anyway and it was cooling and tasted wonderful and he felt it going into his blood.

A young woman came and sat at a table near the sidewalk. She was pretty and wore her ponytail tucked down through the back of a baseball cap and Nick looked at her and knew she was much more than just pretty and hoped the man she was waiting for was a good man and deserving of her. And Nick thought, "I've seen you, lovely, and the Sawtooth Mountains belong to you and all the world belongs to you and you belong to this hour and this day."

Nick went back to writing and fell into his story and got lost in it. He wrote the story but it wrote itself too and when he stopped writing, he looked up and the woman was still there and she was looking at the man who had joined her—her expression intense but happy—nodding her head up and down.

Nick smiled too, and thought about a time of his own when he was with a young woman who was also pretty, but in a different way, but pretty and strong, yet delicate too. It was up in Michigan, where he took her on a lake on a spring day and he paddled the rowboat out to the middle of the lake and let the boat float aimlessly as they ate a lunch of French bread with Jambon, Saucisson, and Pâté, with sliced apples and oranges—a veritable feast—and a crisp Chardonnay that was not fruity but oaky, which he liked very much.

He remembered her smile when she opened his rucksack with the lunch items in it… a smile that lit up her face like a Christmas tree as if she had just opened a present she never expected that was the very thing she had always hoped for. And this young woman said to him in the rowboat that spring day, "That's just amazing, Nick! You're so thoughtful! How did you know all of these are my favorites?" And he liked that very much.

He watched the pretty woman with the baseball cap talk to the man, and the man reached across the glass-topped table and took the woman's hand and pulled it gently towards him across the tabletop that sparkled in the morning light.

As the man looked in her eyes, he brought his other hand from below the table and moved it across the tabletop, and dropped a ring on it right in front of the woman's left ring finger. She hadn't noticed since she was looking intently at the man, but when she heard the ring tinkle down on the table, she looked down and saw it. She stared at it for a few seconds with a blank stare, like she was trying to comprehend what it was and what it meant.

The man started to say something, "Tina, you are the love of my life. Will you. . ."

But he couldn't finish because she sprang from her seat, jumped around and almost over the table, and flung her arms around the man's neck. A glass of water tipped over and crashed onto the tile floor, and everyone there turned to see her put her hands on the man's face and pull his lips to hers. After a not-so-short and very enthusiastic kiss, she took her baseball cap off and playfully put it on the man's head.

The man finished his question, "…marry me?"

The woman bent down and whispered into his ear. Nick could read her lips: "Yes! Yes! A thousand times yes!" she said. The man's expression softened, and his lips curled into a smile.

The woman pulled her head away from his, looked at the ball cap again, reached up, and spun it slightly, so its bill pointed sideways and laughed a good hearty laugh.

A waitress tending a nearby table called out, "Hey Tina! Don't forget the ring!"

Everybody laughed and then applauded.

They had lost themselves in each other.

Yes, love in the time of blood-letting was something special. It came upon you slowly and then suddenly, and you knew it the moment you felt it. It was exciting and pure and true and something you could count on like money in your pocket next to your rabbit's foot. Love in the time of blood-letting never disappointed, but increasingly fulfilled, and brought a special kind of joy to those who experienced it that regular-folks who had never blood-let could never know.

Why blood-letting? Nick Adams knew the answer to that since…

Daniel's daydream was interrupted when he heard footsteps fast approaching across the hardwood floor.

"So, do you want to play catch?" Daniel asked the four-year-old boy who really was who had just jumped on him on the easy chair.

"Yeah!"

"Christina," Daniel called out. "I'm taking your son down to the beach to toss the ball around."

Christina came into the room holding a kitchen towel, dropped it, and picked up her son. "You're gonna play catch with G-dad Dan?" she asked.

"Yeah!" the boy who really was replied. "We're goin' to the beach. I wanna swim in the ocean too!"

"We know who he takes after," Christina smiled at Daniel. "I'll just stay here and take care of sweet baby-girl Gracie all by my lonesome," she mock complained all whimpering like.

It was September and still very warm, and Daniel strapped Joey into the car safety seat in the back of his SUV. Daniel and Joey said hello to Mary, the park entrance booth attendant, and Daniel flashed her his membership card. Soon he and the boy who really was were playing catch on the beach.

It was a beautiful evening, and there were several people on the beach and some out on the jetty tanning themselves or just hanging out. Then someone called out, "There! There it is! I told you! See! It's a dolphin!"

Joey wanted to see the dolphin, and so did many others, so a little crowd gathered at the water's edge to see if they could see it.

A fin poked out of the water several yards beyond the jetty. Then another one. The crowd was talking and laughing and pointing. The fins were out past the jetty where the water was deep enough, and the fins came up several times, first swimming left in front of the rocks and then swimming right.

Daniel said to Joey, "Here, young man. Climb on my back, and we'll go get a closer look."

The boy who really was jumped on G-dad Dan's back and Daniel waded out to the jetty—his dark-blue swim trunks hanging almost to his knees—and let him off. Daniel climbed up on the rocks too and looked west over the sea. He thought of a similar evening years ago when he had set out on a swim. But that swim hadn't destroyed him—it made him better.

There were no white streaks in the sky this evening, and the sun was full and yellow-golden and true. And he felt *muy suerte.* Then he looked down to where the dolphins had been seen, and waited.

"There it is!" Joey called out.

One fin surfaced. Daniel saw four indentations on one side of its dorsal fin. Then another larger fin surfaced. Both dolphins snorted, sending spray into the air. People on the jetty ooh-ed and aah-ed. Daniel smiled.

But that wasn't all. The smallest of ripples appeared next to the smaller of the two dorsal fins, and up from it emerged another—but miniature—dorsal fin. "Well, would you look at that?" Daniel mumbled.

"Stay right here," Daniel told the boy who really was. Daniel eased himself off the rocks into the deep water. The people on the jetty murmured amongst themselves like they had just witnessed a wreck on the highway.

"Whatcha doin' there buddy?" one man called out. "You wanna get yourself killed?"

Daniel took a few strokes away from the jetty and started treading water. Then he heard her, "Eh, eh, eh, eh."

Gracie had fully surfaced and now swam up to the not-so-old man as a better man and smiled. Jorge was right beside her, and on her other side, floated the baby fin.

"How you doing, there, Gracie? How you doing, Jorge? I was wondering if you'd ever drop by to visit. It's great seeing you two. Looks like you're doing well."

The dolphins both chattered, "Eh, eh, eh, eh." "EH, EH, EH, EH."

"And it looks like you have a new addition to the family." A little dolphin head poked out of the water right next to Mama's side.

"Congratulations, you two. I'm happy for you. What's the little tyke's name?"

Gracie and Jorge both raised their heads and let them smack down onto the surface, sending gentle splashes of water onto Daniel's face. Daniel laughed. "Okay. I get it. Your little one's name is Splash. That's a good name for a dolphin, I'd say. Gracie, Jorge, and Splash. Very nice."

Daniel treaded water for a few seconds as all three of the dolphins stayed floating in front of him.

"I too have someone I want you to meet," the not-so-old man as a better man said. "Hold on. I'll be right back."

The dolphins turned and swam away in a circle. Daniel doggy-paddled over to the jetty and reached his arms out to the boy who really was. "Come on, Joey. Come meet my friends."

The boy who really was did not hesitate. He eased himself

down the rocks into his G-dad's arms and slid around onto his back and held onto his neck as Daniel doggy-paddled back away from the jetty.

The crowd was going wild now. Most were taking pictures or videos with their phones or scrambling back to shore to get them. Others on the beach had jumped off their towels or abandoned their swim and were descending on the jetty and climbing onto it.

Gracie and Jorge surfaced and back-peddled on their tails to give the boy a show. The boy who really was laughed and pointed and held onto his G-dad's back.

Gracie pulled up to Daniel and Joey and surfaced, the little fin right beside her. Daniel reached out with one hand while treading water with the other and petted Gracie's nose. The boy who really was reached out and touched her.

"This is my grandson, Joey," Daniel beamed. "He's heard a lot about you."

Gracie laughed, "Eh, eh, eh, eh."

"And I have you and Jorge to thank for that," Daniel added.

Jorge eased up to Daniel. Daniel reached down and shook his flipper. Jorge snorted and nodded his head. "You the man, Jorge," Daniel whispered into his ear. "You the man."

Daniel was tempted to climb on Gracie's back just for old times, but instead, reached under her and scratched her belly. They all swam around each other a few times—the boy who really was on Daniel's back and the baby fin close to Gracie—and then said so long.

The sun was close to the horizon. Daniel swam back to the jetty, and Joey climbed back onto the rocks. Daniel turned around and saw his friends surface to see him and the boy one last time. Then Gracie, Jorge, and Splash dove and swam away.

There is never any ending to Honeymoon Island and the

memory of each person and dolphin may differ from that of any other. But we always returned to it no matter who we were or how it was changed or with what difficulties, or ease, it could be reached. Honeymoon Island was always worth it and you received return for whatever you brought to it. But this is how Honeymoon Island was in my later years when we were very rich in having each other and very happy.

FOOTNOTE

† In 1961, Ernest Hemingway was diagnosed with hemochromatosis, a hereditary blood disorder caused by the excessive absorption of iron from foods in the intestinal tract, leading to excessive concentrations of iron in the blood. Hemingway never received treatment for this disease.

Iron acts as an oxidant, which, if present in excess amounts, causes tissues to effectively rust—similar to how a nail rusts. This, of course, impairs cellular and organ function, leading to an array of possible complications such as diabetes, cirrhosis of the liver, liver cancer, depression, suicidal thoughts, hypothyroidism, heart disease, irregular heartbeat, lack of energy, diabetes, joint pain especially in the knuckles, fatigue, general weakness, weight loss, stomach pain, bronze skin pigmentation, and impotence.

If untreated, it could cause severe pain, suffering, and premature death due to heart or liver failure. The disease is much more common in men than in women, and its likelihood increases with age since the body loses its ability to eliminate excess iron as we age. Symptoms in men usually begin in their late 20s and early 30s. It's estimated that 16 million Americans have some degree of elevated iron in the blood. It is not common, but children can have hemochromatosis. Most individuals affected by hemochromatosis are not aware they have the condition because symptoms overlap those of common conditions and do not manifest until later on in life.

In Hemingway's lifetime, there was no direct way of genetically testing for hemochromatosis, and the disease itself was hardly ever diagnosed. However, now there are simple and inexpensive blood tests that will show if someone has too much iron. To this day, doctors still rarely consider it (and didn't consider it in Hemingway's case until very late, and then, never treated him for it)—it takes an average of three doctor visits before it's diagnosed. In addition, there isn't an accepted set range of blood concentrations considered safe or healthy (as there are, for example, for cholesterol, blood pressure, and blood sugar), and each lab that runs the blood tests sets its own healthy range. However, research shows that most of the ranges set by labs are too high. Healthy levels of iron as *serum ferritin (SF)* should be no greater than 90 nanograms/milliliter (one lab stated that an acceptable range was between 30-400 nanograms/milliliter, 400 being way too high for healthy blood). Other blood tests that should be run along with *ferritin* are *Total Iron Binding Capacity (TIBC)* and *Serum Iron (SI)*.

Hemingway's hemochromatosis undoubtedly contributed to or even caused many of his health challenges, including depression and suicidal tendencies. His excessive use of alcohol made his symptoms worse, of course, and probably contributed greatly to his untimely death. It's interesting that the photos of Hemingway when he was recovering from his war wounds in Milan and while living in Paris when he was in his early and mid-20s, showed him to be quite cheerful and vibrant. Photos of him in later years, not always so much.

Clarence Hemingway, Ernie's father, had many of the symptoms of the disease, most notably depression. This undoubtedly affected how he treated his wife and children, which could have influenced Ernie to subconsciously protect himself with overbearing, overcompensating, or other less-than-healthy personality traits. There's a saying, "If mama ain't happy, ain't nobody happy." Could that apply to daddy too?

There's a growing awareness of hemochromatosis, and July (the month Hemingway died) has been proclaimed National Hemochromatosis Awareness Month. Treatments include diet modification, therapeutic phlebotomy (blood-letting), and donating blood regularly. It's interesting to note that some researchers believe that women generally live longer than men because they lose some blood every month during menstruation, thus keeping excessive blood iron at bay. Removing blood from the body works because blood too rich in iron is removed and replaced by the production of young red blood cells that contain small amounts of iron. This makes the average level of iron in the blood come down. Donating blood regularly (as often as once every 56 days) lowers the iron in the blood and reduces the risks of heart attack (up to 88% less risk in male blood donors, but not so in women), depression, diabetes, cancer, and improves emotional wellbeing. Donating blood is good for your heart, liver, brain, and other organs. Regular blood donors are also generally thinner than those who don't donate. If you or someone you know is suffering from any of the symptoms of hemochromatosis, check with a doctor and get the necessary blood tests done.

(For more information go to www.hemochromatosis.org and www.hemochromatosishelp.com.)

Gabe Mirkin, M.D, graduate of Harvard University and Baylor University College of Medicine and a practicing physician for over fifty years, says this about hemochromatosis and Ernest Hemingway:

> You need iron to stay alive because it helps your body carry and use oxygen, and functions in many of the chemical reactions in your body. However, iron is a potent oxidant that can deposit in and damage cells throughout your body. To protect you from being poisoned by too much iron, your intestines stop absorbing iron when you have enough. People with hemochromatosis lack the ability to stop absorbing iron

when they have too much. Iron can accumulate:

• In the brain to make you lose your memory, cause depression, and interfere with every brain function such as thinking reasonably

    • In your pancreas to cause diabetes

    • In your liver to cause cirrhosis

    • In your skin to turn your skin a bronze color

    • In your eyes to cause loss of vision

    • In your joints to cause horrible painful arthritis...

Hemingway's symptoms were incredibly similar to those of his father. Something was damaging every cell in his body. He repeatedly went to doctors for treatment of arthritis, cirrhosis of the liver, severe heart disease, arteriosclerosis, diabetes, depression, and loss of teeth. He spent most of his life treating his total body pain by drinking mixtures of tomato juice and beer, gin and lime, Angostura bitters, or absinthe, and champagne. Something was also damaging his brain. He was so depressed that he was repeatedly given brutal and horrible electric shock therapy. In 1961, he considered suicide and returned to the Mayo Clinic for more electric shock therapy. He lost even more of his memory and finally shot himself. He was driven to suicide by extreme pain, depression, and loss of mental function. Taking a routine family history should have led his doctor to order a simple, readily-available blood test that would have led to the correct diagnosis and treatment...

If iron levels are kept in the normal range, there is no tissue damage and a person with hemochromatosis can live a perfectly normal life. Every few months the doctor does a blood test called ferritin, a measure of how much iron is deposited in the person's tissues. When blood levels of ferritin are too high, the excess iron is easily removed by drawing a pint or two of blood. This blood is perfectly healthy so it can be used in blood banks...

If Hemingway had blood withdrawn every time his tissue levels of iron were too high, he could have avoided all of the horrible pain he suffered and probably would have lived a much longer life. He would not have had to suffer damage to his brain, liver, pancreas, eyes, joints, and skin. His suicide can be explained by the pain of untreated hemochromatosis...

Medical records made available in 1991 prove that Hemingway was finally correctly diagnosed with hemochromatosis just before he died in 1961. Hemochromatosis is most common in people of Irish, Welsh, Scottish, and other northern European descent, and Hemingway was of Celtic heritage. As many as one in every 200 North Americans suffer from this highly treatable genetic defect, and nearly 20 percent of the population carry the recessive genes associated with hemochromatosis. There are several different mutations that cause the disease; the H63D mutation is carried by 13.5 percent of North Americans and the C282Y mutation is carried by 5.4 percent. It is so common that I think the simple test for hemochromatosis should be included in a routine physical. (Used with permission from www.drmirkin.com.)

People still think Ernest had mental issues, and that's why he took his own life. He wasn't perfect, that's for sure, but to slap a label like that on him (and his family) is short-sighted and unfair. Realizing he had battled this affliction part of, and perhaps most of, his life makes what he accomplished even more impressive.

Besides having hemochromatosis, Hemingway suffered many blows to the head—while boxing, in airplane and car crashes, even when a skylight fell on him. In recent years, a lot of attention has been given to Traumatic Brain Injuries (TBI) due to the long-term often devastating effects it can have on people, many of whom play sports (especially American football, boxing, soccer, and other contact sports), and those in the military.

Dr. Kabran Chapek says in his book *Concussion Rescue—A Comprehensive Program to Heal Traumatic Brain Injury*, "Mild traumatic brain injury is a major cause of psychiatric problems, and very few people know it." He says that research shows TBI increases the risk of depression, anxiety, psychosis, PTSD, suicide, drug and alcohol abuse, dementia, aggression, ADHD, and learning problems.

According to the Center for Disease Control (CDC), there are over two million new head injuries in the U.S. each year, and it's estimated that over 80 million people in the U.S. have sustained head injuries over the last forty years. Dr. Chapek goes on to say how TBI can be diagnosed using advanced scanning techniques and gives treatment protocols to help heal the brain and ameliorate the damage. (For more information, go to www.amenclinics.com)

Hemingway's concussions and other less serious blows to his head had to have taken a toll. Those, in combination with his blood disorder, make it even more incredible he did what he did, lived as he lived, and was who he was. If he had known what we know today about these afflictions and had gotten proper advice and treatments, there's no telling what else he would have accomplished. He was, after all, an *aficionado* of life. Truly, he was.

> **Ernest Hemingway wasn't made for defeat.**
> **Hemingway may have been destroyed,**
> **but his spirit will never be defeated.**

HEMINGWAY QUOTES

No one you love is ever truly lost.

Oh, now, now, now, the only now, and above all now, and there is no other now but thou now and now is thy prophet.

When you love you wish to do things for. You wish to sacrifice for. You wish to serve.

But did thee feel the earth move?

Courage is grace under pressure.

But man is not made for defeat. A man can be destroyed but not defeated.

We would be together and have our books and at night be warm in bed together with the windows open and the stars bright.

All you have to do is write one true sentence. Write the truest sentence that you know.

We are all broken—that's how the light gets in.

People were always the limiters of happiness except for the very few that were as good as spring itself.

Try as much as possible to be wholly alive with all your might, and when you laugh, laugh like hell. And when you get angry, get good and angry. Try to be alive. You will be dead soon enough.

Imagination? It is the one thing beside honesty that a good writer must have.

...the hard times will pass, everything will get better and the sun will shine brighter than ever.

Write hard and clear about what hurts.

Go all the way with it. Do not back off. For once, go all the goddamn way with what matters.

There is nothing noble in being superior to your fellow men. True nobility lies in being superior to your former self.

Happiness in intelligent people is the rarest thing I know.

For a true writer, each book should be a new beginning... He should always try for something that has never been done or that others have tried and failed...

The best people possess a feeling for beauty, the courage to take risks, the discipline to tell the truth, the capacity for sacrifice. Ironically, their virtues make them vulnerable; they are often wounded, sometimes destroyed.

You may talk. And I may listen. And miracles might happen.

How little we know of what there is to know.

The writer's job is not to judge, but to seek to understand.

My aim is to put down on paper what I see and what I feel in the best and simplest way.

No tears in the writer, no tears in the reader.

Be fully in the moment, open yourself to the powerful energies dancing around you.

The rain will stop, the night will end, the hurt will fade. Hope is never so lost that it can't be found.

"How did you go bankrupt?" Bill asked. "Two ways," Mike said. "Gradually, then suddenly."

'I thought of Miss Stein... and egotism and mental laziness versus discipline and I thought who is calling who a lost generation?... I thought that all generations were lost by something and always had been and always would be.'

" ...You belong to me and all Paris belongs to me and I belong to this notebook and this pencil... I hope she's gone with a good man, I thought. But I felt sad."

"There is never any ending to Paris and the memory of each person who has lived in it differs from that of any other. We always returned to it no matter who we were or how it was changed or with what difficulties or ease it could be reached. Paris was always worth it and you received return for whatever you brought to it. But this is how Paris was in the early days when we were very poor and very happy."

Brief History of Ernest Hemingway

1899 - Ernest Hemingway is born in Oak Park, Illinois, on July 21, at what is now 339 N. Oak Park Ave., in a second-floor bedroom. See *The Hemingway Foundation*,

www.hemingwaybirthplace.com

1918 - Hemingway tries to enlist in the army but is rejected for poor eyesight. Instead, he volunteers as an ambulance driver and is sent to the Italian Front by the Red Cross. A month later, he gets wounded by mortar and machine-gun fire and later awarded the Italian Silver Medal of Military Valor for dragging a wounded Italian soldier to safety.

1921 - Marries first wife Elizabeth Hadley Richardson September 3, 1921; they move to Paris, arriving December 22, 1921.

1923 - First son John (Mr. Bumby) is born.

1926 - *The Sun Also Rises* is published. The title was inspired by the Bible, Ecclesiastes, Chapter I

> One generation passeth away,
> and another generation cometh:
> but the earth abideth forever.
> The sun also ariseth,
> and the sun goeth down,
> and hasteth to his place where he arose.

1927 - Ernest and Hadley divorce on January 27. Ernest marries Pauline Pfeiffer, a fashion writer, on May 10.

1928 - Hemingway and Pauline move to Key West and have Ernest's second son, Patrick. His father Clarence commits suicide.

1929 - *A Farewell to Arms* is published.

1931 - Hemingway's third son Gregory is born.

1933 - Ernest and Pauline safari in Africa.

1935 - *Green Hills of Africa* is published.

1936 - Meets Martha Gellhorn in Sloppy Joe's bar in Key West around Christmas time.

1937 - Works as a war correspondent during the Spanish Civil War; *To Have and Have Not* is published.

1940 - *For Whom the Bell Tolls* is published; Hemingway divorces Pauline November 4, and marries Martha Gellhorn November 21; volunteers for the Navy and hunts German U-boats off the coast of Cuba in his own outfitted boat *Pilar* (a nickname for Pauline); receives the Bronze Star for his service in 1947.

1944 - Hemingway goes to Europe as a WWII war correspondent and reports on the liberation of Paris; begins relationship with Mary Welsh.

1945 - Divorces Martha Gellhorn, December 21.

1946 - Marries Mary Welsh, March 12.

1950 - Hemingway's novel *Across the River and Into the Trees* is published. It's the most poorly reviewed novel of his career.

1951 - Hemingway's mother Grace dies.

1952 - The novella *The Old Man and the Sea* is published.

1953 - *The Old Man and the Sea* wins the Pulitzer Prize in literature.

1954 - Awarded the Nobel Prize for Literature.

1961 - July 2, Hemingway shoots himself in the head with a shotgun at 7:30 in the morning in the downstairs foyer of his house in Ketchum, Idaho. He's buried in Ketchum Cemetery overlooking the Sawtooth Mountains.

Quotes From The Not-So-Old Man And The Sea

Concentrate on the stroke. Make each stroke better than the last. That's what perfection is. Better than the last. Better than what came before. Each stroke more true to itself.

Feel yourself shoot headlong through the sea, the deepening sea.

Pain is nothing. Dying is nothing. Will is everything.

Perhaps that is why I trust... Or perhaps it is simply because I am lazy.

They looked up at the greatest show on earth and entertained each other with their imagination and stories.

Yes, I would show them all... And I would show *her!*

The stroke. Sure and true. Each stroke better than the last. Each stroke more true to itself.

But the rhythm... The rhythm will restore my luck.

How little we know of what there is to know.

The sea that drives you to sin and the sea that washes them all away.

The nobility is in the try, not the do.

This one time, I'm going to dive in and face it head-on. For once, I have to be true.

Focused, attentive, consuming, unconcerned with outcome.

Relationships aren't so much about liking the things someone does, but not having to put up with things they might do that you just can't stand.

But time does not lie, and it would not lie to him for the rest of his life as much as he wanted it to or thought he deserved.

Ego is the problem: not being able to admit when you're wrong.

Maybe the pain is pushing you towards more. It's shouting at you,

"Get busy! Make something! Make *yourself* something!"

Stop it... What's done is done.

People are stupid. If only I were king.

...no ten-lane highways full of cars going nowhere with drivers pondering nothing.

Suffer enough abuse and a man turns cruel.

Ernie's writing was simple. Almost too simple. It was like Ernie would beat you over the head with a club into liking him.

They would have grown up together—the boy for the first time and the not-so-old man as his father for the second.

Life does not want to die. It is pesky, unrelenting, and covetous. It will push aside almost anything in its way to survive.

You get to heaven if you can recognize hell and face it truly... And that hell is right behind your eyes.

It's a pity instinct can kill you.

After all, every girl loves the bad boy, but teacher's pet, not so much.

I deserve to be anything I am.

I will fight you with everything I have left, even though it is nothing. So bring it on.

If I am to die, so be it. But I will die with dignity.

Perhaps deception is a sin. Perhaps deception is the only sin.

Living is nothing.

Maybe you're not here to learn lessons, but simply to see how much crap you can handle. Maybe you get to heaven in one simple way...You get to heaven if you can recognize hell and face it truly.

A rhythm that was unlike any rhythm he had ever felt before. A rhythm that wasn't helping him to swim faster or think clearer or relax. Rather, a rhythm that was crushing his ego, maiming his pride, and butchering his prejudice. A rhythm that wasn't serving to save his life, but to save his soul.

Ho-hum. Another life? No big deal. It has happened before, it will happen again. Let's just get on with it.

The sound and all that vibration in the air all around him would comfort him and yet at the same time enliven him and make self-evident the fact that there was more to life than what we can know.

As grand as they may appear, even great men have their weaknesses... Which sometimes makes that great man even greater.

Contented, we'd drift off asleep to the sound of water dripping back in the cave, like the ticking of grandmother's clock, the faint echo telling us that the world is still here and this life is as good as it gets.

Life journeys into the unknown. Life struggles. Life triumphs. Life lives.

Funny what a man might do when he's under pressure.

"My son. My son. You're okay, my son. You're okay." His father's finger touched his as he looked him right in the eyes. "My son. My son. I love you, my son. I love you."

But being a girl, they tend to forgive you.

Self-assuredness, on the other hand, is direction without the static. It's smooth sailing. It's freedom. And it not only preserves energy, it focuses it like a laser.

Farmers used to work all day eating bacon and eggs and beef jerky and butter. They did pretty darn good. Built this country up.

Now most men can't even father a child, for crying out loud. Need some blue pill or something. Bunch of politically correct sissies eating soy burgers.

Living is something.

Finish it. Finish strong. Finish true. Finish... with dignity.

*N*OTES

Perhaps you learned something by reading this story. Here's some space to write down anything that moved you. Mr. Barlow is in the process of writing a follow-up to bring to light the life-altering concepts he learned by researching and writing about Ernest Hemingway. Keep an eye out and check our website and Amazon.com for his next book titled,

What I Learned from Writing a Book about Ernest Hemingway
The story behind
The Not-So-Old Man and the Sea
novel and how it may change your life

Kathy's car?"

"Yeah."

"Good. She'll understand," I say. "Go straight to my trailer and look under the big throw-rug in the living room. There's about five thousand dollars spread out under it. Gather up about half of it and take it with you. Can you remember that?"

She nods her head.

"Where's the money?"

"Under the rug . . . living room."

"Right. Then drive straight to Charleston. Don't stop for nobody or nothin'. Don't tell Kathy or your dad or nobody. Got it?"

"Yes."

"Go get a room at the Holiday Inn near the causeway. The round one. You know it?"

"Yeah."

"Stay there until I come for you. Don't use your real name and don't open the door for anyone. Use your middle name, Sarah, and the last name Wilson. When I come for you I'll leave a message that I'm in the lobby with my Sunday bonnet on." She exhales a tense little laugh. "You'll never forget that, now, will you?"

She shakes her head.

"I need some time to clear this up. If I don't they'll just bring me back here or kill me trying. If they get me, they'll forget you. If I win, you'll be safe too. But that may take some time. If I don't come for you in two days, call your dad. He'll know what to do. So stay away. Got that? No more private eye stuff, okay?"

She smiles that enchanted smile and we hug each other tighter and kiss briefly—as if I was the husband leaving for work in the morning. "Now go. I'll be right behind you."

We let go, and she walks to the front door, her high heel shoes clicking on the linoleum covered cement floor. She takes hold of the doorknob and turns it as I say, "And Kaitlin . . ."

She pauses, not turning her head.

"Just don't go and spend all that money on shoes or somethin'," I smile.

She turns her head quickly and looks at me with a glance that's hopeful and a little spiteful and yet, at the same time says, "It should have been you!" A spark shoots up my spine.

"Don't worry, Sam," she says as our eyes linger on each other's. "I'd rather go barefoot."

Read the exciting conclusion at Amazon.com ebook or paperback and

www.ingramcontent.com/pod-product-compliance
Lightning Source LLC
Chambersburg PA
CBHW050147120726
47903CB00002B/532